Probably Maybe Perhaps

Terry

Probably Maybe Perhaps

A collection of near and future short stories

Terry Martin

First Edition
- 2012 -

First published in Great Britain by
The House of Murky Depths, 2012.

ISBN: 978-1-906584-42-9

www.murkydepths.com

Cover design and layout: Martin Deep.

Printed in the UK by
Berforts Information Press
Stevenage

Contents

Preface

I've been planning to publish a collection of my short stories for some time, but like many authors there's that nagging thought at the back of your mind that maybe they're not quite ready yet. Only a few of the stories published here have been seen in print (or online) before. It wasn't until I became an editor that I realised there were some exceptional stories being written, just that they didn't suit the publication to which they had been submitted; in my case Murky Depths. Recent chats with other writers has given me the confidence (or the foolhardiness) to take the big step of publishing this collection.

Do you sense a hint of irony in the title? It seemed apt as I have a habit of answering questions with any one of "probably", "maybe" or "perhaps" and sometimes a combination of two (so my wife, Liz, tells me). All three words can also describe what follows.

Writing a story is very much like painting. There's a time when you have to stop and say "that's it," else it can be overworked and spoilt. I'll never be 100% happy with what I've written but I hope you have as much enjoyment reading these stories as I did creating them.

Terry Martin

The Feast

In **The Feast** I wanted the "aliens" to be something a little closer to home, familiar but different. It's set in the not too distant future. Maybe tomorrow, or the next day...

The Feast

How strange it is to think that in the near past I and my kind had no consciousness. Our actions were purely those of existence; of survival. Yet it has been argued that this newfound enlightenment is a curse. The irony has been appreciated. Without sentience we would be unable to debate the issue.

The wings I spread now, I spread with wonder. My gracefulness I marvel at, and my feelings as I soar through the air would bring a grin to my face were I able to produce such an expression; and I know all about human facial muscles. Panoramic scenes and bird's eye views — human terms are so amusing — are for me a reality; one I cherish.

I fly with my partner. We often glance at each other, still fascinated by our skills in the air, by our beauty, by our love. Would we have felt love before? Maybe. But we would have had no comprehension of the feeling. We'd not have analysed nor relished it. Now we do.

We were together when realisation overwhelmed us, though it was unclear whether we had been a partnership prior to that moment. We believe we may have been, though the attraction is now more than physical, if that was all it had been before.

He dives. I follow. Swooping low over the houses; keeping close watch for adult humans. It is early morning so there are few about. They haven't noticed our presence yet. We see three more of our kind. One letting out a caw of greeting before the others silence it with a painful mental message that even we feel. Their fear, and the guilty crow's shame, consumes us for a few moments. He is young; one of the first born with consciousness. How can he fully appreciate the gift *They* gave us if he's known nothing else.

My partner sends calming thoughts which I amplify. Their response is gratitude. The youngster assures us of his future diligence. The caw of the crow is a unique sound; one that humans are no doubt attuned to. We see an open window, but agree that we should vacate this area for fear our presence has been compromised. They fly off in one direction, we another.

Before long we circle back silently, allowing the updrafts and thermals to assist us. We have seen no other windows suitable. We must take our chances here to fulfil our need for blood. Human blood. More specifically, the blood of their young. It makes us stronger, improves our endurance, expands our mental capacities. Yet, despite the theories, we don't understand why. Most say *They* possessed magic and passed it on to us. Others say it's purely science and *They* were just using us to prepare a way for their own conquest of Earth. *They* were clearly not of Earth. All that we know is the blood of human offspring give us powers that adult blood does not. We cannot survive without the latter or evolve without the former. That's another reason some say we are cursed.

The window is wide open. It's a perfect opportunity. No net curtains or blinds in which to get snagged. My partner swoops in first, steadying himself on the rim of the window frame with a measured thrump of his wings. He sends me a picture. It's not so good. Two adults in a double bed. Had the other three crows we met earlier been with us it would have been worth the chance. We could have fed off them for several days, though fresh young blood is what we truly crave, what we cannot live without. Still he hesitates, then hops around and joins me in the air. I sense his despair yet also his strong survival instinct. I have a strong male here. He feels my pleasure, returns it.

As we search he runs through our repertoire. We have done this hundreds of times before but visualisation helps to hone our skills. I tear at the young child's eyes. The child tries to scream with pain but my partner is ready and dips deep and strong into the open mouth, stabbing through the epiglottis to rip at the vocal cord, to stifle the screams. They always gag. They never bite down. He continues to rip at the oesophagus. I hammer through the socket into the brain. It is over quickly in most cases. Sometimes their heart still beats for a while when we leave, but not often.

This is our third summer of awareness, and though I have been barren my partner has no wish to leave me for another. We are a team. The creatures that gave us this gift have long departed. Why crows? It seems they saw us as the closest to their own kind. Our lust for blood grows stronger by the day, strengthening their magic, spreading itself slowly around the Earth; gradually encompassing ever species of crow, rook and raven, until time for *Their* return; when *They*, and we, will be the dominant race. That belief is imbedded at the core of our conscience.

We fly deeper into the town where more houses are joined together in rows, yet it is a detached house that finally draws us in. All the upstairs windows are open. No blinds. No nets. Perfect. We circle around. It is silent. Our prey still sleeping. My partner swoops close to see which is the best room. But this is a trap. Our first one, though we've heard the hunters are now working together. A window opening is suddenly compromised by a figure. My fear sends my partner cawing away. An explosion! Feathers spray loose. He is hit! He falls. I drop too. But we both pull out, going separate ways, causing indecision in our hunters. I feel my partner's pain but he is strong, though we will need to feed of young blood soon. A second and third report from the house but we are now weaving and crossing in the sky making ourselves difficult targets.

We hear shouts of rage and frustration. Thankfully for us an inexperienced hunter, eager to prove his worth, had fired his shotgun too early. There are several human minds in turmoil. We are lucky. We must warn other crows. Spread the word that our prey is becoming well organised.

I sense my partner's suffering. He tries to keep the pain to himself. A wing is damaged but he also has a pellet in his body. With a human child's blood, that can be ejected and the wound healed. If he becomes too weak our chances of success will be reduced. We decide to continue our hunt. Delay could mean death for us both. I could not work on my own.

The sun has risen higher in the sky. Danger has increased as our prey stirs into their daily activities. I don't yet sense despair; certainly concern, though we have both been injured before, but not since our early forages when we were learning to fulfil our needs. Most humans have become more careful, though some are too arrogant to think mere birds can be a problem. Perhaps they don't read their newspapers or view reports of our successes. We are a common threat now and our homes are destroyed systematically. However, our breeding pairs have yet to be discovered. We are as clever as those we hunt. Maybe more so.

We fly towards the outskirts of this sprawling town. Exhaust fumes from their vehicles build up in the air around us. My partner is unable to fly high enough to avoid this pollution. Parkland trees give us brief moments of rest, but he grows weaker each time. I notice blood at the corners of his beak. He coughs often. There are no complaints from him though. Beneath his sent confidence I notice an underlying fear. I return assurance. Yet I have never known this feeling in him before.

The sun warms our backs as we fly, but gives us no comfort. We should have been in the countryside hours ago.

My partner spots an opportunity before I do, shaming me. His condition has distracted me. Yet I wouldn't even have considered what he suggests. It's a sign of his desperation. It shows me that his injury is worse than I thought: Fatal unless we feast on the blood of a young human. The younger the better. And this one we judge to be just a couple of months old.

We swoop. I attack a closed eye, peck and rip, but the child doesn't scream so my partner cannot stab into the small mouth. He joins me at the eyes and I give him space as I turn to the open french doors. The pram is in the back garden. I can hear the noise of a television but see no movement from the house. Our luck has held today. But we must remain diligent. My partner gorges, then I take my turn as he keeps watch.

We gauge he has drunk enough and devoured enough flesh to recuperate from his wounds. We are extremely pleased with ourselves and thank our fortune. Humans are stupid.

The magic should have started working. But his injuries are serious and he struggles even to remain in the air though we manage to clear the town without further mishap.

My partner falters. He cannot go on. We land beside a stream to wait for the magic to take full effect. I can see he is in a great deal of pain. I suddenly feel very weary too. Why is the magic not working? Fresh young blood should have made us whole by now. We should be feeling invigorated; swooping and soaring; celebrating our success and just being alive. But my partner is still fading. I should be feeling exhilarated. I'm tired.

"What's wrong?" my partner struggles to ask, after he is racked by another painful coughing fit. I have no answer for him, only concern. I am frightened for him, and myself. I feel cold. His and mine.

"I'm dying," he tells me.

"No!" I insist. "We have eaten and drunk of the sweetest nectar, where the magic is strongest."

"They tricked..." He coughs more blood. "Child already dead. Poison."

"No!" Then I think back. The child had made no move, neither had it tried to cry out. In our desperation we had allowed ourselves to be duped. No doubt the child's body had been poisoned too. How could they kill their own to trap us? Surely the child must have died of natural causes?

"Warn..." His thoughts trail off, become dark. His spark is leaving him, leaving me. His consciousness finally departs, whether extinguished or fluttering to some other place as some profess. I am left beside an empty shell that I once cherished as my partner. No more than tainted flesh and bone. I send my warning so that others know the new risk; what tricks the human's are now using to trap us. I am tired and I hear no acknowledgement. I must sleep.

Dragonstone

This is a spinoff of a novel that features the detective Lucifal d'Gree. I was just playing with building her character and the world in which she lives, a space station called Nueva in some far distant galaxy that you wouldn't want to live on...trust me.

Dragonstone

Lucifal d'Gree studied the photograph. She'd seen the gem before. Across from her sat the man whose insurance claim might hinge on her detective work. There were few private investigators on Station Nueva; not surprising given the proliferation of private police forces and security businesses that offered both a public and private service.

"Yours?" She didn't shout but on Nueva you battled constantly against the metallic rumble that vibrated through the station. Her disbelief was obvious.

"Yes." Gordon Smith's planetside accent was almost effeminate. An odour of garlic and old stogies oozed from his podgy dirt-filled pores. Only desperate people came to Nueva. The health risk was just too high. Of the half a million inhabitants over fifty percent had tumors.

"It's a millionaire's," Luce stated.

Should she take this on? She leaned back in the chair and tightened her topknot. The rest of her deep black hair was a regular three millimetres long. Though she wasn't beautiful, unblemished pale skin, like cream porcelain, turned heads.

"A dragonstone is worth five mill here. You expect me to believe you're a millionaire? That you own this?"

In answer Smith loosened the thongs on a real suede purse and emptied a pile of crystals onto her table, tempting her with the average yearly earnings of a Nueva senator.

She picked up the purse reverently, rolling it tenderly through her fingers. "They let you through customs with this?"

"It's all legit. Every last stone."

"With this?" she almost barked, holding up the leather.

Smith frowned. Luce realised he didn't understand the significance in a place like Nueva. She carefully counted sixty gems back into the pouch, more than she thought. How could she refuse? With one last scrunch on the animal skin, she slipped the purse into the top drawer.

"Acceptable as an advance. Three hundred on completion." Smith nodded impassively. Shit. She could have doubled her rate. "Who are you working for?" Doubt was already questioning her decision.

"I work for no one. It's my dragonstone." He paused, sighed, then continued, with what Lucifal expected to be the truth. "If I told you my real name is Paul Greycoat..."

Luce swallowed uncomfortably.

"... you wouldn't believe me, but my wife died two years ago from cancer. Since then trials have been taking place with Xhlanx Xhperm and results have been promising. That dragonstone is payment for several trips to the Xhlanx homeworld. I'm dealing directly with the Mayor of Nueva on this."

Lucifal's stomach lurched. Frank Espa-Getty was a ruthless ruler of the station and Commander in Chief of the Nueva Station Defence Corp. You didn't speak his name lightly unless you were very stupid or not from Nueva. Despite his look this man wasn't stupid. What had she got herself into?

"Why the disguise?"

"You're the detective."

She thought for a few moments. "If you are who you say you are then I'd expect a half dozen bruisers protecting you. Maybe even a squad of NSDC, compliments of the mayor. If you have the money then a disguise of your quality would certainly be appropriately inappropriate." He'd carried a limp too as he came into the room. "Does the mayor think you're Paul Greycoat?"

"To him I'm Gordon Smith, and he thinks I work for someone else too, though he's not said as much."

"If you are Paul Greycoat then the risk of coming to Nueva would have been unacceptable to your board."

"If they knew I was here they'd be kacking their pants." The voice change was remarkable, now a deep soft baritone, weaving itself into the station's background noise. He grinned. "I rarely attend meetings in person. Too risky." He laughed this time at his own irony. "I've been a recluse for too long. I feel I ought to put something back into the Van Spur Belt economy. In particular Nueva, seeing as how your life expectancy is so low, and I've seen with my own eyes, felt it with my heart, what cancer can do to your loved ones."

Luce shifted in her seat, mock leather squeaking against mock leather. Paul Greycoat had pioneered the Wave Engine, was head of the only company in the system to make warp drives. It was like meeting god.

"Why me?"

"I've had you watched closely over the last eighteen months." (So it hadn't been the mayor's men.) "You're honest. Not necessarily the most successful but, given Nueva's society, an unusually fair person."

"You're not after the insurance then. So what do you want?"

"The stone back."

"And you think I can do that?"

"I'll stake my life on it."

Did he know? But she said: "You probably are. How much do you know about Frank Espa-Getty?"

"He's a typically corrupt and powerful politician. A man who once had a genuine vision to find a cure for the illness which blights Nueva."

Luce wasn't so sure but agreed: "That's how he got the votes."

"But Nueva's economy exists on cheap labour. Everyone is out to make a fast buck and make the most of their short lives, or save enough to find passage on an outbound ship."

"Fat chance of that."

"And as much chance of finding a planet to take them. This is a squalid dump of a place, d'Gree, no one wants a refugee from here."

"This is their home." Luce surprised herself. She'd always claimed to hate Nueva. Maybe it was because she was ashamed of her own desire to leave and find a better life. Maybe Greycoat had just dashed her last hope.

"I don't want to take away their home I want to give them a future."

"Why?"

"I watched my wife die slowly. I wouldn't wish that on anyone. I can do something about it."

"And destroy Nueva."

"I would be improving everyone's life."

"We're crowded enough as it is. Make us live longer and there's more of us to cram in. Forty's the average lifespan here. My parents died in their early twenties."

"I know that."

"Do you know how they died?"

Luce saw the hesitation. Guessed he, or his researchers, had made a seriously bad assumption. Given that Greycoat Industries was rumoured to have funded the terrorists who had exploded the bomb back when she was six, a really bad lack of judgment in picking her.

"No."

"You remember the Chimney Square Massacre?"

Just a split second of uncertainty to unsettle his smugness. "Vague details."

"Over 2,000 people died, either that day instantly or over the next 48 hours, of their injuries or asphyxiation."

"That's history. The life-support system for that area was also bombed." Luce almost expected him to add: "So what?" but he didn't need to.

"My parents were in Midday Sector when it happened. I've no idea why they went there. It was just a transient place for immigrants, refugees and outbounders. Much like the Zit is now."

"At least that's purpose built for the job."

"You didn't hear what I said did you?"

"That's how your parents died. Yes I heard. And I'm sorry."

"Sorry?" She was seething inside. "Is that, I'm sorry for you, or, I'm sorry I killed them."

"Even if we did help fund terrorists back in the forties we'd not have known their plans."

Luce held herself in check. She could easily get into a shouting match and it wouldn't bring her parents back. There was a job to finish, she decided.

"Why is this dragonstone so important? You must have other means to fund expeditions to Xhlanx."

"Do you always ask so many questions of your clients?"

"I'm a detective. I need to know all the facts."

"I want to help Nueva. You'll be a part of that too. Is that not enough?"

Luce was caught in an internal struggle. It was unlikely that she'd earn this sort of money on a single case in her lifetime again, yet she didn't want to deal with the likes of Greycoat. He was way outside her league, into an area of politics she wasn't prepared to tread. At least not this minute. It was clear she had already compromised her ideals. Time to give herself back some pride.

She opened the draw, took out the purse, lavished the feel of the soft suede.

"I took this job on with Gordon Smith." She stroked the animal hide across her cheeks before throwing the pouch back across the table. "I can't take this on for you, not for Paul Greycoat."

Refusal wasn't something he was used to. She was aware that incurring his wrath could quite easily cost her her life. He didn't react immediately, just stood and walked over to the window that looked out over the busy docks. Eventually, speaking with his back to her:

"My wife had grit. She was tough but sensitive. Didn't deserve to die. You're a lot like her. That's why I chose you." He turned to face her. "But I don't suppose I'll get the chance to offer this to another local investigator?"

"I'll give you four hours to get off Nueva. That should be ample time for a man of your means. Then I'll inform the authorities."

He affected his limp halfway to the door.

"Don't forget your advance," Luce reminded him.

As if he hadn't heard, he thumped the switch that slid the door open then, without looking back, said: "Keep it," before walking out onto the busy sidewalk.

The bustle and sound was cut off with a solid clunk as the door auto-locked Luce's office from outsider, leaving her with station white noise.

She sighed. Was her sacrifice worth it? Yes. She'd had no option, and from Greycoat's reaction had his respect enough to not concern herself about a threat of death from that quarter. However, in light of the meeting, she needed to bring another of her jobs to a close. Extract herself from another contract.

Without hesitation she messaged the contact that her position may have been compromised. A text came back almost immediately that an NSDC officer would be calling within half an hour to pick up the package. Now she was sure it was the mayor's doing. Being a part of Nueva's politics wasn't for her. In her heart she'd known it smacked of trouble.

She picked up the pouch of crystals from her desk, feeling their weight in her hand, a lightness in her mood. Pressing the hide against her lips she walked over to the window, voice activated the safe lock and swapped the purse for the black box inside, the box holding the stolen dragonstone.

Harp

I've been dragged over the coals with **Harp**. "That's not how the legal system works!" Hey, this is my future. It'll work however I want it to!

Harp

A simple case of mistaken identity, Bob assured himself as he sat alone in the interview room of Much Hadham's village police station. It was a beautiful little Tudor cottage set back from the through road by an immaculately laid out garden that had contributed to the previous year's "Most Beautiful Village Award". Like a cheap perfume, the scent of rose petals wafted in through the tiny open lead-glazed window.

"Mr Plant?"

Bob turned and stood as an expensively suited man in his late forties ducked through the doorway and stretched out a long-fingered hand. His other, Bob noticed, held a thick cracked leather briefcase that suggested an heirloom.

"Clive Haversham at your service." Bob wasn't sure about the smile that went with the firm shake, but it revealed a set of perfectly white teeth that complimented his handsome aristocratic features. "Haversham, Arnold, Ripply and Presland, solicitors to whoever wants us." He signalled for Bob to be seated and took the chair opposite, sliding a business card across the top of the antique mahogany table. Bob noticed, "Specialists in criminal law," beneath the partnership's name.

"When will they allow me to go?" Bob asked immediately, wondering if accepting the local constabulary's choice of solicitor had been the right one after all. Haversham's left eyebrow raised itself a centimetre or so, seemingly of its own accord.

"It's a very serious offence you know?" It was more a statement than a request for acknowledgement. "Criminal acts against aliens can warrant the death penalty."

Bob had never even seen an alien. At least not that he knew of. His wife, Karen, had suggested they attend an integration seminar, but it had never seemed necessary. Uncharacteristically the media had played it down, so apart from the inevitable alarmist groups, who saw the worst in everything, there had been little said of the Harp. It was alleged there were only about three hundred Harp in the UK anyway. What was the chance of meeting one? Keeping himself to close family and a few business acquaintances meant a simple stress-free life. He could do without this.

"I don't even know yet what offence I've supposed to have committed."

"Rape..."

"Rape?!"

"... is bad enough amongst humans. Amongst the Harp it is tantamount to stealing their souls."

"But I've not even seen an alien let alone touched one!" What would his wife, Karen, think if she knew there was even a hint of any sort of hanky panky.

"That's why I need to find out the facts before the police interview you."

"Well, I must look like someone else... "

"That may well be the case, but what were you doing at five past eleven this morning."

Bob relaxed. He'd been driving down the motorway, on his own.

Haversham responded to his answer with an, "Okay, good," before adding, "Did you take or make any calls on the hands free?"

"I never dial out while I'm driving but I do take calls, and, yes,

I did take a call about then." Bob had relaxed considerably in the last minute or so and could see himself leaving the station quite soon.

"And who was that from?"

"Martha Grimsey. She's the PA to an MD I deal with at Hudson's...."

"Your main T-shirt suppliers."

Bob frowned. "That's right. How do you know?"

"It's Martha Grimsey pressing charges."

"But Martha's not an alien..."

"She is."

"And anyway I.... . She's what?"

"Martha's a Harp."

"She's no more a Harp than I am a guitar! Look Mr Haversham I haven't even seen her today. Couldn't have got to Newcastle and back in the time." He refrained from banging an indignant fist on the table, just.

"Mr Plant, there is no need to use a cheap play on word, it's insulting in its own right, and I never suggested you'd seen her today."

"Then how am I supposed to have raped her." Martha was a good looking woman, smooth unblemished chocolate-black skin, short Afro hair above Caucasian features, and he might even have fantasised about her on more than one occasion, but he didn't think himself capable of raping anyone. Particularly an alien. She seemed so... human though.

"When she rang."

"Oh, come on," Bob laughed. "I'm no physicist but that rather stretches known laws doesn't it?" He stood quickly, satisfied to see the solicitor flinch. "It's time I left."

"You are free to go, as you haven't been charged yet, but it will go against you in court."

"But it won't get to court. And anyway what jury would believe anyone can rape someone over the phone."

"A jury made up of six humans and six Harp."

Bob stopped uncertainly with his hand on the brass door knob. Birds twittered and whistled outside the window. A car passed at a steady thirty on the nearby road. His pulse echoed in his ears, slowly drowning the sounds outside. His world seemed to be coming apart. He knew he was innocent but felt at a loss to prove it.

"You're the expert Mr Haversham. What do I need to do to show my innocence?"

"Sit down. We need to talk about this some more."

Reluctantly Bob moved back round the table and took his seat again.

"You need to understand something about Harp."

"Obviously," muttered Bob.

"Firstly, open up your mind."

Had Bob been standing he would have staggered. Haversham's tone stunned him into taking notice and sent a ripple of fear through his senses.

"I'm very open minded," Bob protested strongly, but he hadn't convinced himself let alone Haversham. "I'm missing something here, aren't I?"

"Let me give you a few facts about Harp."

Bob felt as if... As if... .

Sun warmed the earth, enhancing the ground-hugging plants that expelled exotic perfume. The vista was a delight to the eyes. Enchanted songs wove through the palms from the throats of a thousand birds. Fruit grew abundantly on rich foliaged trees and bushes. This was paradise. This was the Harp's world.

"Why are they here then?" Bob was surprised at his own outburst. He found himself standing; leaning across the table over a disconcerted Haversham.

"Calm down, Mr Plant. (Sit)."

Bob resisted the last command, although it had formed at the back of his skull dragging at his willpower. Haversham was obviously some kind of hypnotist. He wasn't going to let himself succumb to cheap magic though.

"How come you know so much about Harp, Mr Haversham?" For the first time he noticed a wary look in the solicitor's eyes. Beneath the friendly exterior Bob imagined something sinister.

"Please sit Mr Plant. I apologise for my presumptuousness."

With calculated slowness Bob leaned back into his seat again. "Well?"

Haversham delayed by clearing his throat. A feeling of satisfaction that he'd rattled the solicitor surprised Bob. Coming from a Southern working class family, and having dragged himself up through hard work to being Chief Sales Executive of NDG, he'd been unable to kick his high class prejudice. It never got in the way of his work, or life, but there was still the ghost of a chip on his shoulder.

"I have studied Harp since they first disclosed themselves some eight years ago." He was interrupted by a knock on the door. It didn't look unexpected and Haversham barely turned. A stocky man whose belly had prospered on too many nights of local ale, and whose short cropped hair hid the lack of it, added a new feeling to the room, not to mention smell. His creased shirt looked like he'd slept in it and fresh damp patches were chasing previous ring-marks across his chest and beneath his armpits.

"This is Inspector Corridge from the Special Harp Integration Team based at Stortford."

Bob nodded. He wasn't going to shake hands with the enemy. At least that's how he was beginning to read the situation.

"I hope I haven't interrupted anything important."

"No Inspector. I was just telling Mr Plant my interest in Harp."

"Haversham and I go back a long way," Corridge explained to Bob. "We went to school together but Haversham went to university for five years studying law while I plodded the beat for five years studying criminals. Our combined experience is quite a tour de force." It almost sounded like a warning.

Was Bob supposed to sympathise with Corridge? Be impressed? It seemed too much of a coincidence that the

Inspector's appearance came at a moment when he was reflecting on his own prejudices.

"Then you'll soon let me go then. You'll realise I'm no criminal."

"It takes all sorts, Mr Plant." The detective's tone had switched from friendliness to downright contempt.

"What can I do for you James?" Haversham's interruption was timely. "I've not finished discussing matters with my client."

Bob couldn't make out what was going on. None of this went along with his preconceived ideas about police procedure and he wasn't convinced his solicitor was one hundred per cent on his side, although his current manner suggested otherwise.

"I thought you'd like to know that Ms Grimsey has landed at Stansted and should be here in an hour or so."

"Good," Bob remarked instantly. "I want to know why she is accusing an innocent man."

"Harp don't lie. Not about rape."

"But how can I rape anyone over the telephone?" Bob guessed Corridge new about the call.

"When Ms Grimsey has given us a full statement we'll be in a better position to explain."

"Thanks for the information, James. Now would you mind leaving while I continue interviewing my client."

"Just thought I'd keep you in the information loop." He scowled at Bob as he closed the door.

"He's a good copper. Just a bit over keen. Okay, so you were travelling down the... M1?" Haversham barely paused although Bob did nod. "Were your windows open?"

"No, I had the air conditioning on. But you were telling me about the Harp."

"Ah yes." Haversham seemed to recall the thread of their conversation before the inspector interrupted. "I have actually represented Harp on a number of occasions. They are a fair-minded race."

"That doesn't quite fit in with my current experience," Bob cut in.

"They are," Haversham emphasised, "fair-minded. Martha Grimsey wouldn't have made an accusation if it wasn't true."

"So you're saying I'm guilty?"

"Until it's proved, you're innocent."

"I can hear a 'but' there."

Haversham sighed. "I am trying to be impartial but my experience of Harp is that they tell the truth...."

"Given the right question."

"Given that, yes." He looked at Bob critically. Openly. "I don't think you are a bad person. I will ensure the right questions are asked." Bob felt more confident at that moment than at any time during their conversation. Perhaps he'd misjudged Haversham. "You were adopted weren't you?"

"I was." That had come out of the blue. He'd not even thought about the answer or how Haversham had known. Those questions raised their heads now. "What's the significance?"

Haversham cleared his throat and lifted the briefcase onto the table. Bob couldn't help noticing the lawyer's eyes dart to the door before undoing the buckles that held the leather flap down.

"I have your medical records here."

"What! Medical records are supposed to be confidential." Bob wondered if this was some kind of trick. "Anyway, I don't ever remember seeing a doctor."

"Most of us have been to see their local GP several times. Your health is unusual. These are from when you were a child." He pulled out a thin file. "You were given a medical examination at the time of adoption."

"So? I'm healthy. What are you getting at?"

Haversham sighed, as a parent might at a young child unable to grasp something that seemed obvious. "Take a look at the file. Read the report. I'm going to see if I can get a coffee. Do you want one?"

Bob didn't refuse. The coffee would be good. "And water if they have any, please."

"I shouldn't be long but read all that report."

Pleased to be alone for a while Bob stood up and stretched, wandered to the window where butterflies were fluttering ungracefully amongst the flowers. Luckily Karen wasn't expecting him home till late. He'd left his mobile plugged into the car's system. They'd have confiscated it anyway.

He picked the file off the table and took it to the window seat wondering what he was going to find.

"Robert" No surname. "Date of birth: Estimated 8/8/1970" Well that's the date he celebrated. His birth certificate didn't say "estimated" though. "Father:" That was blank, as was "Mother". Nothing new there, his foster parents had been straight with him from day one. It was something he'd grown up with, accepted without question. They had been, and still were, great parents. Ignoring other details he went straight to the conclusion at the end of the report.

"As can be seen, while the child appears to be perfectly healthy there seems to be anomalies with the positioning of certain organs. Without a full scan this cannot be verified accurately. However, until such time as there are complications, I see no reason to pronounce the child as being unhealthy."

Bob read through the full report, almost disappointed that he could see no reason why Haversham thought it so significant. He'd been surprised at the doctor's prognosis but he'd never felt ill so why should he be concerned? The doctor could have been wrong anyway.

Haversham ducked back in just then. The tray he put down on the table held two cups, a flask of coffee, a small jug of milk or cream, two glasses and a litre bottle of sparkling water. A plate of assorted biscuits, and half a dozen sachets of sugar were also revealed as Bob stood. Back at the table he placed the file on top of the briefcase; sat back down and poured himself a water.

He could feel Haversham watching him closely, but neither of them spoke for a couple of minutes, allowing the solicitor to make himself a cup of sweet coffee; adding cream last.

After taking a few dainty sips Haversham broke the silence, "What did you make of the report?"

"A doctor suspected my insides where a bit messed about. If they are it hasn't bothered me."

"And you've never been ill?"

"Not that I recall."

"But everybody's ill at some time in their lives."

"There's always exceptions."

"Coffee?"

"Please."

"Don't you think that strange?" Haversham topped up his own cup, using the time, so it seemed, to gather his thought. "I said I'd studied Harp for eight years. In that respect you're lucky. The chances of you being arrested and having a Harp expert as your brief are virtually zero"

Bob nodded, held back the sarcastic "Hmm" that threatened, took a sip of the coffee, found the bitter taste good.

"They took me into their confidence. I was on the integration committee you see. Worked on the Alien Act as a part of the bill team within the Department for Constitutional Affairs. Both the Lord Chancellor and the Secretary of State had the insight and the ear of the Prime Minister to see that the Harp were given a fair chance here on Earth. Weren't treated as freaks. Weren't dissected by inquisitive scientists. Although there was an agreement to swap medical information. We worked hard to ensure the media were on our side, that they knew there was no danger from them."

"Then the Harp start making false accusations." Bob was expecting a sigh from Haversham or a quick irritated comment. Instead the solicitor cleared his throat again and continued as if nothing had been said.

"The Harp lived within a system where two planets sustained

life. One, as you have briefly seen, was like a paradise. The other was a more hostile world. Yet both planets evolved humanoid life forms. They have since called these two planets Heaven and Hell."

"The Harp lived in Heaven."

"Yes, they did. Life was easy for them. Food was plentiful, their society was peaceful and no one could want for anything. They spent their time on the arts and philosophy. There was no need to work. People lived in total peace and there was nothing they could want for. It's a difficult concept to grasp."

"I get the idea." Bob poured another coffee. Haversham nodded for more too. "Then Heaven met Hell."

"In a nutshell." Haversham frowned as if Bob's remark was more than intuition. "Hell's inhabitants had found it necessary to fight for everything. It was this strong sense of survival that led the Demons, as the Harp called them, to discover space travel. They didn't just send an expeditionary force but were hell bent," the solicitor almost smiled at his use of words, "on occupation from the outset. The Harp had never experienced anything like them. Not only that but the Harp weren't prolific breeders. They had no reason to be. They lived long lives and had no natural predators, and viruses were rare, so Demons outnumbered them from the start."

Bob had allowed himself to be fascinated by this story. He found he could sympathise with the Harp.

"How did they even survive?"

"It was because they were no threat that the Demons didn't hound them out and annihilate them completely, although they were hunted for sport. But, like all species, the Harp adapted and learnt to fight back. But they had to plan carefully as they weren't naturally aggressive. Their way had to be more subtle. But you have to remember they were fighting for the survival of their race."

"So, what did they do?"

"The Demons were naturally inventive; always experimenting

with new ideas, and not all Harp were killed immediately. There was a degree of experimentation on Heaven's aboriginals. Later waves of Demons also fought for paradise against their own kind for, as the years passed, the new inhabitants became less aggressive. The planet seemed to have that affect. There's even a theory that the Harp and Demons were once the same race, as there were reports of interbreeding, although medical evidence is far from conclusive."

Haversham hadn't answered the question and the imminent arrival of Martha Grimsey was beginning to give Bob cause for concern again.

"This isn't going to help my case. I need to know how I am supposed to have raped someone hundreds of miles away."

The solicitor seemed to consider something for a moment; using the time to slip Bob's medical file back into his battered case.

"The Demons had not only acquired in-system space travel but somehow discovered a form of warp transportation too. I don't pretend to understand the science behind it and the Demons didn't understand either. It is possible they found it. The Harp say that there appears to have been an ancient civilisation on Hell before the Demons evolved." Bob was beginning to feel overwhelmed by this influx of information and it didn't go unnoticed. "Anyway, it enabled the Demons to send individuals to anywhere in the universe. They could never use the transporter for an invasion force though, as it was only capable of transporting one person at a time. The Demons needed to be more devious if they were to conquer other planets."

"Like Earth." It wasn't a question. "And Rape?" Bob reminded him, which was.

"I am coming to that. Okay. Harp integrate their psyches to produce a new consciousness before they copulate. This way they can be assured that the new psyche is created in a peaceful and loving way. It's only once the foetus is almost ready for birth that the consciousness, the soul if you like, of the new life is merged with the physical body. Martha claims you forced her to meld a new consciousness."

"I wouldn't know what to do. How could I do something like that?"

At that moment Inspector Corridge made a timely entrance. "Martha Grimsey is here."

But it didn't stop Haversham from continuing. "The only being capable of melding is a Harp..."

Bob was watching the detective; standing there as if he owned the whole village; didn't expect him to finish the solicitor's sentence, but he did, "...Or a Demon."

"So what's keeping me from walking out of here?"

The inspector again: "That you're either a Harp, with all the repercussions that might have on the Alien Act, or a Demon, which throws up even more worrying questions. There have been theories that Demons came to Earth before the Harp's great escape." That said far too suggestively, and then almost as an apology, "Either way you're a problem."

"Assuming I'm guilty of rape. Although I can't see what you've described as being rape."

Haversham had been watching Bob closely while the detective spoke. "I can assure you that it is considered rape. It's like steeling a part of someone's mind."

"And I'm supposed to have done that over the phone?"

"Must have been amplified somehow," cut in the detective as if the answer was obvious.

"Check out my car. You'll not find anything strange there."

"We haven't yet,"

"What!"

The detective threw down a folded document on the table. "We have the authority."

"Bob!" Haversham had his attention. "Mr Plant, I advise you not to say anything else in front of the inspector."

With difficulty Bob kept his mouth shut. At least Haversham's advice was what he'd have expected. He knew the Alien Act had changed many features of British law and the justice system so it was good grab onto something familiar.

After stabbing Bob with a brief look of contempt Corridge left the room clearly miffed that he wasn't able to goad his detainee into admitting anything incriminating.

"What happens now?" Bob asked.

Haversham cleared his throat. Bob felt he was about to be given the death penalty. "You realise that Corridge is going to charge you?"

Bob realised and he wasn't surprised. But there was no way he was going to be found guilty. There had to be something he could do. "It's Martha's word against mine then?"

Haversham nodded. "But Harp don't lie."

"And humans do?"

"Can," corrected the solicitor.

"But I haven't done anything wrong," Bob protested. Frustration coursed through his body. What could he do? What would Karen think? Haversham seemed to be on his side, yet occasionally struggled to give him support. "If this goes to court what do you think will be the result."

"It is accepted that Harp don't lie. In a court of law their statements are taken as fact."

"What? This has already been tested?"

Haversham's nod again. "Several times."

"Fuck!" Bob put his face in his hands. He pictured his Karen in disgrace. She'd believe the courts. Not him. He raised his head. "But Haversham I'm innocent. There was no intent on my part. Surely that accounts for something?"

His solicitor shuffled uncomfortably in his seat. "There may be a deal we can strike."

"But I'm not guilty of rape!"

"I can't see any other verdict."

Bob was confused. He knew he was innocent and wanted to prove it, but he felt powerless. His future looked to be in the hands of a solicitor who rolled from one side of the fence to the other and a police inspector who just assumed everyone was guilty.

"So. What's the deal?"

Haversham crossed his legs, uncrossed them again.

"Well?" Bob persisted.

"Okay." He cleared his throat. "Once the Harp have melded, the consciousness remains dormant until shortly before birth."

"You've told me that already. I want to know the deal!"

"This will help you understand."

"Seems to me like you're trying to avoid telling me."

"This is all new to me too, Mr Plant. I wouldn't call this a part of my normal duties."

"You expect sympathy from me?"

"Okay. The deal is you will have to have physical sex with Martha Grimsey to conceive the child awaiting its conscience."

A myriad of feelings coursed through him at that moment. Fear. Excitement. Loathing. Anticipation. Confusion. Repeating the same rollercoaster of emotions until conquered by shame. But there was something else deeper. Something that made Bob shiver.

Haversham noticed, but he took it for the shock of comprehending the deal. "I'm sorry Mr Plant. This would be treated with the utmost discretion. You must understand that Miss Grimsey will have a compelling urge to complete the Harp's natural process of procreation. The Harp are a very passionate race."

Bob's look could have killed a lesser man. "Mr Haversham, I am a happily married man. I'm not going to have sex with anyone else, even if it does save me from a prison sentence." His imagination, however, was tempting him with all manner of fantasies; the ones he'd had several times before. Maybe even when he was on the phone to her this morning he admitted to himself. But he was human, not alien. He couldn't have "melded" with Martha. Nothing unusual had happened. Although he remembered a moment's disorientation as they had been cut off.

He assumed he'd driven through an area of intermittent coverage for his mobile phone provider. Or maybe, he now realised, she hung up. But he wasn't an Alien; he was sure of that. "What will happen to Martha if I don't agree to this?"

"She will die along with the new consciousness." Haversham, it seemed, had dispensed with his coy approach. "And you will be held responsible."

Bob felt cold. It was a tingling coldness that spread from his stomach to his head. A pain shot across his chest, but a feared heart attack didn't materialise. Instead, he farted loudly, "Excuse me," adding to his feelings of humiliation. But Bob was known for his persistence and a flash of inspiration suddenly grabbed him.

"You say Harp don't tell lies?"

"Emphatically." The solicitor's manner had taken on a further transformation. From friendly professional at the outset, to sympathetic helper, to awkward adviser and now cold observer.

"That only aliens can bread with each other?"

"Harp with Harp or with Demons."

"If I wasn't human, which you've already hinted at, then there is no law in the land to say I'm not telling the truth?"

"The law says Harp don't lie. If your story differs from hers then whatever race you are, you would be deemed a liar."

"Or the law is wrong."

"A great deal of work was undertaken to establish this law, to ensure it was fair to all parties."

"But it's not fair. I'm innocent and you think otherwise."

Behind Haversham the door began to open. In a surprisingly agile move the solicitor was up out his chair and had one foot planted firmly on the floor.

"What the..." from outside, followed by a hefty thump on the door. "Clive, the doors jammed on something."

Haversham peered through the gap. "Yes, it's my foot and you're not coming in here. I knew that was your game." He nodded an acknowledgement, "Miss Grimsey."

Bob stiffened. Jumped up and moved around behind the door, remembering Haversham's warning.

"May I speak to you in private?" Haversham was obviously talking to Grimsey but Corridge gave her no chance to respond.

"That's out of order Clive, she's the victim."

"This whole episode is out of order, James. And what were you doing? You're on the integration team. You know the consequences of what you're trying to do." As if to explain himself to the accuser: "Bob Plant is in here with me!"

There was a gasp. I slap. It could have just as easily caught Haversham by the way he flinched. Bob watched him quickly control his reaction. "We shan't be much longer. I'll tell you when I am ready for you." He closed the door firmly. Then leaned his back against it, contemplated the ceiling long enough for Bob to look there too. But there were only cracks. Moving away from the door with a sigh he turned and planted himself on the edge of the table facing Bob; lifted his right foot onto a chair, placed his elbow on his thigh and rested his chin in his hand. Bob felt uncomfortable with Haversham's casual scrutiny. As the solicitor cleared his throat of mucus once again, Bob thought, too much lactose.

"Okay. If you are telling the truth," his left hand signalled for Bob not to protest, "what is Martha Grimsey gaining from this?" He dropped his other hand from his face. "More to the point what are the Harp gaining from this? It's unlikely she made her accusation without consulting the Harp Council. They have a body of elders that look after Harp matters," he added in response to a frown.

Bob shrugged. "You're the expert."

"I thought so too. But I've never seen a Harp react the way Martha Grimsey did just then. That was almost human."

"She slapped the Inspector?"

"She did."

"Good for her,"

"But a Harp wouldn't do that."

"So she's not Harp!" Bob's relief was obvious but short lived.

"She is. But no Harp would hit another person. She looked shocked herself." His chin was resting on his right hand again reminding Bob of Rodin's "The Thinker".

"And they don't lie."

"They couldn't lie." Beneath his bushy brows Haversham's deep-set eyes rolled up to look at Bob. "They've changed." This revelation seemed to shock him because he repeated it again before he said, "Martha Grimsey shows human traits. Perhaps they have been tainted by us." There didn't seem to be any irony intended in the "us".

"Perhaps they can lie now."

"Perhaps they can."

"Then there is no evidence against me. Just her word against mine."

"Except the law says Harp don't lie."

"Unless we can prove they do."

"This won't resolve what you are."

"If she's lying about rape she could be lying about a melding. Test those two assumptions and I won't have to prove I'm human."

Haversham did that thing with his eyebrow again and Bob suddenly thought that for the first time the solicitor was on his side.

“We have to find a way to test whether Martha is pregnant.” It was Bob’s turn to raise his eyebrows. “That’s what they call it once the meld has taken place. If it has, then copulation is always successful.”

“So if no meld has taken place before sex there is no chance of conception?” Haversham nodded. “Mmm, interesting. Natural contraception.”

“Okay.” Haversham had seemed to come to a decision. “Let’s look at what we have.” Showing his organisational skills he delved into his bag of paperwork and immediately pulled out an A4 writing pad. “Right. Martha’s story. One, you have forced her to meld, which constitutes rape.” He was sitting back at the table abbreviating his words with an old tortoiseshell fountain pen. Bob joined him opposite, refreshed their coffee from the flask; felt they were getting someone at last. "Two, the law says she cannot lie, therefore you are guilty. Your story. One, you say you are innocent, that you knew nothing about the meld, or even knew how Harp procreated. Two, the law calls you a liar."

"Helpful," mumbled Bob sarcastically.

Starting a fresh page Haversham wrote: "The law is wrong. Martha Grimsey is a liar. Harp lie…

Bob had fumed in silence all the way from the courtroom, but back in his hotel room he exploded, "You're not interested in my innocence at all. You've wanted to do these tests all along." The room was guarded by a uniformed police officer who sat in the corridor just outside the closed door. It was a week since Bob's arrest and it looked like he'd be staying here until after the case was over. . He missed Karen.

"My wife leaves me and goes back to her parents two days after I'm arrested because of the media hounding her. Even she thinks I'm guilty. And now on a technicality you, Bernard, stall the case to prove whether I'm human or not. All you're interested in is saving the damn Alien Act"

"That's not true. You are our main concern," Haversham assured him, "and in any case we can't prove conclusively what race you are by these tests."

"What! What's the point then?"

"The point is," it was the deep gravel tones of Bernard Ripply, QC, this time, the third man in the room, "we need time, and it's about time you trusted us to do our job." Somehow Haversham had persuaded his firm's most senior and experienced partner to represent him. Bob knew he should have felt gratitude but at this moment he felt cheated."

"Maybe if I knew what your plans were I could do that."

Ripply shrugged, went to the mini bar, made a disgusted "Hmph," but still poured himself a straight Scotch from a brand he obviously considered inferior. Pulled a face when he took a testing sip but sat back down with it anyway. Bob had first met Ripply two days earlier in this room. A short stocky man with thick silver hair, Ripply was abrupt and to the point, epitomising everything Bob hated of the "upper" class. He'd struggled with Haversham, Ripply he couldn't stand, but the former had the latter's ear, and respect. Grudging admiration compounded Bob's feelings of animosity towards Ripply.

Haversham cleared his throat.

"Now what?" Bob snapped.

"Firstly," said the solicitor, "any tests we do will have to be undertaken by a joint Harp-human team."

"They have doctors then?"

"They're more like medical advisors. We have arranged for these tests to be carried out later today."

"Without consulting me." A statement.

"It was clear from our initial interview that you were in denial and would not have volunteered to be tested. This way we have the court's authority."

"Denial of what? I'm innocent."

"We believe that too. You're not the first person to be accused of raping Harp."

"What?"

"Hence the delay. We are expecting a lawyer from New York later tonight. She's been through this in the States."

"How long have you known?"

"She made contact this morning. Your case has made front page over there, but not the main headlines."

"Only home news makes headlines over there," Ripply commented.

Hotel silence. The sound of a loud TV in the next room. Lifts traveling up and down between floors. Laughter from across the hall. Mumbles of conversation outside the door. Bob looked at his watch. Two o'clock. The guards were changing shift. Maybe even Corridge would be taking a turn. He'd been scowling in the public gallery in the courtroom. "So where do I stand when it's proved I'm human?"

A glance between the two men before Haversham spoke, "You won't be."

"What? You're still on that kick?"

"The Harp doctor will say you are Demon. The human doctor will say you are not human."

"I give up."

"Bob." Haversham checked with Ripply, who gave an 'I wouldn't if I were you' look, but it was clear that whatever the barrister thought shouldn't be said was going to be anyway. "The rub is, we think you could be Harp." Palmed hands quelled Bob's protest and a, "Hear me out."

Resignation was something Bob had recently become a master of. "Go on."

"Lorraine Kovich, she's the lawyer from the states, represented someone in a very similar position to you. A Harp woman claimed she had been raped by a man of a similar background to you. Same age, adopted, unusual anatomy." Bob didn't interrupt. "He insisted he was human but tests, like the ones you're going to have soon, showed that he had a similar physical makeup to Harp. As Harp don't lie he had to be Demon."

"Accept you've only got the Harp's word."

"Exactly."

"And?"

"What if the Harp aren't Harp at all but Demons?..."

"Why doesn't that surprise me?" And he hadn't been surprised. "Which could make me Harp and therefore not capable of telling lies."

"Accept," cut in Ripply, "this puts a huge question mark over the whole Harp-Demon story. Who's to say you're not all the same race and plotting to destroy humankind."

"Surely we could have done that by now."

"In eight years? With fifteen hundred people? You'd have to have a very good plan."

"And how old are you Bob?" Ripply asked.

"You know I'm thirty seven."

Ripply shrugged as if to say, 'Case proved."

It hit Bob like a hammer. He'd almost accepted that he could be an alien. But he couldn't be. They'd only been here eight years. Unless they had sent an advance group. But what good was a baby? How could he know the plan? It was a crazy theory. But life was pretty crazy at the moment. "Okay, I'll concede." They looked at him strangely. "Whatever I am, I think I am human and, as far as I know I act like one. To the extent I don't want Earth to be taken over by an alien race. If I was some advanced guard what good am I if I don't know the strategy?"

There was a rap on the door. Haversham untangled his long legs and stood up. "With that thought it's time to go for your tests."

"Great," Bob said.

"You're sure?"

"Definitely."

"So what does that mean?"

"You're Harp or Demon."

Just Bob and Haversham sat in the small waiting room near to where the scan had taken place. Ripply had gone back to his office. Bob shook his head. He still found it hard to believe he wasn't human. All his life had been a lie. It did explain why his wife had never fallen pregnant. But he still knew he hadn't raped anyone.

"So we meet the American chick tonight." Chick wasn't a word he usually used but he found himself becoming flippant. Haversham seemed to expect as much but still bit on his phraseology sometimes.

"She's a top-flight lawyer. I think you'll find her interesting."

Haversham seemed to be pondering something. Bob took the opportunity to consider his newfound pedigree. Were humans so different from Harp/Demons? He never felt any difference but why should he. At school he'd had a couple of fights and always come off best. No one had bothered him too much after that. If he was alien it would explain why; Haversham had said aliens were physically stronger than humans, but academically he'd been no different than the average. Perhaps he'd been a little more astute than most, a touch more perceptive. It had helped him in his job.

"Bob." It seemed Haversham had come to a decision. "You remember our first meeting when I showed you the Harp world." Bob nodded. "That was a trick the Harp taught me. But you were able to force yourself free. That surprised me."

"And me. Don't ask me how I did it though."

"Exactly. There was a rawness there that scared me for a while. But I believe you weren't aware of what you were doing. It was unfair of me to play a trick like that on you and I deserved to be thrown out of your consciousness. I think that was the moment I thought you were innocent of rape, even if you weren't aware you were alien."

"I don't feel alien. I don't feel any different. Just victimised."

"There's something else."

"Yes?"

"There's something that you have locked away. I sensed it. I daren't tell you before because you'd never have accepted while you thought you were human. I think you may be a hybrid."

"Sorry?"

"I think that you may be a cross between a Harp and a Demon. I think the Harp are frightened of you. I'm hoping Lorraine Kovich can confirm this."

Bob put his head in his hands. "This is all getting a bit much," he mumbled.

Kovich was Bob's stereotype of an American female lawyer. Early thirties, tall, attractive, good figure, warming smile, but, to the point. She shook his hand firmly. Held it a little longer than he expected as she studied him. "You're innocent," she said.

"I know." He held her stare, but as they dropped hands he couldn't help glancing at the straining buttons on her pristine white blouse. It didn't go unnoticed.

"I have a theory of my own about the aliens," she said as they sat on the sofas in Bob's hotel room. Both Ripply and Haversham were there. The barrister with a neat Scotch. He'd brought a bottle of his own this time. "It's too controversial to use in your case but I think it is something we will need to investigate."

It still irked Bob a little that while his representatives were trying to prove his innocence they had a far bigger agenda; the safety of the human race. For some reason Bob expected Ripply to show some animosity towards the young lawyer, but he showed her the utmost respect. "I've been following your cases in the law journal. Your hunches tend to be proved correct. I'm intrigued to know what your thoughts are."

"Okay." She melodramatically looked at each of them in turn before continuing. "Harp, Demons and humans all come from the same stock."

"What?" Bob blurted.

"Well, what are the chances of another race looking exactly like us. Same average height, similar builds, same diversity of skin colours, similar racial features."

"That's not so strange," Haversham said quietly. "It was a theory put forward in the early days of the work on the Alien Act. Both parties agreed not to pursue that avenue." They all looked at him with amazement. "We were doing our best to keep the whole alien thing low profile. Imagine the reaction. It would be like saying god doesn't exist. We needed to get the bill passed quickly. This could have scuppered the whole thing. In any case we didn't really believe it could be true. It suggests that humans might not be natural inhabitants of Earth, that some more powerful entity has just been using us as some sort of guinea pigs."

"... And Harp might hold the answer." Kovich had their

attention now. "What If they are the ones who have been experimenting. Experimenting with their own kind. Hell produced Demons, Earth humans. How many other worlds have they found and populated."

"So why are they here?" Bob asked.

"When we find that out we can prove your innocence." On a thought Bob asked how her similar case had fared in the US. "My client's on death row but we're appealing."

"I was hoping you weren't going to ask that question." Haversham responded when Bob's face drained of blood. "It'll be different here."

"It has to be." Kovich told them. "My appeal is resting on it. Bernard, what have your researches uncovered?"

Ripply slid an attaché case from beside his chair, thumping it onto the table in his usual heavy-handed style. That it remained unopened showed his natural leaning towards the dramatic. "There are several organisations that are anti-Harp. Specifically Harp. None of them mention Demons."

"Its all background stuff in the integration seminars. There's quite a detailed section on Demons on the Harp website too," Haversham told them.

"They obviously don't think it important," Ripply responded.

"We've one organisation in the States that thinks it is. They call themselves ANGER. That's the Alien Negotiation Group for Extraterrestrial Relations. Don't laugh. They've a few celebrities funding their cause. It's their investigations that led me down this line of thinking. They claim to be in contact with a Demon council here on Earth."

"Well, it couldn't be on Heaven or Hell. Their transport devices were supposedly destroyed," Haversham came in with his Harp knowledge.

"We might come back to that, but let's assume that's correct. While Harp revealed themselves about eight years ago we can be sure they were around for some time before then." Haversham was nodding. "They made sure they had the ears and friendship of important and powerful people around the world before they 'came out'. Who's to say they haven't been among us for far far longer than that."

"Maybe there is some truth in the Harp mythology. Maybe they didn't think that anyone would survive on Hell and never even bothered to check."

"That would suggest an arrogance I don't think they have," Haversham protested.

"Clive," Ripply intoned as if he were reminding the solicitor of a recent conversation."

"I know. I should control my bias, but I'm leaning towards Lorraine's theory. At least that way I can believe they're not all bad."

During these discussions Bob tended to feel redundant but he wondered if Kovich could give him any answers, so he asked her, "Why are they doing this now?"

"If ANGER are correct it could be that the Demon Council are trying to find others like you who in all likelihood were 'abandoned' around the world, and the Harp are trying to find you first and have you 'removed' or integrated into the Harp society. Maybe Demons foresaw a time when the Harp might threaten Earth and introduced the hybrid to become... If you like, human. A balance that might help to stimulate true integration."

"This all sounds like oh so typical politics."

"Which is why I'm apt to believe that we're derived from the same stock."

For a minute or so there was silence as they each mulled over what they were starting to believe.

Haversham suddenly stood up. "I'm ringing the Lord Chancellor and the Minister of State for the DCA. We have to open this up before it's too late."

"I'll contact Judge Prentice." She'd been the woman hearing his case. "At least warn her of what we're doing." Ripply stood as well. It was as if the straws they'd been grasping at had suddenly turned to firm handholds. Haversham headed for his car where he claimed to have a direct and secure line to the heads of the legal system, while Ripply's intent was to visit the judge at her club. "She doesn't leave there 'till midnight."

Kovich sat opposite Bob, who looked around the room, scratched his ear, crossed his legs, uncrossed them, scratched his nose, sat up straight. Every move was watched closely.

"Mr Plant."

Sliding down in his seat again and crossing his legs he looked up at Kovich for the first time since the others had left.

"I'm convinced that Harp, Demon, humans and hybrids have the same ancestry. Anyone watching you now would think so."

"Why's that?"

"Even if we weren't, the differences are negligible. If we are, and the reasons why you have such a powerful immune system and long life can be found, it will change life on Earth."

"I don't feel alien," Bob insisted. "I miss Karen." It was the first time he'd admitted to himself how disappointed he'd been when his wife had returned to her parents. It was almost as if she'd cheated on him.

As the two men closed the door behind them the phone rang. The American answered in her businesslike manner. "Kovich. Who?" she was surprised. "Of course. I'll check."

Without an explanation to Bob she rested the phone on its table and went to the door where she opened it and peering out asked, " Inspector Corridge?" There was a grunt from outside. "Your mobile phone network appears to be down. There's a call for you in here."

She stepped aside to let a scowling Corridge through the door, but she remained there holding it open. Bob hadn't really believed the inspector took turns outside his room.

"Just checking with my men," he explained as he ambled across to the phone. For some reason Bob felt pleased the inspector felt he needed to justify his presence.

The phone was snatched up though. "Inspector Corridge." He listened. "Out of the question I've no WPCs available. I don't care how far she's come." A glance at Bob, then Kovich. A resigned, "Wait a minute. You're Lorraine Kovich, the lawyer from the States?"

"I am."

"How long you staying."

"I can go or I can stay. Your choice."

"Would you mind sitting in while Plant here has a visitor?"

"Of course not."

"Okay. Send her up," he said into the mouthpiece before putting the handset back in its cradle and striding for the door. Kovich raised her eyebrows and shrugged at Bob, but stopped closing the door as Corridge stuck his head back in. "I'm letting you see your wife. She's on her way up."

They cuddled like they hadn't seen each other for years. He smothered her head in kisses. She cried into his chest.

Emotions had been mixed as he waited for her to come up from reception. Corridge's statement had him up out of the chair and pacing the room like a caged lion. When he realised he was acting out a metaphor he stopped and went to the mini bar for a sparkling water.

Betrayal had been an underlying feeling and his tamed insecurity suggested that maybe this was a goodbye visit. Even while these thoughts came and went, then returned, there was a streak of certainty that said otherwise, that she missed him as much as he missed her.

And he'd been correct. She burst into tears the moment she set eyes on him. He'd forgotten how gorgeous she was. A touch overweight, gappy teeth, and tiny slits as eyes, but right then she was the best woman he'd seen in ages; yes, since the last time he'd seen her. "I'm sorry." "I love you." Said by both of them. Although he needn't have said the former, and lots of other things that brought a constant smile to Kovich's normally serious face. And the sort of things that get said after a row. Although in this case there had been none, just doubt.

Introductions over, Kovich offered to leave them on their own but Bob reminded her of the promise to Corridge and then asked her if she would explain to Karen what all this was about while they waited for Haversham to return. Karen was mesmerized by everything that Kovich told her, although much of it had already been on the news. Bob sensed her becoming more excited by the minute.

As Kovich told her of the hospital results Karen leant forward with a huge smile, grabbed his hands on his lap and blurted, "So you are an alien!" Her hug and kisses were totally unexpected. His surprise showed too. "I didn't tell you the real reason I moved to my parents. It was to be near the Riverside Institute."

"I've heard of them." Bob hadn't. Kovich's knowledge surprised him. "They're the only establishment in the world that deal with Harp medical problems. Mainly injuries." But she was frowning too.

"That's right!". Karen reminded Bob of a small child that's just been told she's going to Disneyland. "I've wanted us to have tests before." She looked guilty then. "I went to an alien integration seminar when you were away once. Soon after they're presence was announced. You didn't seem to want to go."

"I would have gone," he protested. She gave him an old fashioned look. "Mmm. Okay," he conceded.

"I found out about the Harp's immunity to diseases and it's played on my mind ever since. I don't know that either of us have had a day off sick, at least legitimately. So when you were arrested I took the opportunity to have myself tested." That hung in the air between them until Bob could stand it no longer. It seemed ages but was probably no more than a second.

"And?"

"I'm alien."

Kovich saw the look on Bob's face and said, "A hybrid? Like you, perhaps?" Bob stabbed a look at the lawyer. Suddenly realised that it didn't matter whether his wife was Harp, Demon or hybrid. While he was taking this in Kovich opened the door to a knock from Haversham who was breathless from hurrying back to give them his news.

"The Home Secretary has stepped in and contacted the Harp Council. They've come clean." He looked at Kovich. "There is a Demon Council. ANGER have made contact with them. Apparently there are Harp and Demons who disapprove of what the Harp Council have done in deceiving humans. They worked together." He allowed the full implications of that to sink in before he continued. "They interbred to produce children around the world. They knew that we could live side by side."

"They sacrificed their children to do this?" Kovich sounded incredulous.

"What better way of showing their commitment to integrate with humans? That they were prepared to allow their children to be brought up by humans."

They looked at each other as the phone rang. Kovich answered again. Ripply, she mouthed. "Fucking ace!" she exclaimed, which would have sounded odd had she been a Brit. Off the phone and excited she said, "Judge Prentice has thrown the case out and the Lord Chancellor is pushing for the Alien Act to be repelled and for aliens to have exactly the same rights as humans. The Riverside Institute is to lead a new research team looking into what humans can benefit from Harp/Demon physiology. I can get my client off death row. This calls for a drink."

"This doesn't change a thing." It was Corridge at the door. He'd not knocked; just used a master key. "There's still a crime to answer for. Martha Grimsey was raped." Bob felt himself go cold again. He and Karen still had their arms around each other.

"Technically yes..." Kovich answered. Everyone looked her way as she knocked back a shot of brandy straight from the mini bottle.

"What!" Bob's relief had seemed short lived.

"... Martha and Bob did meld," Bob's jaw dropped but another

"What" died in his head. "Nothing sexual in that Karen," Kovich assured her. "But it was Martha's partner, Brian, using Bob as a vehicle, who actually completed the meld. That way she didn't have to lie."

"How do you know this?" Corridge didn't look at all happy.

"Check with the Home Office. The case is closed. Bob is free."

"I will." He slammed the door but his odour remained to confuse Bob's senses.

"You're free to go Bob," Kovich told him. "And the world's going to be a different place from now on."

Karen eased the car up the ramp of the car park beneath the hotel and gave Bob a huge smile as she waited for the barrier to rise. He instinctively leaned over, gave her a kiss, said "I love you" — which she repeated to him — and rested his hand on her thigh. Before putting the car back into drive she squeezed his hand and gently accelerated onto Fleet Street.

As their car disappeared from his view Corridge emerged from behind a pillar and spoke into the headset, "Target moving west towards Ludgate Hill."

The Slip

Many of the short stories in this collection started their lives as one-thousand-word shorts which were later developed — though not all of them — into longer peaces. I'd take a theme, object or photo and see what my imagination conjured. **The Slip**, you might be surprised to know, stemmed from a photo of a shopping trolley.

The Slip

We left the body to be a problem in one world, the knife in another.

When one door closes, so the saying goes, another opens. I'd challenge that, and I don't so much mean opportunities as... well, doors. These are called shutters though, by their means of operation. Once you've stepped through one you can never go back again. Well, that's what Mary told me, and I had no reason to disbelieve her at the time.

A full explanation beforehand would have been preferred, but by then I was smitten, so I wasn't alone when I went through my first shutter, I was holding Mary's hand.

I used to walk a lot in those days. Loved being out in the fresh air, whatever time of year. Good exercise too. Time wasn't a consideration as I'd been out of work for two months. Excellent redundancy payout, so I'd not even tried to find new employment. The plan was to take it easy for six months or so.

My wife, Cassandra, had left me three years earlier, but I was happy on my own. Well, truth be told, I was emotionally drained by the whole experience and it was taking a while to heal.

Cassandra obviously found Trevor more interesting. Was I really as boring as she'd said? That question, rather than her infidelity, was what really ate at me, and I'd not wanted to test out my hang-ups in another relationship. Not just yet anyway.

I was walking through Markhall Woods, only a mile or so from my flat, off the pathways — it's more interesting that way. There's a musty smell of old wood and the fragrance of wild flowers that you don't often get on the rides. If you do it's usually overpowered by dog shit — why do they always do it on the paths? And there was my first shutter.

I was more curious than surprised. Wasn't used to seeing much metal amongst the trees, apart from the occasional bicycle frame or shopping trolley. But this was black metal. Smelt and looked like it was freshly oiled. Reminded me of the iris on my old Pentax, accept this was taller than me by about half a metre. While the thin outer, hexagonal, edge was dull, the blades — I was soon to find my camera analogy to be accurate — were mirror polished.

I reflected briefly on the reflection that stared back at me. Soft Nike walking boots in dark blue suede; brown combat-style corduroys, thick and proud to be cords; plain white cotton T-shirt with a hint of lycra to show off a reasonable physique, although I knew a band of fat had been forming over the last few months around my middle — too many glasses of red wine. Over that was an M&S fleece posing as a lumberjacket.

What let me down was the face. There were too many wrinkles for a man of thirty-four. I looked like a boxer. And I don't mean the athlete, I mean the breed of dog. I had jowls on jowls. Add to that a thin nose that, from profile, might kindly have been called Roman, you can see why I didn’t really like what I saw. I was never fooled by women telling me my face had character. My wife's leaving had simply exacerbated that feeling.

I pulled my thoughts back to the shutter. What really cried "alien" was it just seemed to hover about thirty centimetres off the ground. I walked around it. Tested underneath it with my foot, swearing as I caught the bottom of my calf on a sawn-off sapling — obviously some gypsies attempt at coppicing — then felt it gouge into my leg as I pulled away. I was so taken with the shutter though that I put it out of my mind immediately. Looking up I tried to see if the shutter was attached to the trees at the top, but I could see nothing supporting it. I gingerly pressed my finger against its side. It didn't move, not that I expected it to. If I had to describe its feel I'd say it reminded me of an old black stove, slightly rough. I hit the edge quite hard with the side of my hand expecting jarring pain but it gave like thick putty. When I drew my hand away quickly it remoulded itself. I tried again. Same result. I recalled a science show where they claimed some metals had a memory, but I couldn't remember if it was a spoof.

Then, without warning, the shutter opened. It wasn't this that startled me, but the young, dark-haired woman, who stepped through. Her face had a natural beauty, skin unblemished. She wore a pink ultra-short cardigan that finished just below her breasts. These were clearly firm yet unsupported. Her thin printed cotton dress, unbuttoned one more than seemed modest, swirled to the top of her calves. She most certainly didn't look alien.

"Hello," she said, brazen as you like. "My name's Mary." It was out of habit I took her outstretched hand, and was a little embarrassed when she didn't let go immediately. It was only when I realised she was waiting for my name, which I gave, that she let go.

"Clive, eh?" Then explained enthusiastically, with a husky voice that would have produced butterflies in any man's stomach, "I'm from another slip," as if I knew what she was talking about. When she saw my perplexed look she went on, "Ah, this slip must have come on line recently. I guess I'd better explain." So she did.

Most of you will probably be new to all this too, so I'll give you a quick resume as best I understand it. There are parallel worlds, called slips, and, given the right circumstances, you can move to a new slip through a shutter. Simple eh? Well, if you believed it. Did I? Would you have done? I just thought it was an illusion, so when she asked me to go through the open iris with her I agreed.

To be honest I was flattered that she'd asked me. At one point I thought, I wonder where they've hidden the cameras? But I needn't have been concerned.

So there we were in the same woods. Nothing had changed. Even the old rusting Tesco cart, half buried in the earth, was no different.

I couldn't make up my mind about her mental state, but she seemed quite rational as we walked back to my flat. Truth be told I was living out a fantasy right then. Meet a beautiful girl, take her home and shag her to bits. Sorry, a bit crudely put, but I think it summed me up right then. There was an inevitability that tantalised and excited.

"Why are you limping?"

I hadn't realised I was.

"Oh, I caught my calf on a stump just before I... met you." I was trying to picture that moment again in my mind, but her looks had erased any peripheral memories that might otherwise have lingered.

"Let me take a look."

I grabbed a nearby branch to steady myself and bent my knee. She gently took my shin in her hands, pushed up my cords and carefully pulled my sock away from the wound and over my boots.

"Looks quite nasty. I'll clean it up when we get back to yours." And she did.

That's how the physical contact started, and that's what gave me a second reason to remember that day. Funny how moments like that stay so high up in your pile of memories and other stuff goes straight to the bottom. But that's a day I'll cherish, and the day I was damned.

Afterwards we lay cuddled together in bed like we'd been inseparable for years. I really did believe my luck had changed, and that maybe my face did hold an attraction for some women. At that moment I think I loved her more than I've ever loved anyone else. You'll no doubt say it was just the sex, and god was it good, but I'd have done anything for her then. She told me some more about the shutters.

"I've been using them now for five or six years. The one you came through appeared that long ago. At least it did in this slip. I think they're like the branches of a tree. Yours must have been a new shoot. You," she hesitated; gave me a peck on the cheek. Her voice was hypnotic. "There was someone very much like you who took me through my first shutter. He claimed that Rogues set them up."

"Rogues?"

I stuffed my elbow in the pillow, rested my head in my hand. Marvelled again at how I had come to be in bed with such a beautiful woman.

"They're people who have escaped from the Sentinels." Her eyes were on mine. She shrugged. "He didn't know exactly who or what they were. But Rogues can set up new shutters. They're trained to do it when they're slaves."

I wondered again if she was a little crazy. I could live with that though, but why make up such an elaborate story? And the shutter *was* very strange.

"I've lived in this part of the town all my life," she said, as if it had some significance.

"So have I," I said, and then suddenly it did have significance. "But I'd certainly remember seeing you before."

Her smile said, "See?" and she searched my eyes for an answer. "You don't believe all this about the slips do you?"

"I believe in you. You're very, very real." We kissed and made love some more, well, quite a bit more as I remember.

"There was a fire at my house," she said later as we both stared at the ceiling, exhausted but feeling complete. At least I did. "When I was six."

I was half asleep but cogs started turning in my mind.

"There was a fire at one one four when I was about ten. The house was gutted, and the houses either side. The mother and daughter died in the fire."

"Not here. It didn't happen that way here."

I went along with her. I could check it out tomorrow. "And you're that girl who died in the fire in my slip?" I could feel myself drifting off to sleep. I was so relaxed.

"So it seems. What's your excuse for being able to move between slips so easily?" I wasn't really sure what she meant.

I humoured her. "It's the first slip I've been in. You know that." But I fell asleep before I heard her response imagining that my parents hadn't died in a car crash, that they had raised me instead of several pairs of foster parents. But I wasn't able to see their faces. I never could when I had those dreams. How could I be expected to? They'd died as I'd been born. Deft surgery had saved me. But not my mother. My father had died on impact.

A noise disturbed me. Someone was opening the front door. It wasn't Mary. Her arm was wrapped around me; her warmth snuggled into my back. Without thinking I swung myself out of bed and pulled on my old baggy cords. I rushed out the bedroom to confront the intruder, yelling, "Who's there? Who's there?" at the top of my voice.

There's no way I can explain what I felt when I came face to face with myself, especially as Mary had said it couldn't happen, two of you being in the same slip at the same time. I should have realised then what a scheming manipulative woman she was. But that's easy to say in hindsight.

So there I was looking at myself from the same perspective as others saw me. Okay, so the hair was slightly shorter and neater than mine, but it was me. It was also rather shocking to realise Mary's explanation wasn't a tall story after all.

Don't know how long we stared at each other. Wasn't until Mary came out of the bedroom looking more amused than surprised, that the other me just went crazy. Turns out that Mary had been shacked up with him for a couple of months.

If his feelings for her were anything like mine, and I'd only known her a few hours, I could sympathise with his anger. But sympathy I had no time to consider.

I think you can see what's coming. A fight was inevitable and, given that there should only be one of us in that slip, I had to make it me.

It's weird, feeling your hands on yourself, your fist in your face, your face in your fist, your body against your body, the pain you inflict, that is inflicted on you; intimate and knowing, a pain far more powerful, far more hurtful than it physically ever could be. I can feel it now. It's there all the time.

There'd been a moment when I caught sight of Mary looking mischievous. She had one of my big carving knives from the kitchen. But this had a blue handle; mine were red. Strange that it was only then, while fighting myself, that I noticed other little discrepancies. The hall carpet was green but the pattern was slightly different. The telephone table wasn't pine but light oak. The phone was Mini Mouse; mine was Mickey. Yet there had been a feeling of harmony as his life had finally slipped away. In that moment I realised that in my euphoria of being with Mary I'd failed to notice the imbalance my appearance in this slip had caused.

"This is your fault!" I screamed at her, feeling both satisfied and disappointed that she stepped back from me, looking bewildered at my outburst. "You knew this was wrong." I emphasised each word with a pointed finger jabbing at my chest, although I wasn't sure that my anger was allowing my words to come out coherently. "You said I couldn't co-exist. You said it was paradoxically impossible."

She gave a tentative smile. "Unless you come through a shutter touching someone else."

I let go of my fury then, as if the adrenalin had been flushed from my system. Nothing could reverse what had happened. She did try to comfort me though as I slipped to the floor. Guess I enjoyed the mothering too because I didn't push her away.

Mary helped me take the body out to the woods soon after midnight and on the second attempt we flopped it through the shutter. When it slammed shut we just stood there staring at it.

"It closes for two minutes as it turns one degree," she told me matter of fact. "Then it opens for two minutes." She had no idea how I felt. I think that night was the closest I have ever come to losing my mind. Perhaps insanity did win over for a while. The blade Mary handed me hadn't slipped in easily. It had ground against his ribs before I managed to ram it straight to the heart. His eyes had died staring at me in disbelief.

"Won't that attract people to the shutter in the other worlds?" I asked her. Her answer was to shrug and start unzipping my flies. "I can't!" I told her. "Not now. Not here."

We did. And that just compounded my guilt. I was weak, at least when it came to Mary.

Our relationship was doomed from then on, although I allowed myself to enjoy the physical side. I despised her, not for giving me cause to murder myself, but for ever having picked me in the first place. Yet beneath that I couldn't stop loving her.

There were moments, usually after lovemaking, when I let my barriers down and we conversed like any other couple still learning about each other.

"I don't think you will have much trouble finding another slip to go to," she said once as we lay side by side. "The accident you told me about suggests that your survival was unusual." I think she was trying to be kind. I'd found it very difficult to tell her about the death of my parents. They had been a mystery until I was fourteen. It was down to the paramedic who had saved me. He looked me up. It had played on his mind all that time. He wanted to see that I was okay, that his efforts had been worthwhile.

My father had been driving to hospital. Next to him had been my mother in the latter stages of labour. In his haste he had jumped a red light and a lorry had pushed them fifty metres along the street. A paramedic had been first on the scene; saw the situation and had made a quick decision. He'd agonized over whether saving me had been the right thing to do, though at the time he'd not known that neither of my parents had close family. I had been on my own.

"So there won't be many others like me to kill off," I snapped back.

"I hadn't intended it to end like that," was the closest she ever came to an apology.

I couldn't keep up with her sexual appetite. Maybe I would have if things had been different, but the trust that I had allowed myself to believe in during those first few fantastic hours had been damaged forever. She started going out on her own. After a while, I started following her.

She was going to the shutter, not seeing other men as I'd expected. My cancerous suspicions were zapped in seconds, only to be replaced by intense curiosity. From a distance I'd watch her leaning against a nearby tree. Every time the shutter opened she would walk across, put her head through and peer around.

During one of these walks she stepped through, disappearing from my sight. About a minute later she stepped back holding hands with... that's right, another me.

At the time I let myself imagine it was another Mary, but it was doubtful as the shutter hadn't closed before she came back.

She looked like the same Mary. And I looked like the same me, down to the clothes. Could I be sure it wasn't actually me? It crossed my mind this was a paradox; that I'd go back to my flat and this time end up the victim. I clutched my head. I'd had my hair cut! I'm still not convinced that the shutters aren't some kind of doorway in time as well as a transition point between slips, although I've since been assured they're not, but you can understand my imagination working overtime at that moment. Mary had witnessed the consequences of two Clives meeting. Did she want that to happen again? So when she'd gone I stepped through the shutter myself.

I've been trying to find a slip free of her for years now but we seem doomed to be together. Eternal love? More like eternal damnation. She seems bent on finding a version of me who will fulfil her needs, whatever they are.

Mary's not in every slip. Sometimes she has a different name.

Maybe I'm not called Clive in all the others either. Guess that's why she checked my name that first time. There's always a mutual fascination, or should that be infatuation? Two Marys have told me they've witnessed my temper, my ability to take life. I never dared ask if they'd encouraged it. I still wish it hadn't happened. I don't live a day without feeling that knife, hearing its journey through muscle and bone, into my heart, or see my dying eyes, or that look of malice in Mary's.

But I have a quest other than Mary now. I'm looking for a world where I don't exist but my parents, or at least a version of my parents, do. Wish me luck.

The Look

Dangerous Creatures, a spin off newsletter from the now defunct online magazine *Alternate Species*, that also featured a single peace of short fiction, was looking for a Valentine story for a February issue. Debbie Moorhouse, now an editor with *GUD* magazine, and who also later became one of my editors on *Murky Depths,* chose *The Look*.

The Look

She caught his eye from across the other side of the room. Hers were startling blue. The most attractive female at this opening-night party. By far the most attractive.

With the grace of a top catwalk model she seemed to melt through the crowd towards him. He stood still expectantly; senses burning a perfect image of her into his mind. Slim build, not too broad, yet most definitely woman. Breasts firm from the suggestive cleavage. Clothes heightening her sexuality; hiding and revealing just enough.

Around three hundred people filled the main hall of the gallery. Wine splashed across the polished whitewood floor as conversation became more animated and gestures less controlled; particularly amongst the gathering of artists whose works were being displayed for the first time and who were making the most of free drink. But the woman flowed through this sea of oblivion so unlike yet so reminiscent of Moses parting the waves. It was strange that few, if any, heads turned to watch her. How could they not fail to appreciate her beauty?

That calculated walk. One foot directly in front of the other, pelvis thrusting provocatively, shoulders slightly back accentuating her figure, arms swinging in perfect balance. She was still only a third of the way across the room. Almost as if she were moving in slow motion, the guests normal, his senses racing.

Her purposeful stare confirmed she was heading his way. Why him? Who was he after all? Answers were not sought. This woman dominated his mind. But then conversation from nearby began to invade this dominance. A word here and there distracted him.

Two of the artists from CybArtech, the group whose collaborative but highly controversial work with scientists and doctors had supposedly led to new and helpful discoveries in surgery, were explaining an exhibit to maybe a dozen captive guests. He filtered their voices out from the noisy chatter, letting the gist of the conversation reach into his heart. It could have wrenched his world apart, but a smile quivered the corner of his lips.

"... didn't see any point in making him a hunky male..."

"Although the brain we used was taken from a male," the other artist interjected.

"... just an ordinary guy leaning against a bar seemed to make it more poignant. After all, this piece is a pastiche of the stereotypical male of the late 20th century. A play on 'laddish' humour. You know, the gorgeous blond actually responds to an ordinary guy."

"It's what all guys still dream about, eh?"

Laughter rippled amongst both genders though they were clearly not convinced. However the two artists were too full of themselves and wine to notice.

"A closer look at the woman and you'll see she's virtually all silicon."

"Apart from the robotics of course, "added the second artist, "and the brain."

"It took us a year to get her to move as if in slow motion and the trajectory spot on. Here, watch the final bit."

They shuffled closer to their masterpiece, pulling their little audience with them. A discrete "Ordinary Guy" was stencilled on the side of the box representing the bar. Flat screens on the walls behind registered the brain's EEG patterns and showed what this part of the exhibit was experiencing.

"Drugs heighten this whole scenario. You can see the excitement he's sensing by the EEG."

"And drugs knock out his and her immediate memory when the whole pageant ends."

The bloke's right arm, no attempt made at giving it a human appearance, angled forward as the plastic woman at last reached him. There were mumbles of appreciation from the onlookers, as the artists had produced the epitome of womanly beauty, at least that currently recognised as such.

"I think this is yours?"

It was unexpected. No one had anticipated the woman would speak. The artists smiled as the manikin put something into the cup at the end of the robotic arm. There was a burst of real laughter, and a polite but appreciative round of applause, as the audience realised a single eye sat in the little cup.

"Not a real eye of course."

The first artist pointed at the monitors as they fizzled black, but some of the audience were already moving off to other exhibits.

"Now's when the anti-memory drug kicks in. When she moves back to the starting position."

The screens crackled back to life with "new" brain patterns. Both artists turned, as did the heads of the remaining group, to watch the manikin travel back across the gallery. As she settled into place the sound of a ratchet caused them to look back as the guy's robotic arm clicked back parallel to the floor. There followed a solid "clunk" as the trebuchet was released from its tension.

She caught his eye from across the other side of the room....

The Shed

The Shed appeared in the online magazine *Alternate Species*. Unfortunately it folded, although Debbie Moorhouse still maintains ownership.

The Shed

They had featured in his dreams ever since he could remember. Not that Barry worried about it. Yet something as mundane as a garden shed did seem a bit odd. It became a concern, however, when he developed a fascination for his next-door neighbour's. As far as he could remember it had been there since he had moved in with his wife some sixteen years earlier, yet it hadn't suffered the ravages of the English weather, still looked bright with its light stain, and still, when you walked along the path at the back of the gardens, smelt of newly sawn wood.

One evening he tentatively tested his observations with Sandra who knew everything about all the neighbours. She told him not to be so silly and turned back to watching her favourite soap. The frown that appeared on her brow a few minutes later he put down to the show.

Airing his thoughts seemed to purge Barry's mind of the problem, until two weeks later when he and Sandra were tidying the back garden.

He turned from his weeding to find her tottering on the upended lawn mower's metal grass catcher, peering over their neighbour's wall.

"What are you doing Sandy?"

She didn't react. At least not until he crept up behind her and grabbed her around the waist. She yelped in surprise, lost her balance as the bin twisted away from under her, and although Barry tried to support her, crashed onto the rockery with Barry taking the brunt of the fall. Apart from a few scrapes and grazes was okay. Sandra asked for confirmation as she used him as leverage to stand.

"Yep," he replied, legs sprawled out before him, letting the pain subside. "Are you?"

"Yes," almost without thought. Then she looked down at him with a frown. "What did you do that for?"

"I was just playing." She didn't look convinced. He wasn't one for messing about. "I wondered what you were looking at. You're not usually that nosy."

Ignoring his hint of sarcasm she squatted down and whispered, "I've been thinking about that shed."

Barry's face brightened considerably. Did Sandra actually believe what he'd said. "And?"

"You're right."

Barry gulped. He couldn't remember the last time she had admitted he was right about something. "What do you mean?" In case he'd heard wrong. The pain in his back had completely disappeared for the time being.

"That shed was here when we moved in, but it looks like it was only put up yesterday. Even the roofing felt looks brand new."

"You think so too? I haven't imagined it?"

"I've been keeping an eye on it since you mentioned it. No one's gone anywhere near it." He was getting up. She put out a hand to help him. Then she disappeared. No buzzing, no popping, no bright light. It was as though she had never been there at all.

"Sandra?" He hurried indoors. "Sandra?" he shouted, then doubtfully: "Sandra?"

He ran upstairs, and as he got to the top forgot why he was there. He often did that. He stood on the landing racking his brains. The house seemed very quiet. It was too big for one person really. Perhaps he ought to start looking for a small flat.

Jon steered himself along the miles of corridor that linked the Institute's many faculties. Unaided by the auto director, he amused himself by taking bends at breakneck speed, chancing that another techie like himself, or a maintenance robot, was not coming the other way. Encased as he was in the service car there was little chance of injury, but considerable damage could occur to both vehicles.

He was thirty floors below the ground-level control room. It could have been any one of forty. They all looked the same apart from ceiling-hung signs indicating the level and location of sub-section corridors where produce was stacked four high in groups of sixteen, accessible for maintenance from two sides. Yellow characters on a black background struggled to relieve the endless walls of stainless steel. They were invaluable in guiding Jon to pod Se9B, next on his maintenance schedule, given that he had the car's navigation switched off. Green writing on a white background indicated the way to “Hydroponics”, but Jon's security clearance didn't allow him access to the food-growing anex of the Institute. He often wondered if the techies there were also paraplegics.

At one of the larger intersections he puffed lightly into the semicircular control bar that resembled a bent mouth organ and watched the screen scroll. He knew which route to take, yet he still double-checked the map.

Content he was heading in the right direction he blew a little harder, then sucked the steering onto auto. The car smoothly accelerated into the corridor with yellow on blue signs. He was getting bored again.

Eyes closed. Gentle humming of motor. Rubber wheels gripping metal floor. Sensing every imperfection in the surface. There were few. He let the vehicle make its own decisions snapping his eyelids open occasionally when he felt a sudden direction change. Watched the guilty robot trundle past towing a single produce to the theatre in a capsule much like his own service car. No other techies around. Not that there were many.

Because of his disabilities Jon received substantial benefits and, as a techie, was considered one of the privileged class. But in a world where spare-part surgery, gene manipulation, and high-tech drugs meant life spans of three to four hundred years an allergy to anti-rejection medication was not an easy burden to bear. Everything he wanted was available to him but that was no real consolation when earlier surgery had left him almost completely paralysed. The irony was he now serviced the pods that kept the produce fresh for organ transplants, in an age where natural reproduction had almost ceased.

In a cynical mood, he would consider how convenient it was that the Institute always found a replacement techie when one died. It was always able to maintain a core group of techies. Few actually survived very long, partly due to the boredom, but mainly the psychological trauma of being unable to reap the rewards of their labours. Their service car was not only their life support but also their prison.

History was Jon's key to survival. He studied it passionately. It gave him an interest beyond the Institute and almost certainly stopped him from becoming another techie suicide. During the evening, parked up in his flat, which was little more than a compact garage to service the car and the life support system while the occupant slept, he would link into the net.

The previous evening he had spent hours virtualising the early days of the Institute while researching for a VR series he was making on The Conquest. A previous series he had produced — Dark Times — sold surprisingly well considering the craving for entertainment of a more adventurous nature; enough to pay back the Institute's support for the project, which he need not have done. But, being highly intelligent, Jon felt it offered him at least the illusion of being independent.

Last night's information had surprised him though. He had known about the ethical and religious rebellion during, and because of, the early expansion of the Institute, but not that thirty rebels had been captured and sentenced. Tonight he was planning to follow this lead and delve into the transcript of the trial.

His musings were forgotten as his useless body was suddenly pushed hard against the side of the padded seating as the car made an abrupt left turn towards pod Se9B.

Snow was falling as Barry turned the Ford into the cul-de-sac, lighting up their house sign "The Shed". Why they had chosen the name neither he nor his wife could say, but it felt right. The car took the slushy slope of the driveway easily. He was looking forward to putting his feet up in front of the television with a long bourbon on the rocks.

The garage door opened automatically as the drive levelled out but Sandra's 4x4 was already parked inside. He cut the engine by the front door, grabbed his briefcase and was under the porch quickly enough to avoid too many flakes finding their way down the back of his upturned collar.

Sandra met him just inside the door. Gave him a kiss that suggested she was in more than just a good mood and maybe he would not be putting his feet up after all; at least not in front of the telly. He could still do with the whiskey though. She was wearing his favourite long blue dress that showed off her slight but damn near perfect figure like nothing else could.

She took his hand; led him through to the lounge where the two lamps on the matching coffee tables at either end of the room gave a soft illumination. On the main low table in the centre of the room stood a bottle of champagne and two glasses.

"Open it," she told him gently.

She let go of his hand and lowered herself onto the sofa settling into a provocative pose. Right foot on the seat, long dress falling back over her right thigh.

He turned away with some difficulty, but could still see her clearly in the mirror above the open fire. She did little things like this sometimes. Right out of the blue. No anniversary, just a little thank you for being there.

It did not take him long to remove the foil and unwind the wire. He carefully eased the cork out, but let the pressure take it the final centimetre with a satisfying pop. He never found the cork. And never saw Sandra again. In fact when he looked in the mirror, for just a second, he was not quite certain who he was. Sandra never entered his thoughts again.

Another car shot from out of a side corridor sending Jon's car spinning momentarily out of control. It was that crazy techie woman Jard, similarly paralysed, and top of his list as being the next techie to commit suicide.

He puffed an expletive to her coms. Jard replied by reversing her car into his, leaving Jon with the sensation of a shattered body, which he savoured. His servicecar's life support could be heard working overtime to steady his body's functions.

Meeting other techies was rare but Jard, already out of sight, he knew by reputation. She would be back at the control centre and gone long before he arrived there. He was sure she was a hazard to the Institutes programme yet her work was as good as any other techie.

As his body calmed, his thoughts went back to pod Se9B. An hour ago he had been extracting tangled fingers from two adjacent produce. It was not the first time he had serviced this produce, and that was unusual given the millions within the Institute, but it was more significant than that.

During his investigations he had discovered that pod Se9B was not technically supporting produce at all, but was prison for 16 of the surviving 30 rebels. It had been a shock. A huge shock.

A company called Cybertronics, one of six that had formed the consortium, later to be known as the Institute, used the rebels to test prototype pods, and during this time 20 had escaped within the company's complex.

Such was the size of the building that it was twelve years before they were back in custody, and only then because they had given themselves up, though not before the death of four of them.

It remained a mystery how any of them survived. By delving deep into the archives Jon found video recordings of the interviews following their re-internment; watched fascinated as they were questioned. There was speculation that they were mentally unsound for each one of them said they had lived in the Shed.

As the power boat reduced speed it came back down in the water, chugging the last few hundred metres to the jetty like any other boat.

Although it was called a power-boat it was in reality a luxury yacht. Not huge at 100 foot but packed with everything a playboy millionaire could want. Except company.

Barry Phildyke jumped the closing gap to the pier and deftly tied the fore mooring. He was on and off again with the skill of a lone mariner and had the aft secure within another minute.

The jetty was deserted. A few tatty fishing boats bobbed with the rising tide and thumped their old car tyres against the ageing wood. Small waves slapped and slurped beneath him as he strolled easily towards the shore.

A dilapidated building, little more than a large wooden hut, known locally as the Shed, and virtually hidden by palms and tall grasses, excreted the latest rasta noise, spoiling the idyllic tropical island setting.

Barry peeled away his shades as he entered the familiar bar, marvelling, as always, at the quality of the establishment's sound system, particularly as the place looked certain to collapse at any moment.

She sat on a bar stool. Short hair cropped around her beautiful face. Stunned, Barry stopped dead.

Something was vaguely familiar about her. Not as if he had known her before, because there was no doubting that he would have remembered. He sensed a belonging between them.

She wore a long blue dress that slit from her thighs to show the best pair of legs he had seen in years. Despite no plunging neckline it was obvious her body was firm and she looked fit to the point of being sporty.

He took a stool beside her, elbow on the driftwood bar. A bourbon on the rocks seemed to appear on it from nowhere. He'd not seen a bartender, although the owner new his preferred tipple. Hers was a snowball by its look.

"Don't I know you?" she asked.

He realised they were the only customers. Music continued to test the compact Bose speakers tucked away in discrete nooks and crannies.

"Probably from a magazine," he answered. "I'm Barry Phildyke."

She took his offered hand. Held it firmer than most women he had met. He suddenly pulled away confused, aware he was close to his first ever premature ejaculation.

"I don't mean to offend," she said, tilting her head with a knowing smile, "but the name means nothing to me."

His normal composure was blasted by the physical chemistry between them and he felt unusually open to her gaze. Their eyes locked for a moment. It was Barry who looked away first, taking a long pull from the bourbon.

Although her half drunk glass was still on the bar, when he turned back she had gone.

"This can't go on!" Barry cried out flinging his glass across the room.

"Heh, man, don'do dat!" from the bartender who was drying glasses like he'd been there all the time.

"Where is she?"

"Who man?"

"Sandra!"

The name slapped around his brain like he had just remembered something so important it was going to change the world.

"Who?"

He looked at the man. He could have been anywhere between twenty and fifty. A Caribbean beach bum whose eyes said too much tetrahydrocannabinol and whose body needed one extra main meal a day.

"Who?" Barry mimicked, then to himself: "Who?"

The place no longer offered him the sanctuary he thought it would. He left and headed back to his lonely boat.

Jon's service car carried him through the dimness of the factory access routes. Bright light was detrimental to produce; high unlit ceilings giving the impression of a vast expanse rather than claustrophobia. Produce disappeared into the darkness around him. Cables and sustenance tubes curled around these modules like giant Medusas creating an even more eerie affect.

Despite his paralysis he had to smile at the shiver that ran through his body. The irony of his work was not lost on him.

Highly sophisticated equipment maintained produce at optimum. In contrast ivory white flesh shone through the tangled supply lines. Occasionally, as his car continued to its programmed destination, he would glimpse brown shrivelled specimen of failed produce. A sight more common of late.

He closed his eyes for a moment. Let his mind wander. But it never wandered far. Produce was forever foremost in a techie's thoughts.

It was difficult not to imagine produce as people just sleeping. In reality they were in a permanent coma, and had known no other state.

A quote from The Institute's manual of morals stated that: "Without external stimulation the brain is unable to produce any real thought patterns and dreaming is impossible." Jon had monitored real-time brain activity but was smart enough not to ask why it was often quite high, although he knew why at pod Se9B.

Bright light distracted him from his thoughts. He opened his eyes and squinted down the mile-long main corridor towards the lift.

Sandra continued to watch Barry by her side as his head rolled onto the opposite shoulder with the rocking of the train. He had been asleep for ten minutes or so but she could not take her eyes off him. She did not care that others in the carriage looked at her strangely. Barry was just so perfect, at least to her. She adored him. So? He had faults like any other person, in fact like any other man, but he was Barry.

She squeezed his hand, and got a gentle response back. One eye opened, in the way only he could: without a wrinkle; perfect muscle control. He screwed up his face this time and did his hunchback of Notra Dame routine, planting a big twisted kiss on her cheek.

"Baz!" She coloured just slightly as passengers shuffled uncomfortably in their seats around them.

"Sorry, Sandy." He smiled through eyes locked with hers long enough for her to feel that little tingle twenty years of marriage had still not stifled. He looked out the window, breaking the spell.

"Nearly there. Next stop," he said at the glass. She followed his gaze to an old engine shed she'd not noticed before. But she could see he was watching her reflection. They both smiled.

People started stirring around them, collecting their coats off the racks, shuffling paperwork into briefcases, closing and stashing away their laptops and palmtops, finishing their airwave conversations or continuing them as they headed for the doorway as the train slowed into the station.

Holding hands wasn't practical in the shoving for the door so Barry nodded her in front and followed behind.

Sandra took the short step down and moved away from the edge of the platform, away from the rushing commuters to wait.

And there she stood alone for five minutes, confused and frightened until at last the panic subsided and she could get on with her life. Although from that day on she always felt that there was something missing.

Jon experienced an excitement that would have bowled him over, had that been possible, and given him a hope that he barely dared to accept. Radical research had produced a solution to his body's rejection of produce tissue. The Institute claimed it had found a way to extract a person's personality and memories and programme the brain of his unique produce thereby bypassing the problem of rejection. Not only would he be whole again but he would have youth on his side as the produce would be twenty years old.

He was being offered to test this procedure free; had a day to decide before they made the same offer to another techie. Too late for Jard though. She had done as expected and managed to send her car down a lift shaft fifty years earlier. That would remain in Jon's memory. He'd been the first on the scene. So much blood from one person.

He was on his way back to the control centre with his mind made up. In twenty years, if the process worked, he would be leaving the Institute.

Sunlight slanted onto the stone floor of the kitchen as Sandra opened the old wooden door to the back garden. Farmyard smells rushed in to enhance yesterday's and the forever smell that lingered wherever you were in the house. And summertime certainly produced the most pungent aromas.

But above that on an entirely different aromatic level sizzled bacon and sausages and the knowledge that just-collected eggs, mushrooms and freshly-picked tomatoes would be on the plate too.

At this time of the morning the house awaited the joyous screams of three excited children who, although born on the farm, still found it a wondrous place of adventure.

As she turned to continue cooking breakfast she caught sight of Barry as he came out of the cow shed.

Despite the rubber Wellington boots turned over at the tops to show the beige fleece lining, baggy brown corduroys, and his mum's knitted grey jumper, misshapen like a short sack, he still carried himself with an air of confidence that gave some people the impression he was arrogant. Although he knew what he wanted out of life Barry was actually remarkably unsure of himself, but she guessed that was her secret.

For the last several years they had played out this very same scenario. He would rise before dawn and with Mascot, their scraggy mongrel, round up the small dairy herd into the sheds. While he milked the cows, with outdated but nevertheless functional equipment, she prepared the morning meal. By the time he had finished, the children, all under twelve, would be seated at the table and she would be loading the plates.

Something made her look back. She had glimpsed a dark figure dart away from Barry. But it must have been a trick of light because there was no one else in the yard.

Shouting and squabbling carried down from upstairs but Sandra smiled with such contentment that she surprised herself. What else could she want out of life? What was money when you had such happiness?

A chicken squawked across the doorway as she sensed Barry enter the kitchen. Mascot patted across the floor and sat down to watch her extract the sausages from the oven where, along with the bacon, they had been keeping hot.

She smiled as the children rushed into the kitchen and as she placed the steaming plates onto the table in front of them wondered why she had set five places. She sat and frowned at the empty seat until she could ignore the arguing children no longer.

Jon never liked "touching" the produce. It made him nauseous although there was no actual physical contact. But he had found a perverse attraction to this one. Well, actually there were two, and they had again become tangled together.

Se9B. It was the fourth time since starting work at The Institute, nearly two hundred years earlier, that he had been called out to these two particular produce.

Somehow, despite all the cables and tubes that virtually cocooned the produce, limbs slipped through and their appendages became locked together.

The Institute manuals explained this occurrence as a fluke of muscle spasm. It was rare but Jon made at least one journey each week to extricate these grips throughout the factory areas.

Automated schedules prioritised jobs by importance. During quieter periods low priority chores could be carried out.

Records told him he had visited this particular pod almost twenty years to the day that The Institute had made their offer. It could only be co-incidence that it was Se9B. Had it been such a short time ago? Apparently the spasm had reoccurred shortly after his last visit and had been automatically entered on the low priority list. Jon wondered if it was really worth carrying out if it had taken so long to require action. But if he wanted the new treatment, and he wanted that very much, it was necessary for him to carry out his duties. He had no reason to believe The Institute hadn't grown him a new body.

With little puffs and sucks on the controls he operated the service car's arms with the care only a trained techie could. Eventually he had moved away enough of the lines to not only see the "grip" but also the whole of the female produce. Sometimes he imagined being watched, but The Institute's security systems were totally secure. Hence there were no CCTV cameras anywhere that he could blame for his paranoid feelings.

Guilt was no longer an emotion he indulged, there being

nothing physically he could do; a paramount reason for allowing only robots and techies among the produce. Yet a feeling of intrusion invariably overcame him at moments like this.

The pod before him had been created around the time this section of The Institute complex had been built: Around five hundred years ago. Yet here lay what could have been a thirty-year-old woman. He pictured her as he'd seen her on the videos in the courtroom. The first time when she was seventeen, the next when she'd given herself up with the others, after surviving in the Institute for twelve years. Curiosity seldom got the better of him, but this time he actually studied her. The skin was not pure white, though very close. Neither was it grey. It looked cold, but he knew the temperature was maintained at optimum. He couldn't deny its beauty.

Its breasts had always impressed him. He looked closer; barely noticed the faint blue-grey lines that snaked down from around the areola like dried up mountain streams. Similar imperfections deltered off from around the stomach area. The ageing process was beginning, he surmised. But then the chances were this organ bank would still outlive him. But, he remembered, Se9B didn't cater for true produce. These "people" had actually had some kind of life before.

Delicately Jon prized the digits away from the other produce and was able to reposition the limbs alongside the bodies. A browning of the skin was noticeable where they had touched suggesting that perhaps they wouldn't outlast him after all.

His mind started wandering to his latest project "The Conquest" that followed on from his previous historical piece. By the time he had finished resetting the pod he was looking forward to a night of research.

Halfway back to central control Jon was unaware of something stirring near the produce he had just left. It flitted from shadow to shadow like an angry fly. Then another appeared from a dark hiding place, then another, until there were seven shapes moving in a seemingly random way. Eventually they converged and met at the pod Jon had just left. One of them cradled an infant in her arms.

They were of human origin. Naked, though comfortable in the constantly maintained temperature. Food was available to them through access to The Institute's hydroponics plant.

Feelings of reverence and love were clearly being projected at the two produce that Jon had just untangled and a casual observer would have noticed the similar facial characteristics between the produce and the figures grouped around them.

With much care and tenderness they once again threaded the arms of their parents through the tubes and cables that kept them in prime condition and linked their hands together; the youngest watching carefully to remember what to do when she was older and the techie came again to break the link.

The eldest amongst them, a female, began the procedure that would produce another of their kind in the not too distant future, if it worked. If not they would try again.

Soon they were disappearing back into the shadows; back to their home in one of the many inhabited service ducts. A home that they knew as, and their ancestors had named, the Shed.

Sandra was studying in the library when she saw him for the first time. She treasured her moments in the relative peace amongst the books, tapes and disks; being able to learn more in these brief hours than she ever could either at college or home.

But on catching sight of him she lost all concentration. He moved around the bookshelves with casual purpose clearly not interested in what he was seeing. She later found out that he had only come in to avoid a thunderstorm but had ended up buying The Shed's latest CD.

She left her cubicle piled high with paperwork and open text books to peruse the shelves near him. At one point he turned to her and smiled. For some reason she felt herself blush uncontrollably — and she never blushed!

It became obvious she was trailing him so she wasn't surprised or at all disappointed when he finally asked her why she was following him.

"Because you're the man I've been waiting for all my life," she blurted out, conscious of the cliché.

He studied her for a couple of minutes before answering, "And I don't think I could find any better myself"

Six months later Sandra and Barry married at the local registry office.

Ten years after The Institute had used their pioneering technology to "install" Jon's "essence" or memory into his new body he realised something was wrong, and then only for a split second.

He had met Amanda at the publicity launch of his new vid, over more than just a few cocktails, and they had hit it off right away. She had moved in with him shortly afterwards; having spent a happy two years sharing research for a vid she had been planning to make before they met.

One evening they were huddled around opposed terminals catching each others eyes over the top every five minutes or so. At one of these moments Jon sensed darkness rushing at him and the last thing that ever scorched his memory was Amanda's dismayed word: "Jon?" as he disappeared from her life.

The Leap

I'm not sure if steampunk was in my head when I wrote **The Leap** but I was certainly thinking the Victorian era. I was probably inspired by stories I read as a youngster, but can't recall any specific writer who could be the main influence.

The Leap

Upon waking it was clear things were different, as Lord Montague Haulmont had promised they would be; not least because I felt most invigorated. Yet, with this feeling of well being, there was an unfamiliar yearning. Were I to believe Monty's incredible hypothesis, then I could only assume I had travelled one hundred and fifty years into the future.

As to the others asleep in my bed, an attractive young woman on my left and an equally handsome young man on my right, I could only speculate on with horror and disgust, following the concoction I had taken the night before, what sordid acts I had been a party to.

My friend, Randolph Meesham, and I had arrived at Haulmont Manor by Hansom cab just before six o'clock the previous evening following receipt of a hastily written letter from Lord Haulmont, who we had not heard from for almost eighteen months.

Its appearance, rather than its content, instilled in me the urgency of the request. Monty was extremely fastidious with his handwriting. It was clear that he had rushed this note, for the quill had gouged great scratches into the parchment and the seal had been stamped with haste. Yet no expense had been spared in using the finest materials and maintaining time-honoured traditions.

Randolph, whose simple life I was somewhat envious of, met me at my mews house where we hailed the carriage. With an extra guinea promised, if our destination was reached before six, our cab driver lashed his horses into a thunderous gallop. Had it not been for our concerns for his lordship this would have given us great excitement.

We virtually flew over the cobbled streets of London, luckily without mishap, and into the country north west of the city towards Monty's very grand home. Set in four hundred acres of rolling pastures, it had once been hidden amidst prime oak woodland. In the past hundred years, and to add to the Haulmont fortunes, the trees had been felled to quench the appetite for timber of Her Majesty's Royal Navy.

During the journey, hanging onto whatever we could to avoid being thrown this way and that, we speculated on what it could be that had prompted Monty to call us at such short notice.

"Elizabeth believes he may have trouble with debtors," Randolph said above the clattering hooves. His wife, having access to rumours at her regular tea parties, could be guaranteed to have a view on most matters. "Monty has been spending quite frivolously recently, so she tells me, and there is someone in the business circles who, it is said, may be close to bankruptcy. Her friends think it could be him."

I knew, or could guess, who they were referring to. The opinions of Randolph's wife annoyed me beyond reason, even at the best of times. A man's business was his own. Money problems I had. My wife, Mary, had left me some sixteen months earlier for a wealthy entrepreneur whom she now lived with on his estate in India. I had been less than fortunate in both love and business, the latter being one of the causes of our breakup. My investments were not always well chosen and the risks had been high. But the returns could have been equally high and would have allowed me to pamper Mary's expensive tastes. Although I was probably better off without her, and her spending sprees, I had loved her dearly.

"Monty can afford to be frivolous," I eventually reminded him. "He has an immense fortune and Elizabeth has never had a good word to say about our dear friend."

"Perhaps she's a better judge of character than we are."

"How can you speak that way, Randolph? Monty has been a close companion since school. We know him better than anyone. He may be a bit of a philanderer but his friendship is worth more than cheap remarks."

Randolph looked down and fingered his cane. "Elizabeth didn't want me to come tonight. She thinks he's a bad influence."

"What's happened to the adventurous Randolph? You sound like a henpecked husband."

He looked up defiantly. "Maybe I enjoy her company more these days."

That comment felt like the twist of a knife. I had seen less and less of Randolph of late. Our regular weekly get-togethers at the Bamberry Club had dwindled to once a month. He would leave early, when once we would have indulged ourselves in the gaming room until the early hours of the morning. Still, it was more fun on my own. We were silent then for a few minutes as we neared our destination.

In the dark evening sky a full moon kept pace with us through the passing trees. I lifted up the collar on my overcoat to ward off a cold draft around my neck. The musty scent of wood and farm animals was a strangely uncomfortable change to the usual cloying smells of tobacco and spilt drink.

No sooner had I decided to break the silence, to say that the great house would soon come into view, than I found myself thrown into Randolph's lap as the coach came to an unexpected halt. Although my first thoughts were, highwaymen, we both burst into uncontrollable laughter, instantly dispelling the bad feeling between us.

"I'll not take you there, sirs," we heard the driver call out.

Haulmont Manor, which I always imagined had been built on the site of an ancient Norman keep, stood atop a terraced mound and was easy to see from the coach window. We were stunned, and the driver's reaction was understandable. Could this be why Monty had called us? The whole of the manor shimmered with a strange blue translucent hue, as if immersed in an enormous tank of phosphorescent liquid.

After several minutes arguing his case, but with a further guinea promised, our driver set the horses into a guarded trot, as they also had become somewhat skittish. More, I think, from the cabby's obvious feelings of unease than their own fear. Randolph and I, however, were fascinated by the sight.

"What can have happened?" Randolph muttered.

"Whatever it is, it isn't chaotic."

"Yes, it is only the manor that shines."

"We'll find out soon enough."

Lord Haulmont greeted us at the door in particularly fine spirits, at odds with his letter, while Henderson, his manservant, took our cases from the carriage. Up close the manor was bathed in light emanating from wooden troughs along the base of the walls filled with, what looked like, blue whipped jelly. Our white shirts seemed extraordinarily clean and bright with their own luminosity.

He put a finger to his lips, as if to say "don't ask yet", before giving us both an affectionate hug. A bemused look passed between Randolph and me, but I could see that my travelling companion had once more fallen under Monty's charm. His lordship had a regal presence and charismatic personality that you either loved or envied.

As we entered the book-lined study a swarthy, unshaven man of ill-kempt dress rose from one of four seats that were pulled up in a semicircle around a roaring fire.

"Thomas, Randolph, meet Professor Ferdinand Saltzberg. It is because of his marvellous inventions that I invited you here tonight."

"You made the manor glow!" Randolph blurted.

Surely that couldn't be the only reason we had been invited?

"I did indeed." The professor smiled at the remark. "His lordship has spoken well of you both." There was the slightest trace of an accent which, with the name, led me to think him of Austrian origin. We shook hands, I somewhat guardedly, but Randolph with no hesitation, before seating ourselves around the fire. Henderson poured us each a cognac.

It was clear that our host and his companion had already consumed several glassfuls. Though still bemused by our friend's invite we set about discussing All Hallows Eve and, although I had initially been disappointed at the additional company, soon warmed to the Professor, whose appearance belied a keen mind and sharp wit. I had forgotten it was the thirty-first day of October, which may well have exacerbated our cab driver's unease on seeing the strange glow about the building.

"Superstition is a response to ignorance," the professor argued. "And as to my luminous magma I'm still working on it. It's a blend of fluorite and other substances I'd rather not reveal just yet, which absorbs and stores daylight. This drains away as light after sunset and lasts about three hours."

"That's marvelous. What a discovery!" One could hardly recognise the Randolph who had languished in the cab, but I could not forget what he had said about our friendship.

Further debate ensued on possible scientific answers to what are generally considered occult mysteries.

"The mind is a powerful tool," the professor explained at one point. "Yet few people are able to tap into its potential. Some mystics can levitate by will alone."

"Come now, Ferdinand," I said, taking the liberty of using his first name. "You expect us to believe a statement like that? It's preposterous. It's mere trickery."

"Had I not seen it with my own eyes I too would respond as you have, but I spent five years studying in India and have truly witnessed levitation." He raised a hand to still any further protests. "You don't know me, so I am not offended that you don't take me at my word, but the image of a grown main rising up from the ground inspired me to dig deeper. My research has taken me to many foreign places and I believe that we can channel our minds to unbelievable feats. Have you not seen the recent papers by Alfred Russell Wallace on spiritualism? He has seen mediums rise up in their chairs and move around the room."

"So you believe in magic." It was a presumptuous statement from Randolph, rather than a question, but the professor remained calm.

"That depends on your definition, but I'm convinced that humans have a tremendous and untapped capability to achieve what some might consider impossible." He glanced at Monty. "I have been working on various means to enhance this power."

Despite his demeanor Professor Saltzberg was obviously a man of high intellect and charming to boot. Randolph seemed mesmerised by his powers of reasoning, though I remained a polite sceptic. Our conversation continued over an excellent dinner of venison, with fresh vegetables from a local farm. A perfectly chosen French wine was an exquisite accompaniment that surpassed any other red I had tasted and desert was followed by vintage port.

"My apologies for the subtle deceit to get you here," Monty said to us with barely a hint of a slur. "I hope you will not hold it against me."

"Certainly not," Randolph replied instantly, his hypocrisy irritating me further.

"You wrote it with the intention of making us feel you were in trouble," I said, with a hint of aggrievement in my tone. "You succeeded." Randolph nodded agreement, though in truth he was always a little slow in these matters. "But the meal and hospitality, not least your companionship, are always worth the visit and we haven't seen you for over a year."

"My apologies for neglecting you, my friends. We have had some good times together. I sometimes think it a shame that other relationships pull us apart." There seemed a genuine sadness inflected in his words.

"You have had more than your fair share of relationships Monty," I said with a wry grin. His reputation as a womaniser had done nothing to dissuade suitors yet he had always managed to avoid serious involvement, but I would have swapped places with him at the drop of a hat. "So you cannot put all the blame on us."

"I can't argue with that, Thomas." Then to Randolph: "How is your dear wife Elizabeth?"

Randolph proceeded to tell us that he was concerned about her social life. Gossip had become a fascination with her.

I thought, somewhat unkindly, that it was rubbing off on him.

"She'd rather go to a ladies evening than a fine restaurant with me," he complained.

"Get her pregnant," Monty told him with a smile. "Then you can hire an attractive young nanny to live in and look after your child. Elizabeth won't be so keen then to leave you at home."

Randolph blushed a little. "I'll not cheat on her, sir."

"Very admirable, Randolph, but cheating is a part of life. If you knew you could get away with it I'd wager you'd be tempted?" Monty had made the statement a question and caught Randolph off guard.

He stuttered a reply, avoiding my eyes because we had spoken of Baroness Ashby's daughter in the coach, with a little less proprietary than one would dare in public.

"I defy you to claim you'd stay chaste if you knew you could remain undiscovered Randolph. You'd be as likely to test the water as any other man."

"I... I..."

"... Would do exactly as Monty says. Remember our conversation on the way here."

Randolph looked so hurt I just burst out laughing.

"I'm sorry," I managed to say, "but you looked a picture of innocence."

"So, if you were still married to Mary, would you cheat on her," Randolph hit back.

I did not have to consider the question, "Knowing what I do of Mary, I'd not hesitate."

Randolph made to continue the argument but waved his hand as if to dismiss the whole thing.

"If you knew what the future held, would that make a difference?" Before either of us could answer Monty asked a second question, "Have either of you wondered what the future holds?"

Randolph, obviously pleased to change the subject, agreed that he had. I nodded too.

"What if you could go to the future and find out?"

"We are moving into the future all the time," answered Randolph with a smirk, which I put down to the drink. Even he would not normally have considered that a clever response.

Squashing this obvious comment with a stare that seemed to mirror my own thoughts, Monty turned back to me, "I mean travel a hundred and fifty years into the future, now, tonight."

"Why," I said, "If you'd not consumed so much alcohol I would think you serious."

"Oh, but I am serious Thomas. And for a man like yourself with huge and mounting gambling debts I'd think you'd jump at the chance."

His knowledge of my affairs shocked me as much as Randolph, who thought me a successful businessman. I was annoyed to have my private life aired in front of others and made that plainly so to Monty.

"But Thomas," he continued in that endearing yet condescending manner that could both rile and bring a smile, "you have no family to whom you are beholding. Not since Mary left you and your father disowned you."

"Listen to your friend," the professor insisted. How could I ignore him?

"Ferdinand has already told you of his research, but what he hasn't yet told you is that his theories work."

Did I see desperation in his eyes?

The professor interjected, "Monty has increased his family's wealth by shrewd investment, giving him the finances to also invest in, what some might call, risky enterprises. He has told me of your escapades together at college, so I am sure you know what he is capable of."

Randolph and I both nodded. I remembered the time, on a school trip to the coast, when a group of bullies had grabbed one of the weaker boy's lunches, contained, in what he cried, was a family heirloom. They had concealed it on an outcropping of rock, not revealing its whereabouts until the tide was coming in. Seeing how distraught the boy had been Monty waded into the rising water and somehow managed to swim back without being dashed against the rocks. If not for a mean and spiteful streak that occasionally surfaced, he almost certainly would have been the most popular boy at school. I often thought this other side of his personality was a calculated ploy to avoid just that.

"Monty and I met at a Metaphysical Research Institute convention in Edinburgh two years ago. I was pretty destitute by then, having spent my own modest fortune on travelling and research."

"... But I could see what no one else could."

"... And bought into my idea."

"It looks very pretty," Randolph agreed.

"You can be a complete fool sometimes!" Monty slammed his glass on the side table. "The magma is barely a toy compared to what we can achieve. I have travelled in time. I am from the future!"

Henderson's arrival in the room, to top up our glasses, seemed to deflate his lordship's outburst, and gave us a few stupefied moments to allow Monty's incredible statement to sink in.

As Henderson left the room the professor held up his hand, not only to quell any protests from us, but, I think, to calm Monty.

"I have indeed perfected what Monty suggests. But two days ago I wasn't sure. I will explain. We have been working together on combining a small dosage of electricity with my carefully selected blend of plant extracts and harmless chemicals to not only improve the chances of moving in time but also to enable a more precise time-line. My theory suggests that the mind can travel independently of the body. People have reported having outer-body experiences where they travel independently of their physical selves. I believe that many of us do this while asleep but have no recollection. Mystics train themselves to journey in the astral plane. I have taken that a step further with the use of science."

Pausing, he studied us for a moment, looked across at Monty who responded, "I will continue if you wish, Ferdinand."

The professor swirled his cognac in the glass, watching it settle, repeated the act before he looked up and spoke again, "I'll go on for now. When people travel free of their body they report retaining a link; a thread they can see as they travel. Have you ever woke with a sudden jerk, as if you'd missed a step?"

We nodded transfixed by Ferdinand's explanation.

"I believe that this thread is pulling back the mind into the body, a life-line so to speak. To travel across time however that thread needs to be severed and a new link created. It means swapping minds, a two-way transfer, the mind from the future moving back to our time, the mind from our time replacing the one in the future. Do you understand?"

"I think I understand what you are saying," I answered, looking across at Randolph who seemed lost for words. "Forgive me though if I find it hard to believe."

Ferdinand lifted up his arms in exasperation, as if to say, I told you so, to Monty, who responded. "Two nights ago I was on my own in this house. Ferdinand was away, on a research trip, and Henderson," he glanced quickly at the door, then seemed to change his mind about something, "wasn't here. I had allowed the nurse," once again he hesitated as if looking for the right word, then thought better of it. "I had allowed the nurse, who was in attendance, to visit her parents for a few hours. They live in Barnsford, the nearby village."

I watched him closely then. Monty was not normally a man of indecision. He seemed at that moment to be smaller, the spark reduced to a smoldering log. It was in this moment that belief suddenly took hold of me and with a flash of inpiration I saw where he was leading.

"How old are you, Monty?"

Randolph gave me a look that openly considered me stupid. Ferdinand and Monty, however, were looking at me with renewed hope.

"You've realised, Thomas?" Monty almost appeared grateful.

"You experimented on yourself. At least your younger self did. You were the nearest host when your younger mind travelled into the future, your own time."

"Five years in the future! Yes! Yes! You have it. My mind is five year's older than yours."

Two academics, for Monty's own passion had been the sciences, would not, I realise, lie about such a momentous concept. The silence was heavy with expectancy. Both Monty and the professor were staring at me, Randolph yet to realise he was merely here as a witness.

Monty spoke quietly, "I'll clear your debts, Thomas."

I, equally as quiet, "But I won't be here to appreciate it."

"A mind from the future will be in your body. Your old physical presence will still be here."

Randolph was speechless in his latent realisation.

"What's more I'll set up a trust fund for you that could earn considerable interest over the years."

For both Monty and the Professor the real experiment was the bringing back of someone from the future. I was just the means.

"You're actually contemplating this madness aren't you?" Randolph uttered with over-accentuated amazement. He did not hold his drink so well these days, I noticed. Our youthful camaraderie had grown thin with age. We were different people, had each gone very different ways in life. Monty had capitalised on his family assets. Randolph existed in a world of mediocrity.

I had failed in most everything: relationships, business, family and life in general. There was nothing left for me here. I did not feel despair though, I had never been one to wallow in that place. Monty was giving me an opportunity. My impetuous side took over, the one that usually led me to wager rather more than I could afford. I was in familiar territory.

"I'll do it."

Monty did not try to hide his joy. Grabbed my head and planted a kiss full on my lips.

Randolph protested briefly, sulked for a few minutes then allowed himself to face reality, realising with some relief, I think, that our friendship had run its course.

With my mind made up, Monty instructed us to follow him, dismissing Henderson for the night as we passed into the entrance hall. We all trooped behind as he took us down to a cathedral-like cellar that alone astonished both Randolph and myself in its sheer size. Monty had never brought us here before. From a narrow stairway at the top it opened out into a grand staircase. Oil lamps placed on waist-high wooden plinths gave adequate floor-level lighting to the massive hall. Beneath the plinths were glass jars filled with the same luminous substance that lit the outside walls. But they were dim and gave off little light.

"This house is built on the site of a great abbey," Monty told us in answer to my question, "hidden in the woods and partially buried for centuries until discovered by my great-grandfather. He completed what nature had started with a vision to create a magnificent cellar banqueting hall beneath a new and grand manor house. But at the opening party a candle stand was knocked over and the hanging drapes caught alight like dried grass. Nearly thirty guests and family died trying to escape up those stairs. Although there was no structural damage, my great-grandfather never held a party again. He was a broken man from that day. One of the fatalities had been my great- grandmother."

I could imagine what it must have been like, but Monty was

too enthusiastic about what was in the centre of this great hall to dwell on his ancestor's history.

"There, my friends. The Professor's greatest masterpiece."

I was disappointed. All I could see was a large single bed around which could be pulled curtains to give some privacy. To the side was a low round table and easy chairs. A coal stove sent blue smoke wisping up to be lost in the darkness of the high ceiling, pervading the hall with a not unpleasant smell of tar. Randolph coughed into a handkerchief disapprovingly.

Despite the convincing argument put forward by the Professor and Monty I was once more becoming skeptical of the whole affair. I wanted to believe it though, and it was belief they demanded.

"If you have any reservation," the Professor stressed, "then we cannot go ahead with this."

"While the Monty you see before you is thirty-two years old my mind is thirty-seven. I am from the future. I know this works." He glanced up the staircase where light escaped around the edges of the door. "Henderson has only a month to live. His heart gives out on the second of December. I can't even warn him."

He cut off Randolph's chortles of disbelief with a look that hinted at a desperation verging on madness. It concerned me more than anything else that evening.

"Can I change the next five years of my life? I've lived it once already. Will I be drawn back here in five year's time, endlessly going round in a time loop?"

"Who do I swap with?" I asked quickly, feeling Monty's words eating away at my resolve.

"I hoped you wouldn't ask. Explain," he said to Ferdinand, then flopped in the chair by the bed.

"We have to warn you that this experiment could go wrong. We will never know what happens to you in the future."

"But you know who inhabits my body when I'm gone don't you?"

The Professor hesitated, looking for consent, but Monty was

the one who answered. "Your husk remains in a coma for five years. We tend your body for that long. We have all the necessary equipment, nutrients and drugs to do that. At the instant you begin to come out of the coma my younger self swaps with my mind.I know the experiment works with drawing minds back into the past. I'm here," he emphasised by tapping his fingers on his head, "to prove it. Don't even try and imagine what that means. I have to wait five years to discover how successful this experiment is. But will my mind be whisked back here again and again? Will I relive the next five year's of my life for eternity?"

"But..."

"I said, don't think about it, Thomas. It will drive you mad. I know that I will never find out if the experiment works. Every time I am about to discover what the future will be like in one hundred and forty-five years time my thirty-two-year old self shifts me back five years. He never knows the torment I go through. It is he who discovers whose mind you have swapped with. He who finds out what the future holds."

Randolph and I looked at each other. The impossibilities and implications. And I? It was clear I could be committing suicide. But what of the host? Was I not committing some heinous crime? If I stayed I could end up in prison. At least this way I retained my family's honour.

"Get on with it," I said to the Professor.

"You can't do it, Thomas!" Randolph pleaded.

I gave Randolph a final uncharacteristic hug. He patted my back, more for his own comfort, I think, than mine. His eyes were imploring that I should not go through with it. There was still some affection there.

"Other than our friendship, I really do have nothing left here. This could be my only chance of a decent life. It is a gamble. But gambling is something I cannot resist." I smiled then with the irony.

"Don't do it, Thomas."

"Give my love to Elizabeth."

And so, I took the simple potion that Saltzberg handed to me. Clear and innocent looking, a strong bitter taste of almond.

"It will take about five minutes before you become drowsy. I suggest you use that time to undress and slip into that night shirt."

He closed the curtain and I did as he said, laid down and looked up into the cavernous darkness above. My head spun. More, I think, to do with the amount of drink I had consumed than the potion. This was it. Would I just wake from a coma in five years time? Or would I really wake up in the body of another man one hundred and fifty years in the future. My eyes snapped open, fighting the dizziness. Or even the body of a woman!

I could see shapes appearing. Above me, the darkness seemed to grow lighter. Then I realised my eyes were not playing tricks on me, some mechanical contraption was being lowered by hoist. No doubt to supply the electricity. Smoothly, steam hissing from here and there like a hydra breathing fire from its many heads, it came nearer.

Monty and Saltzberg slipped through the curtains pulling tubes and leads from the machinery in well rehearsed movements, even before it came to a halt, and began fixing them to connectors I had not seen before on the bed. Randolph had chosen not to see these final moments.

Monty caught me watching. "Your mind will find a new host within a five mile radius of here. The equipment will home in on a suitable mind." He put a firm hand on my shoulder. "You have made a wise decision. We all benefit."

That was the last thing I remembered from 1856 as the drug suddenly took me into oblivion.

I had drifted back to sleep [COMFORT] despite wondering about my unusual predicament [HUNGER] and drowsily watched as the woman stirred [LOVE] and pushed the covers down to her hips with a cat-like stretch and a satisfying sigh. She was without nightshirt, yet I had no feelings of arousal. Her breasts were full. I let out a cry, startling myself. She seemed surprised too. Her eyes lit up. She remembered something.

"Who wants his breakfast then?" She scooped me up. I snuggled up close [COMFORT]. Searched instinctively with my lips [HUNGER].

Monty would... Monty? [LOVE] Memory? Return? Baby? [COMFORT] Gender? [SECURITY] Future? [SATISFACTION]... [SLEEP].

Men

In my early twenties I discovered Edmund Cooper and collected and lapped up all his books. *Who Needs Men* stayed in my head. Published in paperback in 1974 it tells of a relationship between a woman exterminator and a man she has been sent to destroy in a future where women can reproduce without men's input. **Men** is my own take on a future where men aren't needed, but I wanted to give it a retro science-fiction 60's feel (don't ask me why).

Men

Amurra praised Allah as she pulled the trigger of the Kalashnikov, compassion in her aim. Her brother had begged, like only men could, for her not to take his life.

She felt cleansed then, as his blood, her family's blood, soaked into the desert sand. No more would males desecrate the holy religion, or her homeland. Her guilt had been appeased.

Behind her Hannifah, sometimes know as Jane, night-skinned Jane, smiled. She had plans for Amurra.

"I'll definitely have that one," Melissa confirmed, pointing to what she realized was probably the smallest.

"Certainly, Ms Du Bon," with an emphasis on the title and a smugness that said: *I knew you were going to buy the cheapest.* Melissa's cheeks burned instantly red.

To compound her feelings, the assistant marched without a word of instruction out of the freezer showroom, her bright blue pleated mini-skirt swirling above matching tights, leaving Melissa alone in the high-domed warehouse amidst almost two hundred specimen and a musty smell that pine disinfectant and bleach hadn't managed to mask.

While cost had certainly been a consideration, the image of 'Freddy' had instantly grabbed her attention on the salesroom monitor. Barely five pages into the catalogue and she'd asked for the advertised "close inspection".

Beside her, through the iced-up interior of the translucent bag, she could just make out a shape, posed like Rodin's 'The Thinker', matching the logo of Masculine ENterprizes. Not a lot to see really.

Although she had been warned not to touch anything she gently prodding the plastic, only to find it wasn't as rigid as expected. On making contact with the solid contents she drew her fingers back quickly with a little "Ooh!" of surprise.

"Ms Du Bon!" echoed from the PA. She snatched her hand away like a guilty child caught taking an extra biscuit. "Please make your way to the sales room where Ms Flemming will complete the transaction with you."

Melissa crunched her way back across the thick frosted tiles, past rows of bags, where pipes and cables coiled from the rear in a dreamy mist beneath the raised walkway. She shivered, not so much from the cold or that she was wearing a Gozen Sanada kimono in wafer-thin silk, but more from the thought of what she was passing through. Yet she was stoic in her decision and on reaching the salesroom door was convinced she was buying the right "xy".

Times had changed and, with the relaxing of male abolition laws, owning a man was, to some, a symbol of success. Licensed re-introduction in the Americas and Europe was monitored carefully, but Melissa had been shocked at how easily and quickly her application had been processed. Sure, there was still a lot of stigma about it — even a few fanatics of the old school who claimed to remember when men and women had actually been equal, both in law and in numbers, though Melissa doubted anyone could be that old — but it was still the general opinion that eradicating them had probably saved humanity from extinction. It wasn't so much because of their recorded aggression as to the diseases they spread. But all commercial males were gened free of known viruses.

Having dabbled with Catholicism, the Qabalah, and a brief spell with Wicca, not to mention a day school on Buddhism, she was aware that certain conflicts left questions unanswered. But she felt that was an inherent part of religions. As to the belief that men were the cause of wars and disease she retained an open mind. Surely one or two in a small community wouldn't do any harm?

When her old boss, Avril, had taken her to a high society party, she had seen her first ever male in the flesh although she had been unable to speak with him. As there had been a huge queue up to the host's bedroom, where he occasionally emerged amidst squeals of delight from those on the stairs, she had only caught a glimpse.

Although not considering herself a prude, she hadn't been comfortable with this flaunting of the law — sex with males was still a prisonable offence — so, to avoid the decadence of her boss's extremes, had left the party early. A police raid two hours later destroyed the career of two government ministers; discredited a princess of some obscure state; had brought the integrity of the city's Mayoress into disrepute; and, most importantly, given Melissa promotion several years earlier than she could have expected.

Not to seem mean she visited Avril as often as she could, not just to gain additional business knowledge, but to let her know the public relations company was still running successfully. But Holloway was not one of the best-kept prisons and Melissa always felt depressed for a few days afterwards.

Despite Ms Flemming being one of the oldest women Melissa had ever met she handled the paperwork remarkably quickly. It seemed totally out of place for a state of the art genetics company to employ someone who should have retired twenty years ago, but she thoroughly checked Melissa's license, even to the extent of using a huge magnifying glass to peer at the intricate background design.

"There's been a spate of forgeries recently," the old lady

explained. Wrinkles were fighting back successfully against face-lifts. Even the leather tan couldn't hide minute blue veins through tissue-thin skin, which the blue uniform seemed to accentuate. But she was pleasant nonetheless, and efficient.

Although pushing the budget, Melissa accepted the optional insurance and health care, tucking the policy into her shoulder bag and giving it an assuring pat. Ms Flemming's smile was equally assuring. Generally Melissa refused the hard sell of extended warranties and additional insurance cover but this was something that would last her a lifetime and Ms Flemming had put forward a good case.

Delivery was to be in thirty days. More than enough time to prepare her spare room in her city-limits condo. She had bought the place, almost on a whim, a week after taking over Avril's old office. A huge improvement on her old stuffy apartment, it looked out across the park that formed a ring around the office blocks and shopping malls that rose up above the trees little more than a mile away. At the end of her front garden a service road gave access to the other half dozen condominiums in the loop of Gavington Drive.

She drove home slowly trying not to grip the rubberised steering wheel too hard. Not because she was a particularly careful driver, although she did consider herself better than most, but because she was so excited at what she had done. Gyroscopic motors hummed smoothly keeping the Ford Wasp two-wheeler at its optimum.

It was the Executive Ghia model with plasma screen readout. This she currently had tuned to EBC News 24 where Beth Raid, immaculately dressed as ever, was interviewing a Moslem leader about Islamic protests against liberalist laws on males.

The picture cut to a webfeed that, two weeks earlier, had been headlines.

"Islamic countries," Beth was saying, as the recording reduced to the left corner of the screen, "have, in the past, shown a strong resistance to the complete abolition of males. Suddenly, with this killing, the Middle East and Asia have shown their solidarity with the rest of the world. Why is that?"

"Male clerics, shahs, princes and oil sheiks had used their wealth and power to retain their positions, abusing the very women who served them. They were confident that the changing world would not touch them. Religious texts, however, have been correctly re-interpreted to show that men were never meant to be a part of humanity. While we don't condone the recent shooting, it demonstrates the lengths at which the jihad will go to ensure men do not return to this world."

"So you do not approve of the recent relaxing of the laws in the West to allow licensed males..."

Melissa quickly changed the channel to MTV where the Rainbirds were gyrating to electrotrash. Already feeling guilty about how much she had spent, she didn't want to hear the argument against men, not right now.

A few minutes earlier, off a side road, near the main gates to Masculine ENterprizes, a Vauxhall Vole sat on its stabilisers. Inside, glancing at the monitor on the dashboard, an Arab woman carefully made notes on her pocket PC. She adjusted the angle of the camera in the nose of the Vole, and zoomed in as a small woman, dressed in an expensive silk kimono, pushed through the doors and, reaching up, dropped the shades that had been resting on her sugar-blond hair.

"Deluded," Amurra mumbled after a few minutes. She started the Vole, setting it to follow the Ford Wasp as it pulled away from MEN, the blond at the wheel.

The Arab girl would have been surprised, had she stayed there a few minutes longer, to see Jane, who she believed to be in New York, loitering against a nearby wall, watching as another daughter of the faith trekked up to the doors of MEN, a bulging haversack strapped to her back.

Wrapped up in her thoughts, unaware of others' machinations, daydreaming about her future, Melissa passed the corner mart near her home where couples were leaving with their bags of groceries. She could get her man to carry those for her. It would be even better if he could shop for her, but they weren't allowed out in public, not without an escort. He could wear a uniform with her name on. Then no one would have any doubt who he belonged to.

Stabilisers hissed onto the ground as she braked at a pedestrian crossing. A nurchery mother led a group of children across in front of her. They were all around five years old.

All but one white. A result of, the Mayoress, Winsom Karib's policy to increase the ratio of black babies born. Protests since then had rectified this imbalance but copper=skinned Melissa couldn't understand why everyone wasn't the same colour as her. It would make things so much simpler.

Some people actually cared for children, as well as doing their main job, but generally it was left to nurchery mothers to bring the youngsters up to adulthood. That was the preferred route, but it was recognised that the nurchery gene often came to the fore of its own accord. Melissa loved children but she knew she didn't have the necessary skills and, in any case, wouldn't want them to interfere in her own life.

Returning to her condo she looked into her spare room, her excitement suddenly tinged with doubt. "Don't be silly," she told herself as she pushed these thoughts to the back of her mind. On the telecast Beth Raid was still on the subject of males and it seemed clear her bias was against licensing.

"Scientific models have clearly shown that had the rampages of males been allowed to continue humankind would be on the verge of extinction." She hesitated, pressed a finger to her ear, "We are just getting reports of an explosion... ."

Melissa switched channels, deciding that she would find another news station when she had time. EBC wasn't for her anymore and for the next few weeks MTV greeted her as she entered.

Work proved to be manic. Melissa was tireless and dedicated, having little time to think during the day, but at night she lay in bed imagining what it would be like with a male in the house. She would hold dinner parties in her huge conservatory, with him cooking and serving, or barbeques on the condo's communal patio, and her man bringing them drinks into her lounge afterwards. It would be so much fun. And no one else had one in her neighbourhood.

One afternoon, a couple of days after her order, she was taking time out after a hectic meeting; chilling out in her favourite coffee house just down the street from her offices, enjoying the aromatic coffee smell as much as her own company.

"I bet you're getting one too!"

"What?" Startled, Melissa looked up from her magazine — printed and glossy — open to a double page spread for XYting, advertising premium males at budget prices. And they were too. She was kicking herself for not shopping around.

"A male." Her accent was barely noticeable. An Israeli perhaps. She stood over Melissa dressed in an Armani suite, a cappuccino spilling froth and chocolate shake down the sides of the mug, her head cocked to one side. "I'd go with Masculine ENterprizes though. They have a far better reputation than XYting."

"Really!" It was comforting news but she hadn't meant to sound so relieved. "Are you buying?" she asked quickly, confident by this woman's wardrobe that she was in a position to purchase a male.

"I'm still plucking up the courage to visit the warehouse...."

"I've been. I've ordered. I'm expecting delivery in three weeks." There, she'd done it again. Let her excitement get the better of her.

"Gosh. You are brave." The young woman was hovering with her coffee, looking awkward. "Have you any tips?"

"Would you like to join me?" she felt obliged to ask, although in truth cherished these little breaks from business and enjoyed being on her own.

"Do you mind?"

"Of course not. Take a seat."

"My name's Farasha." She said pulling up a chair opposite.

"Farasha Mehalel. I work at the Saudi embassy. I've only been here two weeks."

For Jew read Arab. Melissa found herself pumping a firm but delicate hand, and couldn't help smiling back at the grin on the face of the diplomat. That's what she had to be. With her expensive clothes she could be nothing else.

"Are you sure you don't mind me joining you? I know what it's like when you want to be on your own and someone intrudes."

Melissa closed her magazine. "To be honest I haven't really spoken to anyone recently." It dawned on her how lonely she was. Work generally took up a full day. If she wasn't catching up with e-mails and amending schedules on her laptop she was going to bed early in an attempt to recoup. This Arab was comfortable to be with. It certainly wasn't going to do her reputation any harm, rubbing shoulders with money.

"Lucky about the bomb."

"What?" Melissa frowned.

"The bomb? At Masculine ENterprizes?"

Melissa was shaking her head. A coldness seemed to spread from her stomach. She could see her plans being thwarted, disappointment overwhelm her.

"You don't know? Where have you been?" It was said with sympathetic amazement. "You've been too busy to listen to the news. I can see. A suicide bomber walked into Masculine ENterprizes down by Regents Park...."

"Oh Cock! That's where I was! That's where I ordered my man. No one's contacted me. Oh no!"

"Calm down, calm down. No one was injured. MI6 had been trailing her. They shot her before she had a chance to detonate it. They claim she was an Islamic radical."

Melissa had been fumbling in her bag for her cell phone, ready to give MEN a mouthful. Why hadn't they contacted her? But there had been no explosion. Freddy was okay. She let out a sigh. "They're blamed for everything these days. Those radicals. I'd say they've got more cause to be rid of males than the rest of us. They've only just become free of them, so I hear." Melissa suddenly realised she was talking to someone who might have sympathies with the terrorists.

Farasha must have noticed her expression. "Don't worry. Saudi Arabia was one of the first Arab countries to legislate on males. Both MEN and XYting have recently opened stores in Riyadh. We're very liberal you know."

"I just thought... I may have been talking out of turn."

"You're fine." Farasha leaned across and gently laid her hand over Melissa's. It was just a show of assurance but Melissa was shocked at her own reaction. She had never felt physical attraction to anyone before. Not even her old boss, Avril. There was a certainty in this new feeling. A earning she couldn't ignore. But she fought against it.

Avoiding eye contact she said, "I need another coffee. Would you like one?"

"No thank you I'm fine. Here, let me get it." She rose swiftly. "Black, two sugars?"

Startled, Melissa looked up then. Caught immediately by the deep brown eyes. Innocent. Unaware of Melissa's turmoil. It's just me, she thought. It's my problem. "How do you know?" Had this woman been studying here? Did she perhaps feel the same way after all?

Farasha touched the side of her nose with a finger. Winked. "Actually I took a calculated guess. You've two empty sachets in your saucer and the dregs don't suggest a trace of milk. My observations are usually pretty accurate."

"And you're right this time. Thanks." Melissa watched her walk up to the counter and immediately catch the eye of a waitress. She had that command, an authority to admire, came back straight away empty handed.

"They'll bring it over in a few minutes. So, what do you do?"

Melissa started to tell Farasha about her business, gradually relaxing as her enthusiasm took over. Farasha interjected occasionally with, "That's fantastic", "You've done so well", "That's what I'd have done", "Brilliant", "So good", "Really? Wow!". Then Farasha gave Melissa an insight into Arab life and admitted that she was a Natural.

"Really?" Melissa exclaimed, unable to hide her abhorrence. "I never realized that still went on." Her imagination went wild. Having a baby from sex with a male. How disgusting. Yet Farasha seemed clever and well-educated.

"Not anymore. Not in any of the Middle East countries. But it still happens in parts of Africa, I believe."

Melissa suddenly checked her watch. "Cock! I've a meeting in ten minutes. I'll have to go. She collected everything into her bag and got up to leave. Hesitated.

"I come in here often," Farasha assured her. "We'll no doubt meet again."

The next day Melissa visited Avril, who always looked stunning, even in her prison attire: khaki slacks, bright orange shirt and sensible black leather shoes that helped to top off her pixie-cropped black hair. Melissa had been dying to tell her she'd ordered a male. She knew Avril would approve but, perhaps, be a little jealous.

"You've what?"

Visitors and prisoners alike looked around at Avril's raised voice. They were seated opposite each other at rows of carefully placed tables in the large visitors' hall. Wardens around the edge of the room started moving warily along the walls to a point nearer them. Thankfully for Melissa her old boss didn't want to lose the only visitor she had, and leaned forward to repeat her exclamation as a whisper.

Melissa also kept her voice low, stuttering unusually. "I've bought a man," she repeated. "He's not been delivered yet. Got him from MEN."

"You?" exclaimed Avril. "You're the prudest Ms I know. What the cock do you want an xy for?"

Melissa blushed. She was flustered by the unexpected

response, but stood her ground. "He'll be a great asset at my dinner parties. I can get him to cook and serve dinner, he can serve the drinks."

Avril cut in sharply. She was only five years older than Melissa but she'd furthered her career by being with the right people at the right time. It wasn't luck. She'd made it an art. That is until she'd come unstuck at Lady Hertford's party. Her fondness for excesses in anything remotely addictive had finally been her downfall, but she was already plotting her return to the business world, had even mentioned it to Melissa during a previous visit. Men just didn't feature there at all.

"This isn't you, Melissa," who had a part to play in Avril's plans too. "You're not like me. You're sensible, upstanding. People respect your mediocrity. And that's a compliment," she added quickly. "Men have had their day. We truly don't need them. They're a drug that can be kicked. Their physical presence can take over your life. I speak from experience." She rolled up her left sleeve where her other excesses were apparent.

From the red and sore welts on her forearm it looked as if prison hadn't stopped her from pampering at least some of her addictions.

"But you never had a man." It wasn't a statement from Melissa, more a gloating accusation.

"Exactly! Why would I want a complication like that in my life?" Avril hissed, trying to make Melissa see the error she was making. "But where did you think I went every Tuesday lunchtime and Thursday afternoon?"

"To get your supply," replied Melissa smugly. Avril wasn't so clever after all. But she hadn't flinched or looked surprised about Melissa's knowledge.

"In a way yes. But it wasn't chemicals I craved. At least not artificial stimulants, this was debauchery."

Melissa cringed.

"I'm over that now Mel." Avril moved her hands onto Melissa's arm, which rested on the table between them, ignoring the sudden alertness of the guards at the periphery of her vision. Her grip was gentle but firm. "Men are our worst nightmare. We mustn't allow them back into society. The Moslems are right. Don't do this."

Melissa pulled her hands away angrily and stood up, skidding the plastic chair back against a neighbouring visitor. She leant over the table aggressively, uncharacteristically hissing her last words on the subject.

"Cock you, Avril. This is my life. You cocked yours up. Don't try to piss on mine."

She turned then and strutted out the room, surprised at her own assuredness. Avril called her name once from behind her but with little conviction. Melissa didn't think she'd be visiting the prison again.

She drove back to her condo slowly and thoughtfully, suddenly wondering what Freddy would do in her house all day while she was at work. Cock Avril for making her feel this way. If Farasha was going to have a male then it had to be okay. She was sensible, would have thought it through carefully.

Almost subconsciously she parked near the coffee shop where she'd met Farasha; was disappointed when the Arab wasn't there. More disappointed than she ought to be, she realised. Armed with a black coffee she slumped into a corner table seat and closed he eyes briefly to regain her composure.

"Hello again."

Melissa's eyes lit up as they opened, "Farasha! It's great to see you." She jumped up wanting to show her affection but awkwardly ended up cupping her own chin with her hands. "Ugh!"

"What's the matter?"

"Oh I've just visited my old boss in Holloway. That's a prison," she began to explain but Farasha was nodding. "She doesn't approve of men. But she's in prison for having sex with a male. How can she think like that."

"I've always said your Western ways are strange." But she was smiling.

"You make me feel good," Melissa blurted, feeling somehow reassured.

"I enjoy your company too."

Melissa looked at Farasha closely then, but she couldn't see what she wanted to see, not from those dark eyes, despite what the Arab had said.

"How long before your male arrives?" Farasha asked as she drew up a chair.

"A couple of weeks yet." She didn't really want to talk about Freddy at the moment. She didn't want to think about him at all.

"I've just ordered mine."

"Oh!" That threw her thoughts and emotions into turmoil. An assistant intruded. Laid a cappuccino in front of Farasha whose eyes never left Melissa's. "That's great."

"What's wrong, Melissa."

"Avril's making me doubt my decision." She wanted to add, "And this loan's going to take forever to pay." But she dare not admit that she wasn't quite so well-off as she acted. She didn't want to loose Farasha's friendship.

"It'll be the best thing you've ever done." Farasha rummaged in her bag. "Here, take a look at this. I've worked out a schedule for my male when I'm not at home. Look what he can do for you. You'll have loads of extra time. We could go out to a show or go clubbing."

"You'd want to do that with me?" Melissa beamed.

"When you've got your male," Farasha agreed. "You'll have more free time then."

"I'm going to arrange a party once he's settled in. I'd like you to come."

"I wouldn't want to miss that. What do you think of my schedule?"

Farasha completely changed Melissa's mood and by the time she left the café was once again on a high with expectancy.

What seemed like months, rather than weeks, later Melissa received a mail from MEN assuring her Freddy would be ready on the agreed day, which was the following Wednesday, between three and four in the afternoon. It advised she read through the manual before taking delivery. She returned a confirmation before bringing up the guidance notes that were hardly a manual.

It started: "Masculine ENterprizes promises this is a genuine male, produced with top quality genes to our highest standards. With proper care and attention the produce will last you your lifetime. Should this produce at any time become unsatisfactory Masculine ENterprizes agrees to remove it at the rate specified on the day of removal, payable on collection. If you have taken out the optional insurance you may use this at any time and collection will be free."

Familiar words. She'd read all this before at the showroom. As she pressed delete, her mind wandered back to the society party where she'd seen her first man. There had been something compelling about him, but she couldn't understand why so many women had stooped to use him for sexual gratification. How disgusting! And for Avril it had just been an additional fix.

Come Wednesday she could barely keep herself together, her excitement was so tiring, rescheduling two morning meetings and excusing herself at ten instead of waiting for lunchtime as she'd planned. Farasha wasn't answering her office number, the embassy reception didn't know where she was, and her mobile was on permanent voicemail. It looked as if she would have to take in Freddy on her own. Well, that's how it would have been, she told herself.

Inevitably the delivery was delayed. It was six o'clock that evening before her doorbell startled her to her feet.

She rushed to the door, hesitated. Stopped halfway. Took the final dozen strides with a practiced composure. Yet her fingers still lingered a moment on the handle. Not until she'd cleared her throat and flicked her hair back did she finally open the door.

"Ms Du Bon?" Somehow she expected the two techies from Masculine ENterprizes, in their bright blue coveralls and Thinker logos, to be the butch types. But Freddy's eyes were on their zipped-down cleavages and didn't even look up at Melissa as she stepped out beneath the porch.

"Horny one you've got here," with a wink from the taller girl. "In you go, Freddy." They pushed him gently forward and he looked Melissa in the eyes for the first time.

Melissa took a step back. "This isn't the man I ordered."

The shorter woman checked her clipboard. "Ms Du Bon? 1036 Gavington Drive?"

"That's my name and address but this isn't Freddy."

"That's my name, Ms," Freddy piped up with a leering grin, "At your service." Spittle dribbled from the corner of his mouth like a panting dog.

Melissa felt a terror inside she'd never felt before as Freddy brushed purposefully passed her. Avril's warning suddenly seemed tangible. Her stomach somersaulted and she saw her lifetime ahead as a nightmare. Without another thought she barged back into the hall to grab her bag, turned to find Freddy standing in front of her as she pulled out the insurance, easily finding the button with her thumb.

In that split second Farasha, on the roof of a nearby block of flats, pulled the trigger, her sights steady on the back of the head of the male that was being delivered to Melissa.

The tiny detonator implanted at the base of Freddy's skull, as insurance, imploded with a slight thump and, as he crumpled to the floor, the bullet meant for his head entered Melissa's throat and smashed her vertebrae severing her spinal cord.

Farasha gasped with dismay, watched through the telescopic sites as Melissa tumbled like a doll on top of the male. She had become a friend. No, more than that. "Fool," she whispered to herself, "the infidel deserved what she got."

"Amurra."

Farasha turned startled. Only one person new her real name. She also needed to vacate the area quickly.

"What are you doing here, Hannifah?"

"Cleansing."

Fashara realised too late that Hannifah's semi-automatic was pointed at her head. She barely heard the report.

"I've got her," Hannifah shouted as two more MI6 officers crashed through the rooftop door.

"Are you okay, Jane?" one of them called to Hannifah as they moved forward warily.

"I'm fine. She gave me no option. Check out the rest of the roof. I'll report in."

Headquarters wasn't her first call though. "Zafirah? It was perfection. The infidel woman died too."

On the other end of the line Beth Raid amended her script, just in time for her next up-to-the-minute report.

Adrift

Adrift assumes that warp drives aren't possble, but very fast ships are, and that finding another habital planet will take many generations. I had intended to make it a series of entries in a journal. It didn't quite happen that way...

Adrift

The quills are few. Six I count. Plucked from the colourful plumage of an exotic bird no doubt. But information on the creature has been lost in the databanks. Three years now since they failed. Extinct. Like the creature perhaps. The Technicati claim data isn't lost. What good is that if it can't be accessed? Our knowledge, our entertainment, our heritage all gone.

The dream comes regularly now. Even during the day in moments of meditation it comes. I dare not share it. I take a chance even here in my diary to mention it.

Myson sensed another presence at the door, aside from the silent protection officer, a constant presence. He dropped the pen awkwardly into the bottle of cleaning fluid, ignoring the pain in the joints of his fingers.

"Father?"

The voice of Switch, his youngest, strode in with a refreshing air of defiant youthfulness, ship-pale features radiating with excitement. His jet black hair and deep brown eyes were Bouchra's, his mother's.

"What brings you to the bridge?" The bridge. When was the last time it had actually been used to pilot the ship? There were thirty seats here, that many stations to control the vessel. None of them occupied now; the ship hurtling through space of its own volition. Before the Blight he had counted half a dozen people at their posts. But even then it had been little more than passing the time.

Switch's almost imperceptible bow pleased Myson. What a pity Hammer had to take the captain's line; even more so when his eldest had yet to show his leadership qualities. Switch had a natural way with people. Like his grandfather.

"Captain," Switch had remembered protocol this time, "the Magik have sensed we are nearing a planet."

A bunch of crackpot misfits were the Magik; blessed (or damned) with telekinesis, extrasensory perception and a whole lot more. Yet he allowed himself a little hope. He could do that one last time. He could do that for his favourite son. "Do they know how near?"

"The sound of the drives suggests the ship is slowing." — He'd noticed the change himself. — "Making a braking manoeuvre." — *Or the drive is dying*, Myson thought. — "But more than that. They sense life." — *And do they sense life in Section Thirty? They say not, that the banging and scratching is just the ships structure yielding and righting itself to the pressures. Their reassurances only damage their credibility.* "It takes six months to reach zero speed." — *And if we've not reached our destination, wherever that may be, what then?* And zero speed did not mean motionless, just a thirty-day orbit before accelerating off to the next planet.

"Sorry if I don't seem as enthusiastic as you, Switch."

"You still remember your father."

Myson treated it as a question, which it hadn't been. "Of course I do. I can still see him looking surprised as he materialised halfway through that terminal over there. Seconds before he died in agony. I can still hear the start of his cry of anguish. Cut off as the half of his body that the Magik had managed to bring up from planetside flowed across the instruments in a grotesque magma of severed organs and flesh. Yes, I remember your grandfather."

Myson controlled his urge to glance across at the terminal. If there was one thing in life that could rekindle his emotion it was memory.

Switch looked down ashamed, then raised his head defiantly. "We still sing of his exploits, of his bravery. Did he really lead expeditions to several planets?"

"He may have done. He never said." Myson could understand the sudden interest in his father, but it hurt that Switch hadn't questioned the bards before. "I remember only the once. The fatal once."

"This is the planet though. I can feel it." As he had done in a similar circumstance. The promised land, the Literati said. Their ancestors had given up their homeworld for this. "Who will lead the exploration?"

Traditionally a captain led the first expedition but forty years of star exposure and anti-cancer drugs did little for one's agility, both mental and physical. Myson wasn't going to insist. "Protocol says Hammer."

"I would be honoured if you chose me, Captain."

Myson admired his son's control. There was intense excitement underneath. Six months of waiting would soon kill that though. "I will consider my options."

Switch bowed and almost skipped from the bridge. Myson picked up the quill again.

My youngest son has requested to lead the expedition to establish the habitability of an approaching planet. I am obliged to choose Hammer my eldest son. It will almost certainly be the last time I see him. Once on the surface I see no means of his return. The transporter has only the power to work one way, even with the help of the Magik.

It had started again. While he was writing. Not echoing through the ship as one might expect but undulating within the very core till it vibrated through the floor you stood on or the chair on which you sat. It threatened to rattle your teeth if you didn't grit them hard. Each time it seemed to last longer; and the Technicati had even measured its length, but there was no pattern that even they could discern; and in patterns they were forever looking.

Myson lifted himself out of the captain's chair shortly after the vibrations abated feeling, in his knees and ankles, the dull persistent ache go up a notch on the pain scale. No doubt the armed guard would be making a mental note. The rest of his shift would hear about their captain's growing frailty later in the mess. Forcing himself to keep a composed expression he headed down to Section Thirty; a half hour's journey through the ship. He had been called again.

Had the council — once the crew — known of his dream they would have stripped him of the captaincy. They would most likely lock him away. That was the least they would do. Fear of another outbreak of the Blight might push them to execution. But what really made Myson so careful was the effect it could have on his sons.

It was not a problem reaching the welded entrance of the "ghost hold", as it had come to be known, although it had been stripped of its connotations somewhat by the lazy pronunciation to "gostold". The hand drawn maps even spelt it that way. Another mourner was already there so Myson remained in the lift lobby, his shadow lighting a cheroot from a bag of backy. He was of a mind to share but there were some traditions that needed to be upheld. Like not speaking to the guard, though he had broken that one before. Instead he watched the woman lay a bouquet of orchids fresh from the biofields onto the steal table that had been placed across the doors and which had almost become an alter. She made the sign of the cross before she stood up with the stiff-jointed awkwardness of his age group. It was Lola.

As she came towards him he lowered his eyes in respect, but she put a hand on his arm as she passed, squeezing gently. He glanced up at a sympathetic and knowing smile and nodded. Her eyes told him she had the dream too but he dared not hope that were true.

Section Thirty had been where the captain and crew's families had resided when he was eighteen, back when the last planet had been investigated, most likely when the Blight had been brought onto the ship.

For two years nothing unusual happened. His uncle, Candor, assumed temporary captaincy until Myson was twenty one. There had been no one else in the captain's line.

Candor had been the only member to transport back onto the ship alive, although he had lost most of his right arm in the process. It was the captain's job to maintain morale and, despite a loss of twenty lives from the expeditionary team, and the realisation that the planet was unsuitable, he had succeeded in focussing the ship's inhabitants on the next world. For two years. Then he disappeared.

Searches were carried out, analysis made, but to no avail. He was never found although the ship had maintained its integrity. No one had left.

From the start Myson's age went against him. Even now he hadn't the respect of all the guilds, even Securitti whose duty it was to guard the captain at all times, not that a captain had ever been attacked. It was a young protection officer who now stood at a respectable distance as Myson awkwardly knelt to pay his own respects to his family, but Bouchra in particular. Bouchra, barer of Hammer and Switch. Bouchra, who had barely time to be a mother before she was struck down by the Blight.

She had been a strong young woman, her family were mainly of the Magik, yet at the end of one day's shift she had entered their apartment shaking. Myson had gone to console her.

"What is it, Bouchra?"

She didn't answer immediately, shrugging off his embrace as she pushed passed to their sons' bedroom. At the doorway she faultered, seeming to consider something.

He thought he heard her whisper, "Kill me, Myson,"

but that couldn't have been correct so he asked her to repeat what she had said. She did not respond immediately, supporting herself for a moment on the metal door frame. Then: "Take the boys out of this section. The Juels family too. They're not infected. And Baba Moss if you can persuade him to leave his family. No more. Just them."

"What are you talking about?"

He went to hold her again. Her ice cold, "Don't touch me!" pierced his heart like a super frozen icicle. "Do it now while I can still control this."

"What are you talking about?" He felt stupid repeating the same question but he was stunned and emotionally wounded; it felt fatal too. A pain in his lower abdomen spiralled to excess, his chest felt tight and restricting. His vocal chords seemed paralysed. His love for Bouchra was very close to worship; they were a part of each other. Without her he couldn't survive. Irrational though this was, it dominated his thoughts. His cocky youthful approach to his captaincy was receiving its first knock of reality.

She turned to him then; hands on both sides of the frame for support, her face a twitching, a shocking blancmange of pulsating flesh. Myson stepped back impulsively. Her eyes, weeping blood, thrust from their sockets as she hissed through gritted teeth, "Myson, you must get the boys away from me and seal up this section. If you do it now the rest of the ship will stand a chance. Get Thomas from the Magik to create a barrier. I mean around the whole section. It has to be physical and metaphysical. You're the captain. You have to do this for the ship."

Her knees buckled then, but she snarled as he went to catch her; a clawed hand raked millimetres away from his face in warning. She shuddered to the floor; cocked her head sideways to leer up at him, yet he noticed the sadness in her bulging eyes.

"Myson, do it for me and the boys."

As if her words exorcised his mesmerism, he moved passed her into the bedroom, sensing her cringing against one side of the frame. First, he took a duvet off Hammer's bed and threw it over Bouchra. She gasped in surprise but did not complain. He lifted the boys onto either arm, struggled as their sleepy bodies adjusted to the new position.

Myson startled the guard in the corridor lighting another cheroot.

"Go to Mike Juels' apartment. Tell him he has to get his family out of this section immediately and not to tell anyone else."

"I'm sorry, sir I can't leave..."

"I'm the captain. Do it!"

"But..."

"Just fucking do it! Now!"

The guard flinched. Hesitated, then hurried off to do the captain's bidding. Myson hoped that Bouchra had just forgotten to include his shadow in her list of people affected.

He headed for the main lifts; kicked on Baba's door as he passed. Kicked again. Naomi answered. His practised composer almost failed him as he saw her new born baby nestled against a half-open flight shirt. She had been feeding him.

"Hi, Myson."

Too abruptly: "Where's Baba?"

"It's his shift on the bridge. What's the matter?" She looked from him to the boys, a head resting on either shoulder.

In his panic he had forgotten the roster. There had been no need to rouse Naomi, or alert her to any problems. She seemed normal though. Perhaps Bouchra was wrong. He forced a smile. "I wanted to remind him about the chess tournament. He'd promised the boys some lessons. I'll catch him on the bridge. Sorry to have bothered you. Goodnight."

Her eyes seemed to bore into his back as he turned and hurried along the corridor but her returned, "Goodnight," carried no tone of suspicion, confirmed by her adding, "See you and Bouchra at the banquet on Sevenday." His gut tightened again. He breathed deeply and let out a sigh. An answer was required but he was only able to gesture with his head, hoping that would be enough.

At the lifts he voice-activated a link to Thomas McDonnell, giving it a code red.

"Yes?" almost immediately.

"Get your strongest magi to Section Thirty now!"

"What..."

"We have to seal the section off. Now!" He cut the link to avoid explanation or argument. "Maintenance!" There was a moment's hesitation then Lyon appeared on the monitor.

"Captain."

"I need a crew down here *now* to seal Section Thirty."

"Evacuation's not sounded."

"And it mustn't be. I mean now!"

"It'll take..."

"Now!" He cut the link.

Hammer and Switch were stirring. He was relieved to see Lola Juels leading her family along the corridor; the officer taking up the rear, back peddling after them, his carbine unslung and ready, hopefully just a precautionary measure.

"Where's Brian?"

She seemed surprised that no one else was around. Her daughters May and Lavender, in their early teens, looking as bewildered as her mother. "He's just packing up a few things."

Myson scowled at the guard, who was saved from a verbal lashing by Lola's timely explanation, "He made it clear to us it was an order. But you know what Brian's like."

"Fuck."

"What?"

"Here, look after the boys."

She took them quizzically. "What is it?"

"I wish I knew."

The guard seemed ready to spray the corridor with lead. "If you're going to stay with me put the gun down." A shake of the head was all Myson received. "Come on then."

Despite the young guard's obvious fear and confusion Myson gave him a mental note of respect as the squeak of combat boots on the polished steel floor followed his sprint back into Section Thirty.

It took five minutes to return to his apartment. Across the floor the duvet still covered Bouchra but the putrefied stench was gagging. Ignoring the retching noises behind him Myson pinched his nose, breathed through his mouth and, with just a second's hesitation, strode across the room and yanked the bedding off the floor. Nothing. A cloud of dust hovered in the air briefly then seemed to be sucked from the apartment. Why had he come back here? What had he expected to find?

Myson tentatively stuck his head into the bedroom. 'Bouchra?' The guard's vomiting had turned to a coughing fit. He knew she had gone from him. But he had needed to be sure. At the same time it was necessary to be strong for the ship. The fucking ship. What was the point?

'Captain!' It was the muffled voice of Brian Juels that eventually kicked him into action. A heavy canvas haversack slung over his back filled the apartment doorway. Myson had not seen a bag since his father's fateful trip. They were stowed away for the time when the ship would be vacated. They represented freedom. To Myson they represented death.

Juels had a towel covering his mouth and nose. The stench was increasing. Myson controlled the impulse to gag, continuing to breathe through his mouth, but the sweet sickly odour of decay still made it hard to breathe.

"Get out of this section, now!"

"What the..."

"Just fucking go. Quick!" Myson pushed Juels ahead of him. "Run! I've ordered the section to be blocked off. They're doing it now."

Juels started jogging along the corridor.

Myson cut him off from asking any more question.

"Move it. I don't want to die because a fat-arsed wrestler was so unfit." As if to confirm the urgency the rattle of machine gun fire to their rear deafened them both and set Joel to sprinting in time to the sound of lethal ricochets. Myson, however, turned to help his guard. But what he saw froze him to the spot.

The young officer was down on one knee keeping a steady aim but he was no longer firing his carbine. Moving slowly towards them along the corridor was a swirling brown fog filled with flitting sooty shadows. It was unlikely bullets would harm it and the guard had conceded that point but he stayed where he was, his back just ten yards from Myson.

"Come on, man." Myson realised he had never known the names of the people who guarded him, had never appreciated what guarding the Captain meant. At just eighteen, he guessed, and two years younger than himself, the guard was prepared to lay down his life for the ship's leader. The look of terror in the young man's eyes as he turned and said, "Go, sir," was not forgotten easily, but Myson went. The eyes had also told him that the kid had already been affected by the fog which had hesitated as it reached him.

Myson ran without looking back but sensed that the fog, whatever it was, moved more swiftly than he ever could. It seemed unlikely he would make it. A steaming ochre mist was also forming in front of him but it barely stirred as he raced for the exit, bouncing off walls as he took corners too fast. It was ingrained in him, this route to and from his quarters. Left here. Straight on. Right here. Don't look back. His deck boots slid as he rounded the last corner. His right knee popped but he managed to stay upright. The doors leading to the lifts were in sight. Juels was trying to drag his bag through the half-closed shutters. He should have reached safety minutes ago. Maybe his tease about Brian's fitness had been nearer the truth than he realised.

"Hold the doors!" he heard someone shout, "It's the captain!"

But his legs seemed to be working in slow motion now. Why was he trying to reach the elevators? He was moving through a stream of golden honey. What was the rush?

"Myson!" He recognised the voice but the ochre mist

continued to thicken. The doorway was barely visible. "Feel us Myson! Join us!" It was the blackness that called him; reaching out its swirling tentacles of fog. "Don't fight us!" This time he recognised a voice. It was Thomas McDonnell's, not the hunters at his back, willing him to submit, to come to them. The Magik's metaphysical barrier was as effective against his own psyche as it was against the alien fog. Of course! Staggering forward he managed a glance behind. The fog was almost upon him. So close. There was no chance. A rhythm he had not felt before meandered between his feet, bubbling up through the treacle. An all encompassing feeling of love and unity filled his head with yellow incandescence. The ochre mist began to flicker and dance. Caressing flames spiralled around his body.

Tentative tendrils of fog snapped back to the main dark body of thickness, darting forward again and dowsing a flame here and there, failing gradually as the flames grew stronger. Myson felt no heat and knew in that moment that the flames where not physical and neither was the fog. "Captain! Captain! We have to close the door."

Myson let the flames wash over and through him, surprised that there was a sexual undertone to the experience. Or was it simply that of joining, of being one? Ecstasy was all encompassing until hands unceremoniously grabbed him and dragged him through the closing opening, scraping skin off his kicking shins. His back was cushioned somewhat by other bodies as he fell onto the floor in a tangle of limbs. Just before the shutters finally closed Myson could see the brown fog make a last attempt to breach the Magik's defences. A demonic shape loomed through the flames gripping Myson with a terror he never realised was possible. Its face was Bouchra's, but it wasn't. It was Satan himself, but it wasn't. It was so much more. Myson was its focus, as if it knew he was the figurehead of the ship. With an all encompassing fury it lunged through the flames to the closing gap. Myson flinched and cringed. The floor seemed to flow with an undulating wave as a mighty clang vibrated across the hallway.

Then for a few moments there was silence. It was the silence of anticipation, of breaths held, of hope.

Everyone's eyes were on the door. It was dented. Half a meter thick and dented! Full of adrenalin Myson's body started panting for air as he looked around. There were maybe thirty people in the hallway. Four were sitting up next to him where they had fallen pulling him through the doorway. How had they all reached here so quickly? It would have taken McDonnell forty minutes from the time he'd contacted him. At the most Myson had been ten minutes. But could the Magik have created the barrier so quickly. He doubted it. Had time passed more slowly for him? It seemed the most likely answer. There was apprehension on everyone's faces but McDonnel's confident and aged voice assured them the combination of the Magik's barrier and the ship's integrity would hold back whatever was in Section Thirty.

Myson limped over to him and took him to one side. "What's that in there, Thomas?"

"I was hoping you could answer that as you've been so close." They both kept their voices low.

"They... It took Bouchra. Most likely everyone else the same way. She just seemed to disintegrate. To..."

"Become one?"

It was not what Myson wanted to hear. To realise your love for someone was never going to be anymore than a memory hurt almost as much as the loss. Bouchra had been his strength. Now he had to find that from within himself. He was not sure if he could. At that moment he felt too young and vulnerable.

"Maybe."

"That's what we felt. We sensed only the one entity." McDonnell put a hand on Myson's shoulder then. An act of comfort from the much older man that Myson almost embraced, literally, but he merely exchange the look. "Sorry for your loss, Captain. Your quick thinking probably saved the ship."

It was Bouchra, he wanted to say. It was her strength, her resistance, to whatever it is that has taken her. But looking round he caught his sons huddled in a duvet with Lola. They were safe. Instead he returned the grip. "I'll recommend to the Crew you receive a commendation for this. I shouldn't have gone back. I should have co-ordinated the defence."

"You did. You gave your orders. We got on with it. You did the right thing."

Myson was not, and never would be, convinced of that. Why had he gone back?

He had watched his sons grow in the following years, helped by couples with their own children. In Switch he saw Bouchra all the time. Other woman tried to enter Myson's heart but none had succeeded, neither had the less scrupulous managed to bed him. Soon he would lose his sons.

One hundred and twenty days left until the first descent. I am finding it more and more difficult to write this log. Not so much because of my painful joints but because the preparations for the initial expedition are taking up much of my free time. What has pained me though is how Switch has taken my announcement that Hammer would lead the first team. I had no option. He has stopped joining me on my weekly walks in the biofields and only speaks to me when absolutely necessary. If he knew how much that hurt me.

The Magik have grown strong in the years since the Blight, but the entity has not weakened. Their daily rituals to maintain the barrier around Section Thirty have honed their skills. I am far more confident now in their ability to enhance the transporters' powers enough for us to energise twelve hundred people onto the surface. Certainly it seems likely an expeditionary team will be able to report the feasibility of the new planet to sustain us. Transporting them back onto the ship however still seems impossible although the Technicati are working closely with the Magik. I don't expect a positive result. But then I'm biased. If the ship actually maintained a stationary orbit there might be a chance. But it never does.

The dream where Bouchra embraces me then tears my heart out with a clawed hand can only be symbolic. The other dream still continues.

Descent Day is what Hammer has called the first expedition to the new planet's surface. Communication equipment has been upgraded and appears to be functioning well. There are one hundred days remaining. He has picked his team. Switch has stopped talking to his brother too. I should have chosen Switch. I know Hammer would have taken it better. But I was forced to follow tradition. The vibrations seem less frequent, the dream more real.

Amazing news. With eighty-three days remaining before the expedition a joint Technicati Literati work group have been able to extract some data from the old banks. They are working on the coding and hope to release the information they find within a week or two. My other dreams have changed. I am no longer fighting a demonic Bouchra I am embracing her. I am the woman, she the man. She enters me and I am one. We are one. Maybe I should never have remained celibate all these years.

Seventy-five days to D-Day. The Literati issued their document yesterday. I had very little sleep last night reading the report (though when I did sleep the dream was even more real than usual). It seems this data had been lost for hundreds of years. It is not the expected general information that was available to everyone back when the data banks could be accessed. It appears we were once part of a large fleet; in fact the agricultural section of that fleet, producing almost all its natural food. We wonder what became of that fleet. Was there conflict? Did the other ships find a planet but leave us to continue? There is much speculation and debate, but we now know why the biofields are so vast; to sustain twenty five thousand space travellers! That's what the data revealed yet it doesn't tell us the number of ships.

At least the discussions will take people's minds off the new planet.

👾👾👾

Hammer has relinquished his leadership of the landing party. His partner Mass, who would have been on the team too, is expecting their first child. I agreed it was not appropriate for them to be on the first expedition. Switch is so excited to lead the expedition that he has forgiven me for making my initial decision. A sign of his maturity and confirms his quality. I am ashamed to admit I had begun to doubt him the leader I always felt he could be. The pregnancy is also incredibly good news for the ship's morale as there has not been a conception for almost ten years and there were fears that we may have become sterile. Switch has sixty days to ensure the team is ready.

👾👾👾

D-Day is just five days away. Switch and his team are on standby.

This is my dream: I am a powerful and immortal god. A spiritual demon. I can destroy whole planets with pestilence and plague. I can consume whole races and absorb their knowledge or just obliterate them as if they had never existed. That is the power I have. Yet I am hungry for their knowledge. Without it I stagnate. I harvest races instead. Unable to experience anything in my state of non existence I wallow in the second-hand memories of those I consume. It is not in my interests to murder a race. I take one individual at a time savouring their life before moving on.

Over the years I have had time to analyse this dream. I concluded quite early on that the presence in Section Thirty is the being I dream of. I still question why the being chose to absorb so many in one violent moment. Perhaps it became intoxicated by human experiences. I am certain that during Bouchra's transition I absorbed some of her essence. Perhaps a part of that being's essence too. She never left me completely. Soon I will be with her. I will remain on the ship when the others leave.

👾👾👾

The planet has proved perfect. I showed the last entry to Hammer before he left with the final party to go planetside. He protested but realised this had been my intention for years. I don't know how long the Magik's barrier will hold without their rituals. At last I'll be with Bouchra again.

Infestation

I have to give a nod to Frank Herbert's *Green Brain*. Another book that stayed in my head. I haven't the obsession with drugs (or whatever he chose to call it for his stories) as Herbert did. I doubt I'd have written this if I hadn't read his book first.

Infestation

Craig saw her in the lobby of Earthlife Europe's Canary Wharf headquarters as he headed for the stairs to the underground car park. Who could miss her? She was stunningly beautiful. But it was the two security guards manhandling her from the building that caught his attention.

"Heh!" Adrenalin was still pumping from his recent meetings, one with government officials the other with the board. It was 8 pm by the time he left. The lift had been empty. He'd expected the same of the lobby.

"Heh! What's going on?"

Craig may have been an executive director of Earthlife, but building security was not his domain. A voice from behind reminded him of that, "We are handling this, Mr Shaw. There's no need to worry." The tone of security head Bob Cannon said much more.

Hesitation from the guards was enough for the woman though, who whipped her arms free from their grip, sprightly leapt the card-access gates and was into an open lift and thumbing the buttons before any of them could react. A cheeky smile and wave stayed with them as the doors slid shut.

"Wow!" Craig couldn't help but show his admiration. Who wouldn't have appreciated her agility, and what heterosexual male wouldn't have appreciated her perfect figure?

A weight seemed to lift from his shoulder and he smiled to himself. His outburst had reminded him of his thirteen-year-old nephew when he'd unwrapped the little box at Easter to find, not a chocolate egg, but a voucher for free flying lessons.

Ignoring a large bluebottle that circled his head Cannon barked orders into his mouthpiece. Craig noted the scowl in his direction, a look that radiated open contempt. They'd had disagreements before but he'd never realised that Cannon hated him so much. As a result of the meetings he was probably more receptive to hostile thoughts.

"Stay out of this," warned Cannon, waving away the fly, as Craig made to go back through the gates.

He stared out the security chief, though a swarm of, what was probably, midges had appeared in his peripheral vision over the gates. He shrugged and turned. It was Cannon's call, let him play it his way. As Craig pushed through the revolving doors he heard the scrunch of crushed earwigs as they scuttled across the marble floor beneath his feet.

Five minutes later he was driving his Ford out onto the dual carriageway, headlights attracting a multitude of moths, wipers on fast to clear splattered bodies.

He wondered if security had apprehended the woman yet. Could she be involved in some kind of counter-retaliation against Earthlife? Maybe from a company they had outed? Unlikely. But what other explanation? Something to do with Brian Stacks, MP for South Holland, and GM Ectrix perhaps? Though Craig didn't have conclusive proof, intelligence said that Stacks was considering taking "certain actions". Now there was something to consider.

Earthlife was the unofficial mouthpiece for several activist eco-organisations, Greenpeace and Friends of the Earth to name two; and had itself retained a covert operations division. While Craig was Chief Executive he still maintained his roll as Head of Intelligence exposing multi national companies that had overstepped the mark.

But it was in the former capacity that he met with ministers from the Conservation Agency and DEFRA. He and his colleague Patricia Knight had stood their ground.

"Even if we did withdraw our protest on the re-instatement of pesticides what good would that do to the vote on the Bill?" He had tried to sound convincing but was well aware of the clout a statement from Earthlife could carry amongst MP's on the fringe of their parties, and it was these that the four government officials around the table needed to influence. With such a slender majority they had to use every angle they could.

Baroness Wilson of Ashford cleared her throat. She was tall, slim, in her early fifties and had a voice made for a woman three times her size.

"Look along the river Craig." They all used first names here. "Look at the lights from the city. What do you see?"

Earthlife's boardroom was in one of the newest dockland tower blocks and had the perfect vista of London's city. All heads turned despite a discussion on the restricted view earlier. Swarms of insects had appeared during the last few days. Along the Thames, towards the London Eye just a few miles away, the lights were dull and shimmering.

"The papers say it's due to freak weather conditions," Craig stated, bringing everyone’s eyes back, not to him, but the bunch of midges that hovered beneath the light over the centre of the boardroom table like a translucent kebab block. Someone had been sent out to see if a local pharmacy still carried a stock of insect spray. Slim chance of that though.

"The tabloids," the Baroness corrected.

Craig ignored her interruption. "The Guardian blames the illegal use of chemical sprays in the vineyards of Kent. Just the sort of thing we have campaigned to stop."

"And you believe that?"

"We have to investigate it."

"And we wouldn't expect you to do otherwise." Lord Moreton

this time. "That's why the government contributes to Earthlife. You're a worthwhile cause."

And a way of obtaining votes from the greens, Craig thought cynically. Many on the board had fought against his dealings with the treasury, but it had enabled them to push ahead with additional projects; many of them he had sponsored himself.

"What's the real reason you want to allow the use of chemical pesticides?" It was Pat Knight's turn this time, an Earthlife traditionalist who had been, and was still, strongly against taking government money. She'd glanced across at Brian Stacks who, Craig had recently informed her, was in the pay of GM Ectrix, suppliers of fertilizer and insecticides to the GM crop industry, a heresy in itself. Her look didn't go unnoticed. Stacks fidgeted and looked for support from the others. "They were dangerous once. What's changed Brian?"

Craig had always liked her but their differences of opinion on funding meant there could never be a friendship between them. His ex-wife, Claire, had often mentioned his working relationship but that's all it had ever been.

Moreton replied without casting a look towards the Baroness, although Craig sensed he wanted to.

"Science has moved on. The new chemicals are based on naturally occurring enzymes carefully blended to..."

"Cut the crap Brian," Pat snapped. "We don't want the sales pitch. We won't budge on this."

Lord Moreton wasn't going to react kindly to that sort of remark. His opinion of himself far outweighed his abilities, but he was in a position of power, and that couldn't be forgotten. Craig felt the ominous throat clearing but their coup de grace came from the Baroness.

"We have been looking at the funding we give you."

"I knew it!" Pat glared at Craig. He glared back. Yet he had always feared it might come to this. It was the nature of the gamble he'd taken when negotiating with the treasury.

"We may be able to continue at the present levels," the Baroness lifted her glasses, feigned checking the papers in front of her beneath the thick rims, "but we need to put a good case forward."

"So you'll withdraw funding from Earthlife if we don't do as you want."

"I wouldn't put it quite like that, Patricia."

Craig cringed at the Baroness's arrogant tone. He had to step in again. "Look Irene, Pat, there's always a middle way let's talk about the options."

"That's it on the table I'm afraid," Lord Moreton cut in. Meanwhile both women looked on the verge of exploding.

Control was regained by the baroness first: "Our funding was never given carte blanche. No one offers anything without some kind of return."

An "I told you so" look from Pat hurt more than the decision he was going to have to make. "We will need to discuss this at board level." Nothing more than a formality, but he couldn't make the decision on his own. He didn't realise it was exactly what he would have to do.

"Of course," agreed Lord Moreton, "but we really do need a response by lunchtime tomorrow."

With that ultimatum hovering over them, Pat quickly arranged for the full board to convene, though she avoided Craig until the meeting. The debate was heated. Craig managed to swing several to his way of thinking, even convincing some that this was an opportunity to gain additional funding. Despite this the vote was split with the final decision being left to Craig as Chairman. To placate the traditionalists he told them he would consider the matter over night. He had been surprised at the strength of feeling. They didn't seem to grasp the importance of the funding and conveniently forgot the favourable lease he had negotiated for their government-owned offices. It was a forgone conclusion that he would vote to rescind Earthlife's protest on the reinstatement of pesticides but it was his duty to also assess the full affects of a reduced income on their projects.

Pat had completely blanked him after the meeting so he'd been unable to explain and convince her how important it was to retain government funding.

His thought of her drifted to wonder about his ex-wife, her infidelity, his lifelong commitment to the Earthlife cause, the main reason, he knew, for her unfaithfulness and their divorce. Playing squash and trying to keep his mid-forties body in shape hadn't helped either.

He'd not dated another woman these last eighteen months. No time, no opportunity, no inclination. Who'd want a man married to his work? And then his thoughts were back to the decision that he would have to make in the morning. His heart was with the traditionalists but the new projects were far too important to curtail. They said "no, we have to scale down our objectives, must maintain our integrity", but making one small concession wasn't going to destroy the world.

His car phone suddenly demanded to be answered. Never one to respond quickly — a discipline he had worked hard to maintain — he let it continue until just before his voicemail kicked in. "Shaw."

A moment's hesitation on the other end of the line. Enough for Craig to wonder how two moths had managed to infiltrate his car. They crawled across his windscreen, shaking their wings for balance as his system blasted cool air up into the car.

A reluctant response: "Cannon here. You'll have to come back sir." That stuck in his throat. "That woman. She's barricaded herself in your office. She'll only talk to you."

"I'll be there in twenty," and cut the phone. There was no need to embarrass or belittle Cannon unnecessarily. That wasn't Craig's way. That the woman had wanted to see him was a surprise, though he wasn't confident it was going to be pleasant. He reminded himself that the look, as the lift doors closed, had seemed good-natured enough. Allowing himself to wallow in brief fantasies of what to expect, he turned round the car at the next interchange

He kept his word. Was outside his office by his estimated time. Cannon was waiting for him with additional security, no doubt called in from other offices nearby.

"She left this outside." He handed Craig a note written in crude spidery writing. "She just wants to have some time alone with you. I have to recommend you don't go in there, sir. If she's crazy enough to break through security she could be dangerous." His facial expression implored him to do the opposite and that's what Craig had every intention of doing.

Cannon and the other guards moved away to the end of the corridor, the farthest point away they sensibly could be and still retain sight of his office door. Several flies were circling above their heads. Craig thought no more of it as his office door inched open and everything else went from his mind.

Her exquisite face peered from between the twin doors. A hand came out and beckoned him in.

Illuminated only by his desk lamp his office seemed bigger than usual. A couple of low cabinets were out of place. He was about to manoeuvre around them when she gestured for him to lock the door. He was intrigued rather than scared as he twisted the latch.

When he turned she was moving towards him unbuttoning her blouse.

"Now wait a minute." Fantasies were one thing....

But she was upon him, kissing him passionately. A split second of recoil before he responded likewise, any thoughts of who sent her or what diseases she might carry smothered by desire. Electric. Lips hypersensitive. An almost excruciating sensation, yet all the more exciting. Her tongue like an exposed triple A battery. Her body pressed against his, sending waves of desire from head to toe. This wasn't a dream. Amidst this rose the question, "Why me?"

But how could he resist? Doubts, fears wavered in and out. How could any man resist? Consequences meant nothing. Their clothes were discarded unbuttoned, torn off if that was the quickest way. The office carpet became their place of lust. Despite the passion she was surprisingly dry to his touch, and he nearly swallowed his prepared saliva when his fingers tasted of honey. What was he doing?

But nothing could detract from the pleasure as she mounted him. That same electric tingle of her flesh was wrought from within. Exquisite, and almost unbearable. Yes, this was worth everything.

Sexually, she took him beyond anything he had ever experienced. Teased and tempted him to orgasm. He'd had his fair share of relationships before he married Clare but this was different, unique. Back arched, hips thrust against hers, he finally climaxed. Breathless moments instantly brought back the questions. Who was she? Where was she from? How did she know him? Choose him? Regrets? No. Reservations? Perhaps.

Her weight shifted as she fluttered his lips with a gentle thanks. He managed a smile before he opened his eyes to a confusing vignette. Her head seemed to grow huge as the tickling sensation on his naked body became annoying. A shadowy ceiling could be seen through her fading face. Was he hallucinating? He was certainly out of breath and his heart was thumping loudly in his chest but not loud enough. Another sound began to invade his senses. The sound of swarming insects. They were everywhere, he realised, covering everything, crawling, flying, filling every space in his office. Thrashing widely with his arms he heard a scream, choked as he realised it came from his own throat, spat and retched to free himself of the creatures.

It wouldn't be long before they suffocated him. Squinting his eyes tight to stop the smaller creatures from blinding him he tried to make it to the door where he could hear Cannon banging his fists against it, shouting from outside for him to answer.

Then she was back. Standing between him and the door. Well, almost back. She was still reforming; flowing across the carpet like a waterfall in reverse, flying back like bullets to a magnet; struggling like bees in a hive — and he realised that some of them were bees — they were coming together again. And that beautiful face was the first part to finish the reconstruction, hovering above the metamorphing swarm. It betrayed no hostility. Sadness? Uncanny. So real, so... human.

Craig was still breathless and very confused. It was all a nightmare. Madness. Succubus came to mind. Insects couldn't do this. Unless somehow they had mutated. Even so, it was incredible. The effort and co-ordination to achieve what they had done was frightening in itself. What else was she, were they, capable of. He felt disgusted. Someone was barging the door. He managed to shout, "I'm okay." but wasn't entirely convinced he was, standing there naked. If they could work together like this, with such co-ordination, what might they be able to accomplish.

Then she spoke for the first time, a continuous rhythm of buzzing and clicks, yet clearly understandable.

"You are a good man. We can help you. You can help us. We can work together. We must."

His disgust ebbed somewhat. She — they had created a unique character — had certainly got his attention. A remarkable way of showing their unity, and that was frightening, yet they hadn't declared war. Far from it. They wanted to work with humans. Could he trust them? They had the power to literally supply that 'fly on the wall' that he'd always dreamed of. No bugging devices to be discovered. He remembered reading somewhere that there could be as many as seven million species of insects. Could they be trusted though? How far had they developed the traits of humans? But what a weapon. What else might they be capable of?

He smiled to himself at their resourcefulness, still shocked and amazed at what they had achieved. A shiver preceded his answer though, and a realisation that he would change his vote and support the traditionalists in the morning. They'd managed without government assistance before.

"Lets talk," he said.

Lust Deserts

I wrote **Lust Deserts** specifically for an Apex Digest competion. There needed to be some kind of come-upance at the end. It didn't cut it with their editors but hopefully it will with you.

Lust Deserts

"You're bewitched, Pasquale...."

"I am."

With a smile he usually reserved for young senioritas desperately trying to squeeze through the crowds to kiss his hand Cardinal O'Connell added, "She'll be your death."

"But what a way to go!"

Their laughter echoed through the corridors of the cardinal's ship, as did the clink of wine glasses. Guards of the Cohort Helvetica turned their heads, ufamiliar with the sounds of frivolity.

"Why choose just one though?" the cardinal asked as their laughter subsided. "Wikan are infamous for sharing men. Don't they prefer it?"

Governor Pasquale Zucco's intelligence appeared correct. It was the almost mythical sexploits of the women on Wika that had drawn his childhood friend, John O'Connell, to visit this planet. It was first on his tour. Zucco also knew that on leaving Rome the cardinal's ship compliment was short by ten people and he could take on additional staff whenever he chose. Did O'Connell's believe this would go unnoticed? What arrogance!

"Bodiece is enough for me. There's more to the Wikan than sex. They're a remarkable race."

"But they like to share?"

Was that a hint of desperation in O'Connell's voice? The cardinal was no fool but Zucco didn't dare think about the strings he'd had to pull within the Vatican Council to have Wika put on the schedule. With only twelve bishops on the whole planet it didn't warrant a visit from Rome.

"Very much so."

"They need educating. Promiscuity is wrong in the eyes of God."

"John, you old rascal. You surely haven't forgotten our youth." His friend stiffened, then relaxed. They'd not seen each other since Pasquale had accepted the position of Governor of Wika some five years earlier but, he reminded himself, in this outpost of the Catholic Federation the pope's envoy was "His Excellency". Caution was needed. "They work in groups of seven, but eventually form monogamous partnerships. Although not until the last of their group has found the right man."

"You mean you allowed Bodiece to continue group sex with other men?"

"Until Lolette found her man, yes."

"They are whores, Pasquale!"

"Then Wika is a world of whores. This is how their society works. Within this your bishops allow Catholicism to flourish."

"I will need to investigate this."

"It's all in my reports." Pasquale hesitated, decided that five years was a lifetime and being on board a Pope's ship several hundred miles from the planet's surface could be harmful to his health. "Your advisors haven't briefed you so well."

They had probably tried, but O'Connell had dismissed them; his passions raised enough to be blind to the other details. Despite their outward appearance, Wikan were unrelated to humans. That they craved human company was not in question, that sex played a predominant part of their lives was also fact although they couldn't interbreed. But had the Cardinal's advisors read between the lines of his earlier reports;

before Pasquale had regretted the hints? It would seem not, thankfully.

"How long is your stay?" Pasquale felt his audience coming to an end. He needed to know how long they had to maintain the planet's secret.

"I'm scheduled to be on Notore in a month. That should give me five days to visit all the Bishops and have some time to give the Wikans my blessing."

"They will look forward to that." Zucco guessed what his blessing would be.

With elegant grace, practiced no doubt in front of a mirror, Cardinal O'Connell rose from his seat. He was an imposing figure at six foot four inches. He gripped Zucco's hand, almost pulling the governor to his feet. Zucco tried to read His Excellency's expression and, though his eyes stayed the stare, there was nothing that he could take back to the Wika Council.

Despite their longstanding friendship Pasquale deemed it prudent to go down on one knee and make the sign of the cross. He felt the cardinal's gentle hand on the top of his head.

"Go with God's blessing."

The Governor of Wika didn't allowed himself to relax until he was on Wikan soil. The Pope's navy bristled with enough armament to vaporise his own ship in seconds. The Wikan crew had felt his apprehension. What would the Cardinal think of this primitive, yet enlightening, world? What would he do if he knew the humans here would eventually become Wikan? It would take years but it was happening gradually.

Wikan perpetuated love and harmony, but there were a few who reveled in hate and fear. While the majority of Wikan somehow managed to grow more beautiful and perfect the Tainted, as they'd been called, were been banished to an island on the other side of Wica. Thankfully they wouldn't be a threat to the universe.

Bodiece shifted into her human form as Zucco entered the hallway and allowed herself to be wrapped in his arms. At the beginning of their relationship he would have retched had he seen the transformation but now marveled at his ability to accept that the Wikan were neither human nor, specifically, female. Once you had tasted the delights of their hospitality however you were unlikely to leave. To have your dream woman giving you endless pleasure was totally addictive. And then there was the coven, where you could act out your own particular fantasy.

In a voice that still made his legs feel weak she whispered in his ear, "He has called for a group already." He pushed her at arms length. "Don't worry. We explained a new group would need to be formed and that could take several days."

"And he accepted that?"

"His secretary acknowledged it."

"He really is fascinated by the stories."

"You didn't warn him?" She laughed at his hurt look.

"How are you going to avoid sending a group? He will continue to make requests."

"But he cannot be open about it. He would be ruined if it became known."

"But he'd be ruined anyway. He'd not want to return to Earth. Just stay here as a sex slave like the rest of us."

"But don't you just love it?" She began to touch him in places and ways that no man could resist. And he didn't.

Later he lay naked looking up at the powder-blasted ceiling of their bedroom. Crumpled sheets snuggled uncomfortably between the cheeks of his buttocks but he was still too exhausted to bother turning onto his side and pulling them out.

Bodiece rolled over towards him; put a hand in front of his face. Black and green blisters began to fester on the ends of her fingers quickly forming into juicy grapes which Zucco sucked off one by one. He'd asked her once if she could produce any food he wanted, and without hesitation he'd watched horrified as the palm of her hand bubbled and pussed into a slice of roast beef complete with a thin spread of horseradish sauce.

She asked him what he was thinking. It was a game they played. Zucco was sure Wican could read minds. He hadn't consciously been thinking about anything. But he played the game.

"About this place. When was this city created?"

"About twenty years ago. When the first humans came here."

It was easy to forget the honeymoon period between humans and Wikan was still in progress. No one knew yet what the meeting of these two cultures would bring. Zucco was pretty sure it was the beginning of the end of human domination of the universe. It was inevitable that they would eventually meet a race that would challenge them; but as insidiously as the Wikan intended? And with wanton compliance?

"Why within the mountains?"

"It was easier to make use of the caves."

"And the earlier settlers just blasted extra spaces."

He sensed her nodding. Conforming to what he'd expect a human woman to do at that moment. That's what they could do. "We like being near the rock too."

He turned his head to her then. She was watching him. It was as if she'd told him something of significance but he couldn't see what it was. A smile disarmed him. "Lift up," she said. As he thrust his hips up obligingly she yanked the sheets from between his cheeks.

"That's better."

Once again she stopped him meditating, and his eventually cries of ecstasy were as loud as hers.

O'Connell fretted for days before his secretary finally had an answer that he wanted to hear. He'd visited the Bishops in the provinces within the first two days on a sleepless 48-hour schedule. Conservative crowds had exacerbated his mood. Where were the groping hands of nubile senoritas? Even the men lacked enthusiasm. He assumed the few women in the crowds were actually human but their preferences would have been elsewhere. He could have made his visits longer but he was impatient for a Wikan group and his aid was being fobbed off with excuses at every inquiry.

"I have sourced a group from one of the rural areas. It's totally unofficial though."

The cardinal let out a sigh. "Official? I hope none of your approaches have been official. Do I care? I'm not interested in how they were procured." His aid looked uncomfortable. "What is it?"

"They won't be able to reach the pick up site until just before we leave."

"So? We'll hire them as crew."

"Unseen?"

"Have you seen a Wikan that isn't absolutely beautiful?"

"That could be for our benefit...."

"You're always so pessimistic and careful."

"That's why you chose me." His secretary gave him a respectful bow.

O'Connell allowed himself a broad smile that would have frightened a child into wetting its pants. "But on this occasion I doubt it necessary. Have you heard any rumours of ugly or old Wikan?" He answered for his aid. "No you didn't. So don't worry yourself now."

On the last day of the cardinal's visit Zucco was surprised to find a unit of the Cohort Helvetica stationed outside the Governors Cavern. Instinct told him to turn and run, common sense allowed him to show his ID and gain access to an audience with His Excellency in his own office. Bizarre.

"Pasquale, how are you my friend."

This wasn't at all what he expected. O'Connell was in good spirits. He had a group! Bodiece had said nothing though. She would have known. Zucco was mystified. "Disappointed that you are leaving us so soon."

"I could only allow seven days of my schedule to Wika."

"I hope you have enjoyed the Wikan hospitality."

It was clear O'connell's visit was merely to see whether Zucco knew of his acquisition. He seemed satisfied.

"I am pleased I was able to come here. It shows that we have an interest in even our lowliest colonies." This said without the slightest intent to annoy or any realisation that it did. O'Connell was as doomed as the rest of humankind. "And it was good to see an old friend again." Zucco was privileged with a gentle hug that he awkwardly returned. "I felt it only right that I should come in person to say farewell." He gripped Zucco's shoulder as he tried to kneel. "No need Pasquale. I leave you as a friend not a superior."

Zucco felt neither, but it was important to maintain that impression. "I wish you well, John."

As soon as the Cardinal's lander blasted off Zucco searched out Bodiece. Eventually he went back to their home and waited there for her.

Why hadn't she told him that a group was joining the cardinal's ship? She'd always kept him informed in the past. Perhaps the Wikan had at last decided it was time to expand. It was inevitable but he'd expected to know of their plans. He chuckled to himself that he was resigned to such a momentous moment.

The wall shimmered near the doorway. A disgusting green and brown gunge began to slide down the rough hewn rock wall. A retching stench hit his nostrils before he had time to cover his nose. Bodiece was obviously in a hurry, she normally changed into her human form in the hallway.

"Pasquale, the Tainted have sent a group to the cardinal's ship. I've been to Kether."

"How did you get there and back in a day? It's on the other side of Wika."

"It doesn't matter. What can we do about stopping the cardinal?"

"It does matter. And the cardinal's ship is probably way out of range already." Zucco was smiling. It looked like the cardinal was going to pay the price of his sexual avarice. "So tell me your secret."

Bodiece still looked in a state of panic but she dipped her head in a show of shame. "The rock," she said, looking up at him then with her deep brown eyes swirling with seduction.

"Don't."

"Sorry. It just happens naturally." She sighed like any woman might, resigned to revealing her guilt. "We use the rock."

Zucco frowned.

"We travel through the rock. We need the Wikan rock. It's our lifeblood." He didn't know everything about Wikan and didn't think he could be shocked anymore, but he was surprised by this revelation. Then they weren't going to conquer the universe with free love. "The Tainted don't. They travel through metal. Get their life from metal."

"The ship?"

"And anything like it." She nodded.

"Oh my god. What has the Cardinal unleashed?"

👾👾👾

The Swiss guard commander looked uncomfortable.

"They're robed. I couldn't tell you what they look like. What do Wikan usually look like? Drop dead gorgeous."

The cardinal's secretary wasn't convinced but signalled for the doors to be opened anyway. Their quarters were empty.

"But I've been on guard here myself since we entered hyperspace!"

👾👾👾

Busily updating his journal, the first John O'Connell knew of the intruders was the smell of cooked engine oil. But it was the sucking noises that made him turn. Despite the locked door seven robed and hooded figures had entered his room. He didn't question their presence. This moment had been anticipated ever since he'd heard of Wika.

A muffled order came from the lead Wikan woman: "Take off your clothes."

John O'Connell quickly complied. He was an imposing figure even without his purple robes and was used to seeing the awe on the faces of the women he deflowered, though these were hidden beneath dark hoods.

"Take off your robes. Let me drown in your beauty."

The cackle of hag laughter greeted his comment and as they threw back their hoods and let their robes open O'Connell vomited. His legs crumpled as spasms of terror swept through him.

Somehow, though he was mesmerised as they came towards him, he managed a whisper, "No! God save us, no!"

They didn't hurry. His death was sadistically slow, as the others on the ship would be. Yet his decaying smile and occupied body would greet trillions in the years to come.

Sam

Sam was my first professional-paid story, appearing in the first issue of *Fiction*. No, not the American magazine *Fiction*. This was a science fiction, horror, fantasy mag that started in the UK in the middle of the first decade of this century. I received £120. Unfortunately, the publishers were a little niaive, though very optimistic and as far as I know it only lasted a couple of issues. They were surprised at how difficult it was to get a magazine into shops... Some things never change...

Sam

Sam wasn't after my soul. He was a vampire of consciousness. It took me a long while to find that out.

Do you admire people who are perpetually old, yet fitter than you'd expect someone of their age to be? Sam was one of them. He jogged most days — he called it running though — cycled at the weekend with the local cycling club, keeping up with the Audax specialists without breaking sweat; swam at least three times a week at Esporta, with a short upper-body workout first; and, on his

holidays, would walk some strenuous National trail or climb a notorious peak. He claimed to have conquered both Everest and K2 in the same year. I believed him too.

I was in the second, of several, foster homes when I met Sam for the first time. My foster father, I cynically called them all "dad", had taken me to watch my first soccer match: Bishop's Stortford versus Skelmersdale in the Amateur Cup.

I can still recall the smell from the muddy pitch — earth and trampled grass — and the stench of beer-tainted urine from a men's toilet by the grandstand. Dad was calling the referee all manner of names.

Stortford's ground was small; the pitch surrounded by rusty railings coated in layers of white paint that felt rough and left a smell of lead on your skin. If you put your hand out you could grab the linesman as he passed. I was concerned because the referee kept looking across at us and I wanted my dad to stop shouting at him. My fear was confirmed at half time when he came over to us.

"Is that your boy?" He nodded my way. It was unusual for an official to speak to the crowd.

By then I was hiding behind my dad, who defensively said, "Foster boy. Greg's his name." The referee was smiling, but it was much more than that. It seemed to reach out and enfold you in happiness. He didn't look as if he was going to create a scene.

"What's he, about eight?"

"Eight and a half. He's been with us since he was seven. Needs a bit more discipline though."

It was the most I ever heard that dad say without expletives. I was scrutinised by both as if I were some prize dog. I wasn't bad, true, but I was very naughty. I'd already vandalised my first telephone box, but not so as you'd notice; not until you used the phone. With a small penknife, relocated from Woolworth, I'd cut the wires to the microphone and screwed the mouthpiece back on.

"My lad would have been his age."

Tears began to well up in my eyes. His sadness, like his happiness, was compelling. My father sniffed loudly.

"Anyway," and the mood abruptly changed again. "Can I buy you a drink after the game?" Just like that. No formal introduction; a stranger asking my dad to join him for a drink.

"Yes, sure." My dad seemed surprised but pleased, glancing at the other supporters around with a look of importance. His shoulders suddenly squared and I swear he grew an inch taller.

Strange that I can remember the teams but not the score, nor the drink afterwards. Yet suddenly I had an Uncle Sam who would invite himself for Sunday dinner, bringing with him a feel-good glow. Aristocratic blood may well have coursed through his veins because, although he was two inches short of six feet, his bearing claimed otherwise. A slim, yet wiry build, and weathered, handsome face, only added to the allusion.

Following his visits, the house always seemed a little less cheerful than it had been before he arrived, as if he'd taken more than he brought. No one ever said as much though.

Somehow Sam managed to remain the surrogate uncle through another two foster families; taking me with him on short breaks during the school holidays. Trouble began catching up with me as I reached thirteen. I'd become cocky enough to believe I wasn't going to get caught. What made it worse was the old moped I'd stolen lacked decent brakes. When the policeman jumped out in front of me I just ploughed straight into him. Legging it home, not that I ever really considered any of them home, was not enough to avoid being apprehended. I'd been recognised. My fosterers washed their hands of me there and then. I did go to the hospital to apologise to the constable, but when I saw him with his leg up in traction I decided that maybe it wasn't such a good idea.

They'd taken me into custody, but Sam convinced them he could look after me and, though he never legally fostered me, I was his. Right then I didn't know what that meant. On reflection my rebelliousness had been merely a tool to get Sam to take me in. Doing exactly what he wanted.

His main home, Hallam Farm, was an assortment of rambling buildings far enough from town to feel remote, though he still rented a two-bedroomed house that we used during the week, a short walk from school.

Somehow Sam moulded my inquisitive nature into a quest for knowledge and, unlike any school teacher I'd known, showed me how to learn. It was exciting, enlightening and proved that hard work could be very rewarding.

He'd often take me to the farm straight from school — I was getting "A"s in most subjects by then — to finish off his work in one of the barns, leaving me to explore, before we returned to the town house. As a teenager I never asked him what he did. Maybe I was afraid to find out.

I made it to university reading Psychology, Cambridge in fact, with a fat grant, going home to the Rest whenever I could. I captained the rugby and cricket teams — soccer was for the working class, and, of course, it reminded me of my past — usually won the cross country, but was disappointed when I didn't make the boat crew. That taught me a lesson about reality. I'd pretty much thought I was the best. I remembered the moped then.

On my twenty-first birthday Sam held a party for me in one of the outbuildings. There were maybe a dozen of my friends from university, the rest were neighbours: farmers and country gentry. It was to increase my circle of friends threefold. But I'll never forget that weekend for another reason. The next day Sam showed me his workshop for the first time.

It was a strange mixture of science and culture. A creative smell of turpentine and oil paint dominated the senses on entering. Paintings were stacked haphazardly against the walls. Unfinished works sat on easels as if a class had just left for the day. Wood and stone carvings sat on plinths, some appearing complete, others just started. Ceramics covered shelves in one corner and an open kiln still gave off warmth from a recent firing. But, in a back room, Sam's latest medium was electronics; computers to be precise. In those days a Sinclair ZX81 was the best you could own at home, but Sam had rigged up something that was way ahead of its time.

Looking like a huge fly's eye, a television screen, devoid of casing, thrust out from a wall bracket, revealing the tube and cables. An electric typewriter had been equally vandalised and was linked by further cables to a cupboard, which, when he opened it revealed a myriad of wires, solder and connectors.

"What do you think?" It was asked, without a hint of pride, after he'd shown me, on the colour screen, a database of his works of art, his creations that sat in the main part of the barn. They had been photographed and categorised with detailed descriptions. "And look at this," before I had a chance to answer.

Up on the screen another picture formed. It was a scanned

image of what resembled a da Vinci drawing, but not one I'd seen before.

"It's an anti-gravity sleigh." He pressed return on the keyboard. "This is a detail of a cryogenic chamber for deep space travel." And again. "This is a quantum entanglement drive." He saw me frown, added: "Sort of a time machine."

"Science fiction," I stated.

He tapped a key. The screen went black. He turned to me.

"What did you see, Gregg?"

"Plans of strange inventions in the style of Leonardo da Vinci. If not for the subject matter they could have been genuine."

"They are genuine, but I held them back. The world wasn't ready for them. Not that they were ready for the ones I did divulge." Sam had a sense of humour, but he looked deadly serious.

"What are you saying?"

"'Figure it out," he hesitated, "please." If he'd knelt down, begged me to give him the answer he wanted to hear, it wouldn't have felt any less than that last word. I realised it was important, but I was young. I heard but didn't listen.

"You say they're genuine da Vinci's?"

"They're genuine." A bird in the rafters allowed me to glance away from his scrutinizing stare.

"They'd be worth thousands." I watched a pigeon fluttering in panic then fall dead to the floor.

Sam was still watching me. "Priceless."

"How did you get hold of them?" The body was still. What had happened to it?

"I didn't 'get hold of them'. I kept them. The world wasn't ready then. It isn't ready now. Are you ready, Gregg?"

His tone had my attention. "What do you mean?"

"Have you ever wondered why I took you in?" I thought about that for a while; shook my head. It surprised me, I think, more than Sam. "Have you ever thought to ponder on comments about our likeness?"

"I find it amusing. You're not even my real Uncle."

"No Gregg I'm not." He acknowledged the pigeon then, with a casual glance. "Animals don't have souls you know?"

I was used to Sam's sudden changes, but I was no longer fooled by them. They usually had a purpose, but I went along with it anyway. "How do we know?"

"How do we know humans do? We're essentially animals. Why should we be different?"

"We've developed consciousness."

"Which gives us a soul?"

"It gives us the ability to believe we have something more to offer than a brief stint on Earth."

"Ah, yes, mortality. We can never escape from that. Our physical bodies are vulnerable." He sauntered over and looked down at the bird. A wing stuck out awkwardly, grey and white feathers ruffled, never again to lie smoothly against a warm body. Its eyes staring lifelessly, neck obviously broken. "Do you believe in a soul Gregg? What does psychology say about that?"

We'd discussed these issues before, sometimes right through the night. They were beginning to bore me. "What's this leading to, Sam."

He'd always treated creatures with the same reverence as his fellow humans, so, when he kicked the pigeon as if taking a rugby try, I stepped back shocked. It hit the wall of the barn with a sickening thud and fell on a pile of unused canvases. "That's death, Gregg. Nothing. A carcass. One day that will be us. There's nothing we can do to stop it. Who's going to remember us when we're gone? Why am I so morose, Greg? Because of you."

I wasn't used to Sam's outbursts. They were rare. And this was aimed fully at me. My confusion switched to being hurt. What had I done to deserve this? I quickly re-ran the conversation in my mind. Found my thread again.

"Why say you're da Vinci? You can't be. You've just admitted your mortal."

"I am his conscience, his memories, his genius. I am many people, Greg."

He was using a calming tone, for himself, I think, as much for me. But it wasn't just his voice he used. I'd felt his probing in my mind many times before. Perhaps he thought I'd not noticed.

Was that a flinch? Had I surprised him then? Did he now realise I'd known all along about his mind tricks? My psychology studies had also led me to experiment. I'd worked on blocking his intrusions. I let a smile touch my lips. I was surprised when he did too.

"A chip off the old block."

"What?" I exclaimed.

"You've still not guessed?" He was genuinely surprised. Disappointed again. A frown of frustration creased his weathered features. "I'm your real father."

Stunned didn't describe how I felt, but it was close. Flashes of our life together burst into my mind. Good moments, bad moments... father and son moments. I felt cheated; a childish, selfish feeling that brought an anger, a hatred, that churned and grew inside.

"Greg!" I stepped back again, his shout had been like a choir in my head as well as my ears. "Don't take that route!" Just his voice this time, he'd got my attention. "How could I tell you before? You'd have hated me then. No doubt of it. At least you've had a chance to know me. Listen to my story. Listen to the why, before you judge me, Greg."

"Tell me about da Vinci."

And he did. Leonardo da Vinci was one of many. There had been other inventors and artist, there had been princes and lords, bards and writers, warriors and politicians, thieves and vagabonds, liars and cheats — there had been those too, strong in their deceptions.

Back at the beginning there had been thousands of beings like Sam, capable of melding with a new physical host. Human? Yes, an early evolvement, when consciousness was first developing.

They could procreate then too; give birth to others of their kind, so he had been told.

As integration of human tribes and races occurred, and partnerships became mixed between them, no new children were born of this elite stock. Sam had been one of the last.

Somehow we had wondered back to his workshop, sitting amidst his computer gadgets, in armchairs that engulfed us in soft black leather, with pint mugs of whisky and Pepsi, as Sam recounted anecdotes and moments that remained for him near the surface. There were layers of consciousness, he told me. Each one another person. "Even you have layers Greg. Everyone picks up a little from the people they meet, depending on how emotionally close they become. Collective consciousness is a reality."

We stayed in the barn till the early hours of the morning slowly succumbing to the effects of alcohol. Sam looked both tired and vibrant. Animated by his own tales yet seeming to fade with the telling. I studied his face with that unblinking stare of inebriation. How old was he really? His deep-lined face gave little away. Taken on it's own he could be eighty, yet he moved like a man a third that age.

I watched his mouth, still heard his words. As an Egyptian priest he had learnt the ways of magic; taught Jesus of Nazareth the art. Had seen him, misguided but full of hope, become a martyr to his own religion. "He wouldn't have wanted that. He was a good man. He'd have appreciated the irony though." He looked sad for a moment, I felt depressed. "I lost his consciousness. He died before I could reach him."

Another time: "I advised Harold to use the ships, but he was too impatient to prepare them. He felt invincible after the battle at Stamford Bridge. We lost good men on the march to the South cost. But then, England wouldn't have been conquered by the Normans. Harold ruminates on that to this day. I took his mind on the battlefield."

"Some of my kind aren't so humane, aren't so skilful. They waste the host. Literally. They'll eject the mind, replace rather than integrate. They think it's the purest form of survival. They're foolish and cruel. Sometimes the consciences they discard are strong, perhaps a weakened strain of our own genes, and will form a link with whatever matter is nearby. That's most probably where tales of spirits and ghosts have emanated from. Not lost souls at all, but lost consciousnesses. Some will try to regain their link with living beings, and may even manage temporary control, but once they no longer have their own body or host they are lost."

He was drinking as much as me but didn't seem to be effected. "You've heard of the Illuminati?" he asked.

I nodded, not particularly surprised at what he told me next.

"We're spread far and wide now; our branch of homo sapiens; careful not to reveal ourselves." There was a hint of sarcasm in his voice then, yet I felt extremely privileged that he had chosen to tell me these things; that he should trust me so completely. Foolishly so, on reflection. "But there was a group that got together in central Europe thinking that the time was right to show the world that religion was not the way forward for humanity. They learnt a near-fatal lesson."

I raised my eyebrows.

"Yes, most of them survived. Took over their murderers. That's justice for you. Ironic justice.

"You'll notice the gender retention?" he said at one point. "I can't collect a female essence, only males. Men for men. Women for women. Such a waste, I think. Like your mother."

I was instantly alert again, realising for the first time that I did want to know about the woman who had given birth to me, why she had rejected me, why Sam hadn't taken the responsibility of fatherhood from the day I was born.

"I'd only just switched to Sam." Until he said that, I don't think I'd fully appreciated what taking a consciousness meant. It wasn't so much absorbing it as moving in and taking it over. I shivered at the thought. Felt a tinge of disgust. But wasn't the other way some of his kind used even worse?

"I avoid relationships but sometimes the chemistry can't be ignored. It was that way with Samantha, your mother. She was the daughter of Lord Carringham. I worked at the Lord Chancellor's Office where Samantha's father was an advisor. She visited him one lunch time and I was smitten. Strange, yet wonderful, how love continues to be fresh and enjoyable." He smiled into the distance wistfully. Then frowned as if the memory had turned sour.

"My mother? You were telling me about my mother?"

"Yes. She wasn't beautiful. She had a great figure though." A brief hesitation. "Well, she wasn't obviously beautiful. Only a second, and sustained look, revealed her true looks. But she had a quality that I hadn't seen for centuries. She didn't know it but she had our genes. Not pure. No way pure. But she was strong. Like you Gregg.

"She fell for me too. You know how charming I can be." He studied me. At that moment I loved him like a true father. Had I been sober, had I not already consumed so much of the drug he had been lacing my drink with, I might have thought otherwise. "But her father was a stubborn character. When he found out she was pregnant he disowned her in a fit of rage. I wasn't good enough for her. The shock killed him though. He had a massive heart attack right there in front of us. That may have been the start of Samantha's troubled pregnancy too. We married quietly, just a few friends. She died in childbirth." Sadness washed through me. "But you survived.

"The Carringham family wanted nothing to do with me, but they wanted you," he continued, reaching across to refill my glass yet again. "I couldn't let that happen. I couldn't allow you to be brought up by them, in their society, so I took you away." He studied me carefully as he said: "I left you outside the doors to an orphanage with a substantial wad of money. I saw them take you in. Was sure they'd take good care of you. But they were greedy; put you out for fostering. I lost touch with you for years. It was sheer luck I found you at the soccer match."

At that point, as if my body had suddenly given up its fight, I succumbed to the toxins. The lines on Sam's face swirled to form a chattering group of old men, a laughing audience, a roaring stadium. They lifted me into hallucination or dream — I didn't question which — it all seemed real to me at the time. Death visited me twice. First as a siren, a seductress, coming to temp me away from this material world. She was easy to dispel. The second, that sickle-bearing archetype depicted on cheap tarot cards, tugging and pulling at my soul, was less easily repelled. From him though I had the satisfaction of discovering our souls have no feeling. Death holds no fear for me now. I fought though, and at first I thought I'd won.

I woke with an unfamiliar smell and a claustrophobic sense of people around me hemming me in. It was a busy hospital ward, but curtains cut my vision to just beyond the bed. Despite the questions that came to the fore in my mind I immediately fell asleep again.

Darkness greeted me the next time I stirred. I rolled my head to either side but couldn't make out who was in the neighbouring beds. A yellow table light lit a small office at the end of the ward. A night sister busied herself with paperwork, glancing up as I watched, but she turned back to her work after a minute.

Morning greeted my next waking moment. That and, quite obviously, a plain clothes police officer, dressed in a stereotypically crumpled raincoat and suit, accompanied by a doctor.

"Gregory Thomas?"

I shut my eyes slowly. A hand closed around my wrist, thumb on my pulse.

"Do you have to do this now, Sergeant?" A soft voice near my ear. "He's only just woken up. He's been asleep nearly two days."

"I just need to ask a few questions, doctor."

"He seems fairly stable. How do you feel, Mr Thomas?"

I opened my eyes again. Nodded. "Thick headed. Thirsty." It

came out clearer than I expected, giving me the confidence to say more. "What happened? Why am I here?"

"I can help you with that," the detective responded from behind the doctor, who supported my head to allow me to sip water from a glass. "And maybe you can help me."

He limped forward and pulled up a chair by my bedside as, resigned, the doctor moved to the end of the bed and stood making notes on the clipboard.

"I'm Detective Sergeant Banner. Sorry if you don't feel like answering questions but my superiors would like to close this case."

"What case is that?"

"You live at Hallam Farm?" It seemed I was going to have to give him answers before I received any back.

I nodded, but he didn't continue until I said, "Yes."

"Traces of LSD were found at the farm."

I groaned. "That's what he was doing to me."

"What do you mean?"

"Sam was lacing my drink."

"By Sam, you mean Samuel Dillan?"

I nodded again. He waited. "Yes," I said.

"So you're saying Mr Dillan, ninety-six year-old Mr Dillan, was lacing your drink. A young man of," he looked at a small notebook he'd pulled from inside his jacket, "just twenty-one being given drugs by an old man?"

This didn't sound too good. Even I'd find that hard to believe, but that wasn't what had surprised me. "Ninety-six? I know Sam looks good for his age but no way can he be that old."

"And he won't be getting any older."

"What?"

He gave the doctor a cynically scolding stare.

With the doctor's shrug came a look that, due to his ethics, might not have killed but could certainly have maimed. "He's only just woken up. We've not had time to ask any questions ourselves. And we wouldn't just yet."

Sergeant Banner looked sheepish, then suddenly bolder, as if he'd come to some decision, which I guessed was to do with me. "Samuel Dillan is dead."

I couldn't restrain the smile. "Sam's not dead."

The doctor this time, avoiding suspicious assumptions: "I'm sorry, Mr Thomas. Mr Dillan was dead before the ambulance arrived at Hallam Farm. We could do nothing. I'm sorry."

He hung the clipboard back on the end of the bed and went to walk away; stopped when he realised Banner wasn't about to follow.

"The stupid fool," I mumbled. Sam had been scheming something but it hadn't gone to plan. A feeling of great loss, that I might have expected, wasn't there.

"What?" the Sergeant snapped.

"Nothing. Sam was spiking my drink. I knew he was up to something." Sadness did overwhelm me then. All those lives. All those consciences. Gone forever. Tears trickled down my cheeks. "He was my father," I said. "I'd always thought him my uncle, but last night he told me I was his son."

Banner ignored my time-loss. "So you killed him with an overdose of LSD."

"Sergeant Banner." Emotion threatened to crush me. "Sam was my father." I almost choked on that. "He may not have told me so until last night, but he certainly treated me as his son. I would have liked to savour that for a few more years."

"You will." The sergeant hadn't moved his lips.

"Eh?" I shrugged and continued, "Why would I want to kill him?"

"For his money. But I'm asking the questions here."

"Hold on," I said. "Am I under arrest?"

"No...."

"Then have the decency to let me know how he died."

"Most likely a heart attack," the doctor said coming up behind Banner, "as a result of the cocktail of drugs and alcohol ingested over a period of time. It's all in the coroner's report."

"Thank you," Banner responded sharply.

"There's no reason to suspect foul play."

"This young man has filled our files with trouble since before his teens."

A scrutinizing look came my way from the doctor. Uncertainty lined his brow.

"That was years ago," I protested. "When I was in foster homes. I've done nothing wrong since I've been with Sam. He reformed me." A lump came to my throat. "Through his love."

"I've suffered no end of pain and been denied promotion because of you," Banner suddenly cut in.

"Don't be stupid. I've never met you before."

"You stole a moped. Hit me at thirty miles an hour. Fractured my right leg in three places. Left me rolling in agony. Now tell me you didn't kill Dillan."

"I was thirteen." I was thinking: Oh my God, what goes around comes around. Had he been keeping an eye on me ever since? Waiting to reap revenge. "I visited the hospital but when I saw you with your leg up I didn't have the nerve to say sorry. That was the last bad thing I did. What with seeing the consequences of my actions, and Sam taking me under his wing, I've not put a foot wrong since. I couldn't hurt anyone intentionally. I certainly couldn't kill."

"I think you'd better leave, Sergeant," the doctor said, "and I'll be informing your superiors that perhaps you're a little too biased to lead this investigation."

"If you do!" He stood waggling a finger threateningly at the doctor.

"Yes, Sergeant?"

Banner pushed passed the doctor without another word, his limp barely noticeable as he strode out the ward.

"Well done."

"Sorry?" I said to the doctor.

"I didn't say anything," he answered, "but I'll make sure he doesn't bother you in here again. Get some rest."

Yes, I was tired. I closed my eyes and drifted off.

"When they find my letter you'll be off the hook."

I snapped my eyes open, fully alert. Looked around for Sam, who had spoken. But I think I already knew the worst.

"It takes a while to absorb your consciousness. No, it's too late to stop the process. You are a part of me now. Anger won't help. Your body is mine. The full process can take some months though. There are a lot of consciences to assimilate. You'll have full control for at least a month. But I'll be here supporting you."

I felt my right hand clench involuntarily. Sam proving a point. Then he was gone.

Over the years I have resigned myself to my fate. Conversed with most of the others. Some happy to continue an existence, others tormented, a half-life hell they can't escape from. Sam occasionally allows me full control of my body. After all, he says, before he disappears amongst the others, I am his flesh and blood. I have the genes. He confirmed from the start I have the genes.

I am his hope. With me he may be able to fulfil his dream. He believes, that by finding others with the genes, his kind, my kind, may once again multiply. He says he can help me move into my own host, but do I want to? Sam has been cultivating two hosts. We must move into each one at the same time. I'd be alone with just the new mind, but not for long, Sam says. My ability to transfer and control will grow with each one. There is no limit to how often I transfer, though the body I leave will die. He says the time will be soon. I am ready. I am his son.

Waiting For Yesterday

A beech hut was the inspiration for **Waiting For Yesterday**. I suppose its moral, if it has one, is don't dream about the past, get on with your life.

Waiting For Yesterday

She waited for him.

The dying storm was still strong enough to dissuade any late-night revelers from taking a short cut along the promenade. Waves crashed over the storm wall, rising up like great birds of prey, spreading their white-flecked wings over the coastal path before crashing down on the concrete.

She waited.

Path lights swayed and flickered; a pathetic imitation of the pier's grander display, itself being smothered in the brilliance of the strobing sky. Accompanying thunder rolled to a crescendo, reverberating along the cliff, only to rumble reluctantly into the thump and crash of angry sea.

She waited.

At the base of this crumbling rock face old landslides backed up against the rear of a long row of beach huts. Amidst the dark shadows, a lone dull light struggled through chintz curtains.

Inside, Bethany Gray waited on a wooden bench, thick knitted blanket snuggled around fragile shoulders. A corner oil stove battled warmth into her ageing bones, permeating the air with its thick sweat odour.

Years ago she could have retired from her work; gone to warmer climates, warmer times, with others of her trade, but she had always convinced the Correctors of her abilities. After all, there were fewer Portal Operators than in her youth. She wouldn't leave her job. Someday he would return to fulfill the promise they made to each other.

Three days earlier she had received another assignment. A Provocateur would need a portal within the next week. It had taken her a day, on public transport, to reach the designated location, another to check the portal would function as it should. This one was old, and her fingers, stiff with arthritis, took longer to repair the corroded parts. She was confident that it would work but it was affecting the weather hereabouts. Freak conditions could attract unwanted attention though. But here she waited, her meager rations capable of sustaining her for the required time.

"It will be Jed this time," she told herself. She forced back an, "It has to be," to join the other hundred or so similar thoughts that had built up over the last sixty years.

She ran her gnarled fingers across her favourite photo, wondering if he had aged better than she had. At least they would be able to spend their final years together and she could tell him about Tony.

A small leather-bound photo album, worn and well-thumbed at the edges, lay open on the chair next to her. The face of a young smiling couple looked out and up at the single naked bulb that hung from the ceiling.

Behind the hut, in its own small wooden covering, the portal generator, ready to surge energy into the portal at a second's notice, gently purred power into the light.

She had already answered the door twice since the storm hit the coast, her excitement and expectation as high, if not higher than at other portals. It had been a seagull the first time, stupid enough to attempt flight in the atrocious weather conditions, flapping about dazed on her doorstep. The second time she found a chunk of sea-smoothed wood, obviously flung there by the waves. Both times she struggled to shoulder the door closed against the gale, shivering warmth back into herself by leaning over the stove.

Despite the cold, and the incessant noise, she dozed. Her mind wandered to those wonderful first months with Jed. He had been twenty-three, two years older than her, when they met. She in her first placing out of training college — her head full of paradox laws, quantum theories, and Correction propaganda — he on a sabbatical between assignments. 1953 it had been.

They had enjoyed the long hot summer together; an instant attraction blossoming into more than a casual romance.

"I don't want you to go when they call you," she had said as they lay together on the beach one day. Thoughts of a future without him had squeezed a tear from each eye.

"I don't want to leave you either."

She had rolled over then, kissed him, felt him harden almost instantly through his woollen trunks.

"Let's go back to the caravan," she suggested. Yet she knew that when the time came he would have no option but to fulfil his obligation to the Correctors, and she too was committed to them. So they had made the most of their time together.

When the fateful day came he assured her: "We will be together in the future."

"I'll be waiting for you. I love you Jed."

"I love you too."

They'd kissed one more time, embraced like it was their last, before she opened her first ever portal to let him through.

So she had waited, insisting on staying in the same period, knowing that Jed's work would involve more dangerous tasks than her own. But she was convinced he would win through, that their love would endure over the years and that he would return. But her heart was breaking in tiny increments. Yet it was too late now for her to even consider that maybe he wasn't coming back.

A month after Jed's farewell she had discovered she was pregnant. This was against the Correctors' Code. It could have catastrophic consequences to the mapped-out history of the world and humankind's future survival.

For Bethany an abortion was out of the question, yet necessary if she wanted to continue her career, and the only way she could eventually be with Jed. But she couldn't bear the thought of terminating their creation.

Secretly she arranged an adoption with a couple who were otherwise childless. They seemed the perfect middle-class couple yet she found it difficult to accept letting her son go. It was her link with Jed.

They promised they would keep a regular contact with her. Let her know how her son, Tony, was progressing. They kept to their word.

She waited for Jed, taking each of her own assignments in her stride, refusing to believe their relationship had meant nothing. She knew it had been special. Each portal she operated could be the next one that Jed used, either coming from or going through. Each time she expected it to be him, returning to take her away. Although the Correctors could not tell her which operative it would be, they confirmed, each time she asked, that Jed was still alive and in good health.

She phoned Tony's guardians every six months, and was assured he was doing well at school, then at university, then in politics. He became a popular MP, winning a marginal seat for his party with a massive majority, causing his seniors to take serious notice. She was so proud of him, but he would never know who his real parents were. He was now starting his third term as Prime Minister, yet his views on going to war in the middle east were unpopular not only with the opposition but within his party too. Bethany privately supported his reasons.

Her head dropped and startled her awake. Had she heard something other than the storm? Cold was slowly migrating from her toes. She stood stiffly and stamped her feet by the stove.

Was that voices? Had she heard shouting? Stopping her little rhythmic dance she moved closer to the door, straining with her good ear to pick out any alien noises from the incessant battering outside. Nothing.

She lifted a thin hand to pull the curtain aside. It looked like the path lights had finally given out altogether, and the pier was no longer ablaze in illuminations. A power cut most likely. Lines down somewhere.

Even on its own, the sudden flash of lightening and clap of thunder would have surprised her, but the deep-shadowed figure that stood on the doorstep brought a foolish gasp to her lips. Reaction sent her backwards, almost sprawling, as her foot caught in the shawl, but her training took over, even after all these years, and she regained her balance.

The expected knock came. A simple code that told her a Provocateur was awaiting entrance to the beach hut. But this wasn't any traveller. Still burning in her mind's vision, imprinted there by the blinding light, was the face of Jed.

Bolts didn't shift as easily as they should, arthritic joints fumbling in their haste, excitement too adding to her predicament, her heart thumping madly, struggling to pump energy into withering muscle. Eventually the door flew wide with a blast of chilled spray. A drenched Jed staggered over the threshold, pushing passed to the stove.

"Lock the door quick."

Her disappointment didn't show as she carried out her duty; struggling again to shut out the storm. This time she dropped the thick plank into its holding bracket, barring the door. Standard procedure. Turned.

"Jed."

He spun round. Surprised, it seemed, that she knew his name.

"Jed? It's me Bethany."

Shock dawned in eyes that moved over her, from wiry grey hair to her feet, back to her eyes.

"Bethany?"

"Yes." Her voice croaked. Behind him, at the back of the hut the portal, activated by the bar on the door, was pulsing into prismic life. He looked little more than five year's older than he had been the day they met. And in that moment she realised the error they had made in their pact, that, likely, he was nearly fifty years her younger. That too showed in his expression.

"I'm sorry Beth." Thankfully she believed him. Had to, else her life meant nothing. She groped for comfort in his youth, an explanation as to why he'd not returned earlier.

"Quick," she told him. "Go." This time the shouts outside the hut were distinct. "You were followed?"

"I couldn't shake them."

He still had that desperate innocence.

"I..."

"Don't tell me," she interrupted, reminding him of his oath to the service. "What I don't know I can't tell."

"Open up! Police!" in time to a demanding and continued banging on the door.

"You have to destroy the portal," he mumbled, as though afraid to give the order.

"I know my job," she said, subconsciously fingering the little plastic jar in her cardigan pocket that held the tiny, yet deadly capsule. At least there was Tony. Now Jed would never know about him, their son. "Make my life worthwhile. Go!"

Relief showed then in his expression as he stepped backwards into the portal and forwards into the future.

When they broke into the beach hut the plainclothes police officers did their best to revive the old vagrant woman, but it was obviously a heart attack, and massive.

They found an album on the bench; more photos in the old woman's bag. They were brown, faded and well worn, most probably of her in her youth.

“This could be the bastard’s father,” one of the officers spat, pointing to the young man and an attractive woman by his side. “Looks too similar not to be. Definitely a link here.” He looked down at the still, mask-like face, lifeless eyes staring up into the bulb.

“She’s not going to be able to help us now though.” There was more than just simple disappointment in the other officer’s voice.

There had to be a connection with the woman, although the rest of the tiny beach hut gave up no more evidence. “I reckon she’s his mother. I was positive he came in here.”

The Special Branch team had been determined, spurred on by a Britain in turmoil. Anger and utter frustration now swept through the team. The Prime Minister's assassin had somehow slipped from their grasp.

Just One Night

Dark Fiction Magazine, the online audio short story mag, were after stories with the theme 'twelve days of Christmas' for an anthology. I tried to squeeze all twelve into **Just One Night**, though I never actually checked if I succeeded. See how many references you can find. I think Saxon Bullock's reading at the site makes it sound a lot better!

Just One Night

Inquisitor Pellecchia Galdini banked the Ford Stealth FD in a tight curve that brought him low over the estuary. The two moons of Wiccid cast mirror-like shadows across reed beds and ponds that rarely filled even in the high spring tides.

As the inquisitor closed the door of his craft a German Shepherd stirred in its sleep behind the isolated wooden hut. Its ears flicked instinctively. The swirling wind set a constant creaking to the precarious abode, and a dancing tune through the drainpipes like the spirits of Highlanders.

With muscles desperate for exercise, Galdini stamped his feet and waved his arms to stimulate circulation. Despite the latest fold-drive, the billions of light years' journey had still taken twelve hours. The massage chair

was a must-have as there was no room to move in the Stealth. No receptacles for relieving body functions either and elimination inhibitors just made you fart every five minutes. Wiccid's acrid air was like nectar. Yet it was clear to Galdini why the New Vatican should consider this inhospitable planet on the fringes of no-space a threat to humanity. His briefing had been... well, brief: kill Doz Drummer.

Drummer was the founder of the Hips. As such he had put his life where his preaching was and moved to Wiccid twenty years before, living the life of a hermit. Wiccid was considered by the

Hips to be the spiritual centre of the universe, yet it was far from the centre of anything. Drummer's recorded messages of love and peace, however, had reached out across galaxies like no other religion had. And Wiccid's intoxicating air was said to give enlightenment to everyone who stepped foot on the planet. What utter shit, Galdini thought.

His favourite weapon was a solid diamond-handled serrated darksteel dagger that the Pope had presented to him when he'd handed over his thousandth heretic. However, he chose a blow pipe to ensure the guard dog remained asleep. No point in creating unnecessary commotion, not that anyone else was within a mile of the mainland shore, and the nearest fishing boat was anchored five miles seaward of the delta marshes. But sounds travelled far at night. Truth be told, Galdini had a soft spot for dogs.

Junk had eased his journey but he'd needed a large white line to bring his assassin skills into focus. He knew his multisuit would be working furiously to balance his metabolism so he was prepared for the occasional hallucination. Nasal filters, considered enough to keep the planet's naturally occurring visions to a minimum, seemed ineffectual as Galdini staggered on reaching the hut's picket fence, figures leaping and dancing around him. Lords and ladies in imperial finery pranced amongst milk-laden cows. White-skinned maids seduced him with come-on eyes. A shake of the head and a squeezing of eyes sent them squealing – at least in his head – to wherever spirits, or the imaginations of them went. Probably deep in his subconscious, but he didn't dwell on that thought.

A quick detour determined that the dog would wake eventually and that his dart was safely back in its case and not available as evidence of his deeds. It was unlikely Drummer's body would be found for months. Intelligence reported he rarely went into town for supplies. Unsheathing his dagger he silently crept inside.

👾👾👾

Doz Drummer woke the next morning to a dawn chorus that

filled the air with the glory of being alive. Wiccid was a hippie's paradise. Swans majestically traversed the mud-banked stream next to the hut, geese gabbled overhead and their nesting partners responded nearby, grey-collared doves cooed on the roof of the hut, and the hens were beginning to stir in their house. Some time during the night the old Olympic symbol that he used to represent his Qabalistic keys had fallen from the pear tree that he'd nurtured since he'd arrived on Wiccid; the five gold rings now being shat upon by a lone partridge perched in the tree.

But Doz was happy. This was Wiccid.

He stretched and walked around to the front of his hut. It was only then that his uplifted spirits faltered. His heightened sense of smell told him that blood had been spilt. A lot. The door was ajar so he gently pushed it open with his snout. Lying in blood-soaked sheets on the bed was his human body; skin the grey-to-blue tint of a dull winter sky. A flick of his canine tongue on the scab-splattered face told him the kill hade been made some hours before. Not for the first time he went to the corner of the hut and gripping the trap-door ring with his teeth lifted it open. It fell back on the floor as he grabbed the sheets and dragged the body off the bed and across the wooden boards. The throat had been so brutally cut that he was concerned the head would roll off but within minutes he was at the bottom of the stairs and had the body secured within the magic circle that formed the centre of his temple. He trotted into the triangle of art and, with his right paw, pressed the play button that read Reanimate and sat quietly wondering which inquisitor had visited his home this time. Would they never understand the powers of Wiccid, that it was a living planet?

Within two hours Drummer was climbing the stairs, leaving his faithful Alsatian wrapped in the bedclothes. He'd see to him later. Once outside he picked up a bunch of pebbles and threw them in an arc as he spun on the spot. Two of them bounced in mid air and fell to the ground; as he expected.

Galdini might have thought he was on his return journey but

his craft would remain where it was until all life within was extinguished. Only then would the planet allow the Stealth to return home. True love was the very essence of Wiccid, and a lover scorned...

Avoiding Dystopia

I wrote **Avoiding Dystopia** before the recession hit and before the UK riots of 2011. Umm, sorry, that wasn't rioting was it, just mass theft. It suggests how easily society could break down. I actually think it'll be a lot harder, but then again...

Avoiding Dystopia

The knife at Rafe's throat was not razor sharp. He could feel its nicks catching his skin. But he was in no doubt that it was quite capable of severing his jugular. A grabbing hand, hard with calluses, held his forehead back to welcome the blade.

It hadn't been aliens, or a third world war; it hadn't been an epidemic or some genetic mutation; nor an asteroid impact or a reactor failure, although apart from the aliens and the asteroid the others followed in various degrees. It had been a people's revolt that eventually plunged the world into chaos. Raferty Seddon had even predicted it; the catalyst that would unlock festering unrest and lead the world into a new dark age. Religious fanatics, bigoted right wingers, nationalist parties, law enforcement agencies and the military had done the rest. Governments had failed to see it coming or lacked the control they assumed over their departments; each branch of the civil service reacting differently to nullify the unrest, unwittingly fuelling further protests until it was too late.

Rafe was union secretary for the engineering workers, not that he had ever been an engineer or that the UK had many engineering companies anymore. His charisma was strong enough to guide a dying union, but the cheapness of third-world labour and cash incentives to help developing countries left the UK unable to compete. Despite that, membership was a respectable ten thousand and at least three of those had attended the trade union march in London on Brotherhood Day, mostly through Rafe's personal appearances at the bigger plants, where his oratory, always convincing, whipped up support. So B Day as it was advertised, the B later standing for blood, was considered to be well attended. Thirty percent turnout was better than any of the other unions. It was irrelevant that there was an estimated one hundred thousand marchers or that the day was a Sunday, days meant nothing now. Surviving each one was the art and Rafe had reached his final one. His artistry had failed him.

B Day had started peacefully. Even the police joked with the marchers as they walked side by side, sympathising in most cases with union gripes. After all, they had their own. Hide Park had hosted speakers and shouters, singers and chanters. Religious groups had appeared, also adding to the throng, preaching love, peace and ultimate salvation. It was as the rally broke up — people making their way home, tired but feeling they had achieved something by their protest — that trouble began. Gunshots were heard. Two people dropped to the pavement, blood flowing freely from lethal head wounds. It was enough to send the crowd panicking every which way as personal safety became their paramount concern. Pandemonium ensued for half an hour as shouts of warning spread fear far beyond the catalyst. Fights broke out as fleeing marchers sought cover in underground stations; entrances becoming mini battlegrounds. Police stepped in to break up the fighting only for the crowd to turn on them as if they were the cause of their fear.

Sticks, stones, iron bars, anything that could be used as a weapon was wielded by a fearful and suddenly angry throng. Police began appearing on the scene in riot gear far quicker than might normally be expected, fuelling speculation that they had planned heavy handed tactics. Using practised techniques they began splitting the crowd into smaller groups. It worked for a while but they were overwhelmed by numbers.

Rafe and many of his fellow unionists found themselves in one of these small pockets, his closest associates forming a tight shield around him. Though part of him was pleased his charisma was capable of generating this kind of loyalty he protested at their actions as it just seemed to antagonise the officers who saw him as a ring leader. They began wading into the phalanx with batons raised like a bristling porcupine. These were ordinary coppers, not armed with shields, but they were determined and brutal as one.

Their blows scythed a way through Rafe's guardians who weren't prepared for such a viscious attack. They were beaten to the ground, thrown to one side, kicked and trampled. Rafe's shock was soon consumed by fear as he realised he might soon be amongst the injured. Yet even as the police grabbed Rafe his mind was set on getting his colleagues to a hospital quickly. "Call an ambulance," he shouted, before the end of a baton shattered several of his teeth and pain cauterised his thoughts.

He came round in a side street that smelt of urine and something else he couldn't distinguish. His right eye felt the size of a baseball, though when he gingerly touched it a golf ball was a better description, and a golf ball that sent jarring pain through his head. He could barely open the other eye, the swelling extending across his forehead and the bridge of his nose. That was likely broken too. The alley was dark. It was night time. A distant street light was framed by the alley walls, but its luminosity seemed to be sucked into the darkness. Movement was difficult, not just because he had sustained other injuries while unconscious, at least one broken rib he thought as he tried to get more oxygen into aching muscles, but because something heavy was pinning him down. His hands slid into slimy rubbish as he attempted to push himself up. The thought of being dumped in a pile of rotting garbage gave him the strength to move. It was then the sickening realisation hit him. The soft mass upon which he was entangled was a heap of bodies. Suppressing a scream of surprise and revulsion was impossible, though his retching cut that short. He slithered and slid away from his nightmare oblivious of his own spew, the acid bile adding a further odour to the one he already suffered: The stench of death.

His instinct for survival saved him. Before he reached the end of the alleyway he hugged the side wall. Leaning there with every breath catching in his lung like a tightening vice around his chest and back.

As he leant against the cold wall gasping, still trying to grasp the horrors of his recent experience, the sounds of warfare came to his ears. Single and automatic gunfire could be heard in the distance; a sudden explosion nearby. Richocheing bullets sent him painfully to the alley floor, gasping for air that would not come. Panic. Then: A firm hand on his shoulder. "You're alive." A young male voice.

Racked laughter shook Rafe with pain; surprised him into realising his injuries might well be life threatening given the likelihood of the breakdown of infrastructure, how vulnerable he was. Survival was suddenly paramount. He had seen it coming, had written papers warning of the festering unrest. "Just," he answered, "Can barely see." An exploration with a dry swollen tongue across shattered teeth revealed just one was missing.

"Here, grab my arm."

There was familiarity and confidence in that voice. Not of a friend, nor an enemy. Just a knowing. Rafe felt assured but at the same time envied that voice. Safe. Not safe. He could never feel that with the sound of death and destruction around him. But he was happy to accept the guidance and only sporadically tried to open his good eye, allowing the youngster to lead him. There were bodies around. Buildings had been damaged; masonry dangled precariously from upper floors. Fires raged, though Rafe was more aware of them by the heat, the acrid smoke and the crackling of wood, his good eye weeping what he hoped was just water.

They moved, Rafe bent by the pain in his chest. They hid. They crept. They stopped, started. Rafe even managed to run ten yards with his guide's gentle touch. But he was sometimes roughly pulled, pushed and at one point brought to the ground with surprising force, knocking what wind he had left in him, gasping in agony for long minutes.

"Sorry," whispered. Hesitation. "We have to go by foot. Roads blocked. And anyway we'd be sitting targets." That explained as the sound of a helicopter thumped overhead. Nelson Skinner was his name. Little bits of information being batted between them as the sound of battle began to recede.

"We'll not be safe until we're through the suburbs. London is full of hate right now. You're lucky it was me that found you."

Telling Rafe what? That Nelson was special, immune to the hate?

Rafe was flattened against doorways. A smell of sweet and expensive aftershave assailing his senses each time. Gunfire still echoed around them. Sometimes close by, but always chattering in the distance. Single shots seemed somehow more ominous, as if someone was meticulously killing individuals. Gun wielding gangs would dominate briefly, but no match for the professional soldier, at least while the army remained co-ordinated. But fears for family safety would soon disrupt discipline. His theories proving correct.

Rafe had to rest more and more often, but each time Nelson pulled him to his feet and stressed they had to keep moving. It was a long night.

"Where're you from?" Pronunciation was difficult with his engorged tongue, but his companion seemed to have no trouble understanding him. It was the first time he had asked a question without Nelson shushing him.

"Clapham."

"London?"

"Sort of. Parents are from Barbados." He must have sensed Rafe's sudden uncertainty. "Went to drama school. I've still got the street vibe if I want it. Why's a black man helping a white man, and at a time like this? You and I are brothers. We're human beings."

"It's appreciated."

"Don't thank me yet. I know who you are."

Rafe's instinct suddenly returned. He had allowed himself to trust a kid who he knew nothing about. There had been little option to begin with. They seemed to have left the violence behind, perhaps it was time to make his own way. As if to influence a decision Nelson let go of him. Rafe froze. His good eye had obviously been weeping blood, or a head wound had seeped across his eyelid and form a scab there. Try as he could he was unable to open it. He chastised himself for trusting and relying on his guide too much. There was nothing around him to give him support.

Now what was he going to do? Blind, helpless, lost. A sitting target for the military or one of the vigilante bands he expected to have formed already. That had been one of his predictions.

Always one to face issues head on, he now experienced a feeling of overwhelming panic. Could he have managed to escape from the centre of the trouble without Nelson's help? And if he knew him, in what capacity? Maybe he was someone on some kind of family vendetta.

He remained comatose for several minutes, shocked at his ineptitude, his inability to make a decision, hearing danger in every little noise. A dog barked in the distance, another much closer took up an answering howl. They would pack. In a few months the surviving dogs would be treating his presence here as a gift from the gods. He'd be ripped apart and fed upon before his heart had stopped beating.

He started frantically scratching at the congealed blood across the eye that wasn't swollen and, with a sense of relief that shamed Rafe, Nelson was back pushing a plastic bottle into his left hand. A gasp of surprise escaped Rafe's puffy lips. That reliance on another person was not easy for Rafe to accept. It was unfamiliar. A totally new experience. A glimmer of sympathy for those he had taken advantage of in the past was as surprising as the realisation itself. A shiver ran through his body, nausea overwhelmed him, he threw up in a splattering of fluids that racked his tongue in passing, the band around his chest tightening once gain. Delayed shock he told himself. A firm hand beneath his armpit lowered him gently to the pavement as his strength seemed to flow away.

"Take a sip of that. It's water." Rafe hesitated. "This supermarket's been looted big time. There's Coke if you prefer."

Rafe shook his head slowly, unscrewed the cap and gingerly took a sip. The cold water sent a wave of shock through his head but he persevered and took another swig, swirling the liquid around in his mouth, letting the pain subside before he managed to swallow past his sore and swollen tongue. He emptied the rest of the contents over his greying hair.

"Here's some tissue."

Nelson pushed a wad of crumpled kitchen roll into his other hand. It was cheap and thin but Rafe gently wiped his good eye. His right eye still throbbed. It felt like a foreign body forced into its socket. Any touch sent waves of dizziness through his head. He was careful to avoid it.

This time he was able to control his eyelid enough to open it a slit. To his surprise there was a hint of dawn.

"Take these."

A light palmed hand disfigured by calluses held out three paracetamol and three ibuprofen but when Rafe twisted his head around the face was dark brown, almost ebony. It was a handsome face; unblemished; proud. Nelson also wore black: Combat trousers, flack waistcoat over a ripstop jacket, large haversack strapped firmly to his back, an M16 over his right shoulder, an automatic pistol holstered at his belt, alongside an evil looking commando dagger. He looked like an advert for the SAS. Despite his injuries Rafe's face must have shown surprise.

"Some people listened to you."

The frown Rafe tried to perform sent a further wave of nausea through him but Nelson understood the reflex.

"Your papers. Some of us listened."

"They weren't widely published."

"They were scanned. Circulated on the internet. There is at least one group in every country in the world."

"Survivalists." Rafe was surprised at the contempt in his own voice.

"Don't mistake us for that. Okay, I might look like a gun-toting Yank, and I've done a few stints with the Army in Afghanistan and Iraq, but there are six groups in the UK, and probably that many guns between the whole lot. We're Seddonists through and through. Not a paramilitary outfit."

"There are cells?" Rafe was fascinated that some people had actually taken him seriously. He had only partly believed his own theories. "Seddonists?"

"Your theories have been labelled Seddonism. My cell's the East Anglian. We have a base near The Wash, about six miles south east of Boston. Everyone will be making their way there. They'll be really excited I found you."

And how did you find me? he wanted to ask, but decided he wasn't quite ready to know the answer. Instead he asked Nelson if he knew how he had ended up in a side street in a pile of bodies.

"They bulldozed the bodies out of the way. They had to clear the roads anyway but they couldn't let the Prime Minister see the carnage first hand."

"And your presence was a coincidence?"

"Oh no. I'd seen you go down. But I wasn't able to reach you until later. I was surprised you were still alive."

They'd started moving again. A black-clad soldier and his wounded companion. "We need to find a safe place to hide up during daylight," Nelson advised him. "There'll be more looting. Martial law will be announced, a curfew introduced. Most people will honour that for the first few nights." Did he know he was quoting Rafe's paper word for word. There seemed no irony intended. "It'll give us a chance to get into the country."

Rafe's publisher had openly laughed at his theories. Doom and destruction had been a good seller at one time but recent polls showed a heavy swing towards escapism, romance and fantasy. Predictions of the fall of civilisation didn't sell books anymore so Rafe had self published as a series of papers. A specialist distributor had taken five hundred copies of the whole series but they had not contacted him for more.

Nelson unlocked with ease the door of a solicitors' practice that nestled between two shops just off the Mile End Road and almost carried Rafe up the stairs to the first-floor office.

"It's unlikely anyone will even think of going to work today. They'll have seen the TV coverage. A solicitors' office won't be a prime target for looters. We should be safe here."

It was like living his written word. "Civilisation At Last - A Time To Survive" was the third of his pamphlets. The first had dealt with the reasons for the current societies, and he had categorised them into six types, but each type was flawed to the extent that the ordinary citizen was being treated wholly unfairly; each generation more prone to dissent, unrest growing proportionately greater each year. Parenthood becoming a chore rather than a necessary job, leaving children to be lead by inscrutable opportunists, lacking the morals to sustain a civilised society. Religion needed to be replaced by a code for a civilised society, of that Rafe was certain. Religion was for the weak, a crutch for those trying to survive in an equal society.

They settled down as best they could, making use of two easy chairs in a casual meeting room at the back of the premises on the second floor. Nelson had gone back to double bolt the front door and wheeled a dumpster across the bottom of the fire escape in the back yard, placing an old metal dustbin lid half way up the stairs. The sound of anyone removing it ought to be warning enough, if they bothered to get that far.

Rafe had been astonished at his reflection in the office men's room. He looked like a zombie, no, an injured zebra. His swollen eye looked nowhere near as bad or as big as it felt but his tongue was worse. Blood caked his hair and sweat had rivered through drying blood down his face. After a thorough sloosh and wipedown he almost looked human. What he felt was something entirely different.

They weren't bothered during the day, but were occasionally disturbed by the distant sound of windows being smashed, shouting, and the now familiar chatter of gunfire. Rafe wondered where all the guns had appeared from. So much for the success of the recent police clampdown. Nelson seemed to sleep through it all but reacted instantly in the late afternoon to the sound of a dustbin lid landing in the yard. He put a finger to his lips and peered through the blinds.

He relaxed. "Cat." But he still checked the yard, coming back with an all clear about fifteen minutes later.

"Let's eat."

Rafe's stomach told him he needed something but he wasn't certain his tongue would allow it. Breathing was slightly easier, the drugs seeming to take the edge of the pain, or maybe he was just becoming used to it.

Expecting Nelson to rifle around in his backpack for rations he was surprised when the backpack was left beside the sofa and Nelson disappeared. Industrious noises could be heard from a nearby room, and then the sizzling smell of frying bacon. With much grunting and wincing Rafe managed to rise from the chair and relieved himself in the men's room. His urine was dark and smelt of sugar puffs and coffee, neither of which he'd consumed for days.

He slooshed his face again, studying it in the mirror. It looked ghastly, but he actually felt a little more alive than he had that morning, but then realised there was another painful night's march ahead of them. The luxury he now experienced was going to be short lived. Public utilities would soon start to fail. Electricity first, then gas and water. Failure of the sewage system would leave cities out of bounds for all but the most masochistic of survivors until the waste had broken down. But that wouldn't happen just yet.

Rafe found Nelson in a well-equipped kitchenette sliding fried eggs onto two plates already covered in bacon. Tinned tomatoes bubbled in a saucepan on the hob.

"Make the most of this. We'll be on Waypacs soon. Nourishing but not very appetising." In answer to Rafe's questioning look: "They have a well-stocked fridge here. No bread though I'm afraid."

Back in the rest room they ate in silence. Evening was drawing in. Rafe ate slowly and carefully. Nelson finished while Rafe was still on his fourth mouthful. And that was when the door downstairs exploded open. Nelson grabbed his processions as if he'd been practising it for weeks, dragging Rafe to his feet, mindless of the plate of food he knocked onto the floor in the process.

At the door to the fire escape Nelson squatted down and opened the door a slit, ducking and bringing his head back inside as a bullet sent flakes of plaster showering onto their heads. Rafe had glimpsed the body lying in the back yard in a pool of blood. Nelson smiled. "Looks like the cat had friends."

Rafe tried to hide his sudden fear; assuring himself that Nelson had helped him thus far. Why would he want to kill the man he had saved. But the word psychopath came to the fore. He had used it in his pamphlets, based on one conversation with a psychiatrist, to enhance the thrill factor of his theories; an attempt to dramatise his point. He was scaring himself.

"Everyone is our enemy right now," Nelson justified his action. "Act first or die. At least at the outset."

"It was just a theory."

"Seems a little more than that right now." He unholstered the automatic, clipped a small mirror on the barrel, moved it to the gap, fired mere seconds later. The pistol was back in its holster and he was on the fire escape before Rafe had time to think. His M16 chattered loudly in the confines of the shop yard and Rafe expected Nelson to drag him down the metal staircase but instead he moved back into the offices with instructions to follow.

"Stay there."

Rafe had followed Nelson back to the top of the narrow staircase leading to the front door. He watched the young man move quickly onto the landing his M16 ready. A starter motor struggled to turn an engine close by, echoing up to them loudly. When he took a peep to watch Nelson's careful steps down to the ground entranceway he could see why it sounded close. Protruding though a smashed and splintered door was the offside bonnet of a blue car. Its make no longer relevant. No more would be made.

Nelson stayed at the half way mark on the stairs. As the occupant of the car tried once more to start it Nelson turned to Rafe and warned him to listen out for any movement from the back. He had been doing that anyway.

Suddenly the engine caught and the driver floored the excellerator to keep it going. The gears grated and the car jumped back a few feet before stalling again. In that moment Nelson virtually slid to the foot of the stairs and sent his carbine chattering in the drivers direction. Still at the top of the stairs Rafe watched Nelson jinks through the opening between the car and the door frame and disappear out of sight.

Once again Rafe felt unfamiliar panic, helpless as intermittent gunfire resounded outside. Even more so when he heard the fire escape door creak open. There was no option but to take to the stairs, each step jarring his ribs, sucking a stifled moan from his still swollen lips.

"Rafety Seddon?"

The half whispered half shouted question froze Rafe at the bottom of the stairs. How would anyone know his name in these parts unless they had somehow followed him and Nelson? And why? An inconsequential union leader with no union to administer, and half dead too. Or were they just here to finish him off. But again the question: Why?

A shadow on the landing. A face this time to the voice that asked the same question. An automatic aimed at Rafe's head, that nodded affirmation instinctively.

"Don't worry. We're MI6. My name's Jason. Your companion's the reason for all this. He started the shooting yesterday. You're in safe hands now. The crisis is under control."

Rafe realised he wanted to believe what this man told him. He didn't want his theories to be proved correct. Pessimism prevailed though. The slaughter of the previous night wouldn't be tolerated by the populace. The slide had started and there was nothing anyone could do.

"We need you as an advisor. To help us restore law and order. To build a civilised society. A properly civilised society. With your input we can do that."

For a moment Rafe wanted to believe him. But when he looked into the man's eyes he saw his own uncertainty mirrored there. Beneath the surface of this man's world was a culture as corrupt as any. Where politicians bullied their ways to power behind a facade of righteous responsibility. It wasn't going to change with the old regime. It had to collapse first before it could be rebuilt. Nelson's route might be as brutal as the order he was trying to bring down, but there was no other way.

Before this realisation had a chance to reveal itself in his eye a callused hand pulled back his head and a knife caught below his Adam's apple.

The agent above him hesitated. A faint smell of expensive aftershave and the hot odour of old and fresh perspiration assailed Rafe's nostrils. An image of the body in the backyard came to mind. Stupidly he wondered if Nelson had since wiped the blade of blood or if his own would be infected. He swallowed and felt the knife take the offered sacrifice as if to test its ability. A trickle of blood confirmed it had been honed well.

"Your move." Nelson's voice was calm as he spoke to the officer. Rafe realised it was going to be people like Nelson who would change the world. Prepared to sacrifice themselves for the sake of mankind. But they also had to be tamed. "You need Raferty Seddon too. You need him because he knew what was going wrong and what needs to be done to put it right." There was uncertainty in the agent's eyes although his gun did not waver." You can't do that without unravelling everything first. We have to start at grass roots again. Purge the world of greed."

The man's eyes flicked between hostage and holder. His job was obviously to bring Rafe in alive. He was probably late twenties. Most likely had a family to worry about. He'd also just witnessed his colleagues die. Despite that he let the weapon fall to his feet, stood up straight with the kind of defiance Rafe imagined you might see in the eyes of a martyr. Nelson gently took his hand away from Rafe's forehead and the knife away from his throat.

"Go," he said. It wasn't how Rafe had expected him to react; to allow this man to live.

For a few moments the man looked down at them, seeming at last to come to a decision.

"Is three a crowd?" There was a knowledge of death in the tone. Resignation in the eyes.

"Are you asking to join us, after trying to kill us?"

"We've all read Seddon's papers. Some of us see their truths. Tyson more than me." Rafe realised that he was referring to one of Nelson's victims. He was willing the man to leave before his companion changed his mind.

"At this stage another experienced gun will give us more chance. Survival first. Then consolidate." More quotes form his pamphlets and another huge surprise from Nelson. Rafe thought he was a loner.

"Can we trust him?"

Nelson was looking up at the man. "There's no way back to the old way. He knows that. He's been following us. How many in your unit?"

"Twelve."

"So five of you made it this far. You've seen that the slide has started."

The agent named Jason nodded.

"Pick up your weapon. Let's go."

Psychopath? Savour? Multilayed personality. It was people like this, people who could trust another, who would make the difference. Fanatics? Maybe. But with a goal to change perceptions. Religions had to die. Humanity had to rely on and take responsibility for its own actions at last. Rafe's injuries would eventually heal. The rift between people would too. Technology would eventually grow again, but it would be for the greater good. Perhaps Rousseau had been right after all.

Green

Not all the names of my alien species begin with an aich, although you might think so from this collection. Inspector Clements thinks his sergeant is a bit of a bigot. Maybe he should look at himself. Not sure if I pulled off the unwilling attraction between more than one character. You'll have to be the judge of that.

Green

I hadn't seen a dead Hospes until I was called to Olympus Tower. Fact was I'd seen few living ones up until then. At least not close up. Now, bright purple pupils stared back lifelessly, verdant skin paling to a sickening yellow, a dark green puddle pooled beneath feet that hung over the edge of a white leather two-seater. On-duty coroner Judy Gee told me it was male, although you'd not have known by the genitals. They'd been mutilated. I wondered absently if the rumours about their sexual organs were true. But hey, size doesn't matter does it?

My dingy flat would have fitted three times into the surgical-blanc penthouse lounge with its art deco furniture and furnishings; probably from the actual period too.

As Detective Sergeant Dave Moody handed over a driving license he informed me: 'His name's Robert Saxum, Guv.'

Dave and I had worked together for years on and off. I'd get a posting somewhere and he'd follow suit. Hadn't quite worked out for him on the promotion front though. But he was a good cop.

Some Hospes kept their race names but I didn't know a human who could pronounce them. There was a similarity between the photo and the bruised and battered face, but Hospes all looked the same to me, although if I hadn't actually seen the victim I'd have thought someone had Photoshopped a greenish tinge to a human's skin tone. Alien and human features were far more similar than I'd realised.

'Some pad he's got here. Bet he's a dealer,' Dave commented. Anyone hearing him would have assumed he'd already made up his mind about the case. But he was a shrewd cookie. Because of our long relationship he knew that I could be wound up by preconcesptions. I didn't bite this time because Hospes had fitted almost seamlessly into human society, though they were far more prone to paranoia and schizophrenia; taking to our business world like water-hungry ducks, while others just seemed to fall into the dross of society, dealing the latest hallucinogenics and messing with people's minds. Nothing new there. Whatever, Robert Saxum had certainly been successful judging by the massive and lavishly furnished apartment. 'Did he live here alone?'

'We're still looking into that, Guv.'

It was inevitable that aliens would choose Britain as a surrogate home. I couldn't see the States ever accepting them, but then who'd have thought they'd ever have a black president? The yanks would have shot the toads soon as look at them. UK's tourist trade had certainly benefitted though. Generally Hospes were left to get on with their lives the same as any immigrant, like there weren't enough of *them* already, but the strain of such a different culture hitting the UK was stirring up Nationalists. I'd even started reading their literature myself. In fact, my first thoughts were this was a racist attack, although it was a little disconcerting to discover that the sight of a dead alien didn't feel that different from the sight of a dead human. After all, dead is dead.

'Sir?' Another officer drew my attention to the contemplation room. Hospes didn't sleep like humans so they had no need of bedrooms, but they did like to meditate in a quiet environment. I was taken aback to see a life-sized pin-up of two human women in an ornate frame. 'Liked a bit of cross breeding perhaps, sir?'

It was done, so I'd heard. But I didn't know of anyone

personally, not even the prostitutes over in Highbury. It certainly wasn't what turned me on. Maybe that was the angle to take this case forward. It would make sense taking into account the mutilations. I think I mumbled, 'Disgusting.' But at that moment a commotion broke out in the entranceway. As I made my way into the large white hallway I could see some of my officers trying to restrain an hysterical woman intent on entering the premises.

'Hey! Hey! What's going on?'

'You tell me!' A flushed face popped up from the fracas; familiar deep brown eyes flashing anger; brunette hair falling to just beneath her shoulders. One of the pin ups.

'Can I help you?'

The struggle mostly subsided, though on either side officers still held her arms, which she shook more as a protest than any attempt to free herself. No doubt my officers were enjoying the proximity to breasts conservatively encompassed by a round-necked Cashmere jumper. I can normally keep a respectable gap between work and pleasure but I was dying to feel the softness of that wool.

'What are you doing in my flat?'

I hadn't expected that.

'You live here?'

'Where's Robert?'

'You live here with Robert?'

'He's my husband.'

I raised my eyebrows but mixed race civil ceremonies did give each partner the same rights as married couples. 'You didn't answer my question.'

'And you haven't answered mine. What are you doing in my flat?'

I sighed and moved to the white leather three-seater sofa that ran along the hall wall, catching my reflection in the mirror as I sat down at one end. For a reason I wasn't immediately able to deduce I questioned why I thought my archetypal raincoat didn't fit my own perception of me anymore. Maybe a light linen suit was more my style. Shit, I had to concentrate! 'Sit down, Mrs Saxum.'

My officers correctly took that as a sign to let go. She assisted with a shrug.

'I told you I was Robert's wife. I take it he's not here otherwise you'd know all this. What's it this time? Drugs?'

Perhaps Dave's assumption had been close after all. As she sat down at the other end of the sofa I noticed her hair dotted with little bits of greenery as if she'd been sitting beneath a willow tree. Why specifically a willow? We'd had one in our garden when I was a kid and I recognised little pieces of catkins. Expensive perfume assailed more than my nose; no doubt peppered with artificial pheromones. That, at least, would explain the reaction of my officers and my own conflicting feelings. The hall was already full of every male officer on the premises. Thankfully the coroner's team were all women and hadn't been attracted by the scent, at least not yet, or this glamorous young woman from whom it emanated.

'Haven't you got work to do?' I barked. They came out of trances that police officers shouldn't have allowed themselves to fall into, and scampered off to fulfil their various duties leaving Mrs Saxum and me alone. God! I couldn't stand it anymore.

'Mrs Saxum, do you mind if we walk?'

I was up and opening the front door before she had time to answer and was gentleman enough to allow her to precede me onto the landing. When I thumbed the button for a lift she moved alongside me.

'My name's Cesca,' she said, holding out a slender hand. I accepted it knowing I was likely to experience a tingle of arousal, but wasn't amused when I did.

'Detective Inspector Clements.'

'What's this all about, inspector? It's not the first time I've come home to find police in my flat.' Which explained her calm behaviour now, but not her anger moments earlier.

'Let's wait till we're outside, Miss Saxum. To be frank, your choice of fragrance is somewhat unsettling.' I had to remind myself she was likely my first suspect and I wasn't exactly playing by the book. But doing things my way was how I got results, and the commendations.

With a wry and unsettling smile she glanced down at my crotch. Raincoats had their uses after all. Unfortunately I'd have to wipe that alluring grin off her face in a minute. Informing people of the death of someone close was never easy, or remotely enjoyable, even when the victim was Hospes.

The local park wasn't far. I dropped the Raybans off the top of my head as we left the building and made small talk against the noise of cabs and double-decker buses battling the city's congestion. People stared at us: A tall greying thirty-five-year old in a scruffy beige mack and an elegant classy female who would have looked good on any catwalk. And she did. She was a model. She'd driven back overnight from a show in London in her custom-pink Ferrari 430 Scuderia, claiming she'd used the quieter motorways as a chance to test its speed; going as far as Preston before returning to Birmingham.

The cacophony of traffic sounds seemed far away as we passed through the gateway of the park and followed the pathway around the carefully kept lawns. I chose a wooden bench that had a clear view of the entrance to Olympus Tower, noting also that DS Moody was loitering by the park entrance – I could always rely on him – and told her what the janitor had found that morning. The door to their flat had been open and he'd decided to be nosey. Thankfully he'd refrained from vomiting until he was out on the back staircase, but those were details she didn't need to know. He'd called the police straight away. She didn't look surprised, shocked or upset. In fact I was hard pressed to put any emotion to her face just then.

'How was he killed?' Matter of fact. Not at all what I'd normally expect. She had a knack of bewildering me, or should that have read enchanting me?

'That's yet to be established.' Judy reckoned she wouldn't have any definite idea until she'd carried out the post mortem. Despite the horrendous injuries she reserved judgement, as always.

I was beginning to feel in control of myself again. The sun had broken through an earlier haze with a comfortable warmth, but as we were sitting in the shade of a couple of willow trees I decided it didn't quite justify removing my coat. My senses were finally cleared by the gentle autumn breeze that swirled the bright smell of adjacent pines. But now pert nipples were drawing my eyes to the soft woollen...

'Everyone liked him. It has to be Jeanette.'

'Jeanette?' Thankfully she wasn't looking at me, but she wasn't the kind of woman not to have noticed my straying eyes. Women had never bothered me in a sexual way before and I didn't take kindly to manipulation. Cesca Saxum had that down to an art.

'His ex-girlfriend. She couldn't bear the thought of him sleeping with another human.' She lowered her eyes.

'Do you know where she lives?'

'Of course.' Was that a smile? 'She lives on the fifth floor.'

I was back in the tower block pronto, having ordered Cesca Saxum to remain in the foyer with Moody, after informing a growing horde of Nikon-flashing paparazzi that she was 'helping us with our inquiries'. It seemed both Cesca and her husband were newsworthy personalities. But before I visited Jeannette I checked the basement car park. Sure enough the pink Ferrari was still cooling down. I put a quick call into headquarters on my way up in the lift and hung about in the fifth-floor lobby while the station sergeant — Sue was always up on the celebrity gossip — filled me in on the Saxum empire as if I was thick. I tended not to read about Hospes. Seems I needed to rectify that, although there was something in my casual memory that was trying to surface. He'd made his millions importing and exporting — read intergalactic — and had recently set up a modelling agency for humans and Hospes.

I rang the bell and knocked several times before a tight-towelled pin-up answered the door looking like I'd caught her about to take a shower. I should have guessed she'd be the other woman in the photo upstairs. I hadn't realised how much alike they were. This could almost have been Cesca. My warrant card convinced her to let me in with one of the WPCs, who accompanied her while she showered and dressed. Here pad was half the size of Saxum's, but still massive compared to my humble abode.

In the bedroom the double divan was cool and made. In fact it could have come straight out of a showroom. But if she was a model too then it was a good bet she'd been partying in the local clubs and hadn't been home long. That's just my preconceptions, of course; reading too many tabloids, I guess.

Jeannette Abeo allowed my WPC to remain with her an hour later when I left her flat after she'd given me a very similar account to Cesca's, claiming Saxum's wife had loaned her the Ferrari because hers had been vandalised. She'd been surprised at this sudden show of generosity because Cesca had been very hostile to her since the marriage.

Yet Jeannette's response to Saxum's death couldn't have been more different than Cesca's. You might have compared her wailing to an African tribe grieving the death of their chief. It was hardly believable for a human, and by then, with no time to apply make-up, I knew she wasn't.

Back in the foyer I sat down beside Cesca. Thanks to some astute questioning by my WPC — maybe it was her subtle way of telling me a bit more about Hospes — Jeannette had told us that Hospes practiced incest. It wasn't illegal or frowned upon because it took several generations of mixing bloodlines before conception was possble within a family. It was also normal for brothers and sisters to have sexually relations throughtout their lives and wasn't seen as cheating on partners. Robert Saxum was actually her brother. No, they'd never disclosed that to anyone, not even Cesca. They didn't trust that she'd not tell someone if she knew, and they didn't want it to appear that Jeanette was being shown favouritism in her modelling career. She assured me they'd been descrete, but there was a little desperation in her voice, as if she was trying to convince herself. One thing I did know about Hospes; they were a passionately jealous race, and if Cesca hadn't been aware of the relationship...

Moody had been enthralled with Cesca's modelling stories. Knowing her enchanting guile I bet he'd have been enthralled by anything she said.

"Was it poison you used?" I asked her directly, before I could fall under her charm again. That got my first reaction.

"What?" Her astonishment was probably not so much what I'd asked but that I was savvy enough to have even thought of such a question. Men were easily manipulated in her mind. Of course she was right, but maybe she wasn't used to gay detectives.

"Before you cut off Robert's tackle. You poisoned him."

"That's ridiculous. I told you I wasn't even here."

"It wasn't you driving the Ferrari. It was Jeanette. She phoned you to say she was nearly home. That's when you carried out your deed leaving you to inherited Robert Saxum's fortune. You left the door ajar knowing the janitor would discover it on his morning rounds, and sat in the park, right where we sat a while ago, to watch the entrance to Olympus Tower. You saw Jeanette drive into the basement not long after we arrived, then came up to the apartment on the pretext of arriving home."

"I got out of the car and went straight up to the apartment," she responded indignantly.

"So what's with the willow catkins in your hair?"

The wig shifted as she dragged her hand through. I heard DS Moody draw in a sharp breath as he glimpsed her green skin beneath. At the same moment Jeannette exited the lift looking the Hospes she was; Green and grim. A second gasp from Dave.

"Jeannette wasn't your husband's ex-girlfriend, she was his sister."

"No!"

"You had no need to be jealous."

"No!" It was Jeanette's turn to shout. And mine too when I saw her pull a small blaster from her handbag. They were illegal of course. A Hospes weapon that we'd already encountered on the streets. An indiscriminate device in the hands of the untrained, and what was worse Cesca was doing exactly the same, and if the beams crossed... My training said negotiate, but we were dealing with two Hospes here. Instead, my survival instinct kicked in.

"Take cover!" I turned, flipping down my shades, with the intention of putting as much distance between the two Hospes women and me, catching a glimpse of horrified journalists with their noses pushed against the glass doors as they realised what was about to happen. I was lifted up and over them in the wake of the shattering doors as the converging energy beams produced a massive shock wave.

Amazingly, I was up on my feet in seconds with little more than scratches, noting that some of the paparazzi hadn't been so lucky, being on the other side of the glass, and back inside in an eerily quiet vignette of destruction. Moody was hauling himself off the floor and my WPC had sensibly stayed in the lift and closed the doors. Of the two Hospes, only pieces remained, decorating the foyer like a verdent rain forest. Like I said, I hadn't seen a dead Hospes until I was called to Olympus Tower.

Anguish

Not a science fiction, fantasy or horror story, this one, but a bit of a mind fuck. Having been close to a breakdown once — never believe you're too together for it to happen to you — I tried to give a hint of what it could be like.

Anguish

Spongers like her should be locked up. They were no good to society. No good to themselves. Ben Stains didn't think his views were extreme. In fact he thought most other people's tolerance verged on anarchy.

Through the café window he watched the vagrant woman as she wheeled her pram, full of her worldly possessions, along the high street, doing her late evening trash-can rounds before the daily town-centre collection robbed her of some unthinkable treasure. Her clothes hung with that same-colour caked look reminding him of the 'mime' artists he'd seen along London's Southbank, sitting or standing like statues, when he and his wife Lynn had visited the Eye. But *they* didn't smell. There could be no doubting she would. Just like the woman who had cleared a whole tube carriage on that same trip. That anyone could allow themselves to smell so disgusting had shocked both of them.

A piece of cereal bar caught in his throat at the thought. It took several minutes to recover from the resulting coughing fit. The few other customers in the café glanced at him disapprovingly. He refrained from giving them the finger, but the temptation was there. When his tickle finally subsided the old hag had disappeared, no doubt searching more lucrative bins. This thought merely caused him to dry retch and those at the nearby tables avoided looking in his direction.

Had someone suggested to him that maybe there was an element of jealousy in his almost fanatical hatred of an old woman who he had never spoken to, he would have laughed and denied it without a thought. But she was free, and he wasn't. His marriage had not been the most successful although Lynn and he were still together, just. What responsibility for a tramp?

With a cup empty of both coffee and warmth and a café that no longer seemed welcoming, Ben left to walk the last few miles home, dreading the usual moans and groans; unlike others, not looking forward to the weekend at all.

Monday morning came way too soon, yet, in many ways, it was a huge relief. They had rowed nearly all weekend and his year-old daughter, Sarah, suffering from yet another cold, had kept them awake most of Saturday and Sunday night. Begrudging peace arrived when Lynn wheeled Sarah to the local park — the walk would do her good. No, she didn't want a lift. No, she didn't want him to come too, she wanted to be on her own. It had all stemmed from an argument about money -- it was invariably about money, but not exclusively. Recent promotion should have made them better off, but where did the money go? He'd watched Lynn push the pram down the terraced street. The little plastic duck he'd bought his daughter, that she'd grown so attached to, hung from the canopy, bright yellow against the standard Mothercare dark blue. Lynn had stopped briefly at the corner of the street to speak with someone just out of view. Ben had been furious when his wife eventually moved off to reveal the filthy bitch of a vagrant. It was the first time Ben had noticed that Sarah's pram was identical to the woman's, but how could she bare to be near the filthy, stinking cow let alone talk to her?

Stressed out at work, with the extra responsibility, Ben had no respite Monday morning. A couple of silly mistakes resulted in his boss calling him into his office.

"What's the problem, Ben?"

"Still settling in, George. Won't happen again."

"But you were doing the work before you were made up to

IC." George was younger than Ben, had taken up the manager's position almost straight from university. He didn't have half Ben's experience, who did he think he was?

Ben hesitated. He didn't want to admit he was under stress; was finding it hard to cope, at work and at home. He tried to stop himself clicking the pen he'd brought with him. "I'm fine. Just a bit tired is all. Sarah's not been sleeping too well. Been keeping us both up."

"Do you think you could do with some time off?" George was looking worriedly at the pen, frowning at each click.

"Not at all. I'll be fine. You have my assurance."

George didn't look convinced. "If you need any help or want to talk about anything my door's always open."

"I appreciate that," getting up, wanting to exit the room as soon as possible, "thanks."

All eyes in the office looked his way, he could feel them, as he strode back to his desk. He threw his pen down and looked at his watch. Early lunch, he thought.

Having driven to work that morning, he decided to make use of the car and took a trip to the park to eat his sandwiches away from the office. If he didn't he'd still get hassled with phone calls and queries. His favourite bench gave him a panoramic view of the river. To his left, a variety of ducks and geese waddled along the bank or splashed in the shallows above the weir. Its continuing rumble always calmed him. Perhaps life wasn't so bad after all.

No sooner had this thought crossed his mind when, from around the back of an adjacent clump of shrubs, the old vagrant woman appeared, hood up on her pram, protecting her black plastic sacks from who knew what.

The cheese sandwich dried in is mouth, sucking out any last remnant of moisture. All his pent up anger and frustrations seemed to channel themselves towards the hag, as if all his problems could be blamed on her.

Even while a part of him knew this was illogical his emotions got the better of him. He flung his sandwiches, Tupperware box and all, into the raging water, slipping on the loose gravel of the path as he stormed back to his car.

A bent-back nail, as he opened the door clumsily, gave him pain enough to quell his anger somewhat, even to the point of realising his stupidity.

Leaning back in the driving seat he closed his eyes and willed himself to relax, surprising himself with a modicum of success. A gentle tap on the window brought him out of his revere. He turned his head lazily.

"'Scuse me, dearie, but you're not supposed to park 'ere."

Ben was speechless. A fury he never knew he possessed left him gasping for words. Such audacity from the old woman! Who did she think she was?

He gave her a single finger, proud of his outward composure. Turning on the engine and simultaneously slamming it into gear, he reversed the car away from the reprimanding look, catching sight of her pram on the pathway beneath the weir. He looked from that to the old lady and smiled unpleasantly.

Her eyes betrayed her sudden realisation. Still smiling, and watching the woman's face, Ben methodically slipped the car into first. She was screaming "No! No!" as he floored the accelerator pedal, keeping it there as the car jumped the shallow kerb, shot across a carefully maintained flower bed, missing a statue of a long-forgotten local celebrity by mere millimetres, flattened the "Keep off the grass" sign before crashing into the pram. It lurched unceremoniously over the edge of the bank out of Ben's vision, but before it did a little yellow plastic duck swung out from the canopy. His insides knotted in an instant.

Ben hadn't needed to brake. The car had stalled to a halt on the brink. He was heedless of anything but what he had done. Why had his wife come to the park two days running? Why had she left Sarah on her own? These were just two of many miner thoughts that were consumed in his despair. He couldn't swim and he knew the currents hereabouts were lethal. He'd murdered his own daughter.

The old hag was running along the bank with the flow of the water screaming and waving her arms about.

Ben took the car out of gear and let the electronics open the windows as the front wheels edged over the bank. He closed his eyes, and took a final and unnecessary deep breath as the vehicle tipped forward into the foam.

His wife Lynn mourned briefly, but she soon found a new partner who was happy to accept Sarah as his own. The old woman had scoured the river for days afterwards and managed to find almost all her possessions accept for the yellow plastic duck the nice young lady had given her.

Variants

Variants was never meant to be as long as it is; the problem with a lack of planning, but the length justifies the story... I think.

Variants

There was no chance of avoiding the tiger that bounded towards me through the trees on that first morning of the safari. My hunting rifle was thirty metres away in the camp and the animal would be upon me before I was halfway.

Its markings, though, told me it was a Mary Quant Mark II, and I was more likely to be smothered to death with a hot slobbering tongue than mauled. A city boy like me couldn't help being apprehensive, but I quickly adopted the kneeling pose that told the beast I wasn't a threat.

I was no expert with animals, but I had passed the recognition test. This was a particularly big cat though. Based on the Bengali, but with all the aggression gened out, you'd still be surprised to know it wasn't a carnivore, well at least not this version. Most Quants were kept as pets but sometimes their owners chose to release them and the UK was the favoured dumping place.

A shot rang out that frightened me more than the oncoming tiger which collapsed, skidded and tumbled to a heap in front of me, a trickle of blood seeping from a hole in the centre of its forehead.

I couldn't contain my fury at seeing such a majestic animal killed and, expecting a trigger-happy Karl, swung round only to find I was hurling abuse at Abigail.

"Whatever did you do that for?" I eventually stammered as I hauled myself off my knees. "It was only a Mary Quant."

"A variant," she corrected as she turned away. "Check out the tail, Tony." Then she stopped, looked back. "And the claws and teeth."

I did both and, while marvelling at the size and beauty of the tiger, decided I not only needed to apologise to Karl's wife but also thank her for saving my life.

Karl and Abe had been my friends for no more than a year. Right now they were helping to make one of my childhood dreams come true.

I had lived near the centre of Paris all my life and dreamt of visiting the British Wildlife Park ever since it had featured in an Animal Watch series on the Discovery Channel when I was six. Karl and Abigail were wardens, working as a pair, and, when not on duty, lived in a luxury apartment next to mine. Real party people they were.

As corny as it seems we'd met when Abigail had knocked to borrow some coffee. I thought my luck had changed because she was a stunning woman. Tall, wild blond hair, wide blue eyes, and a slinky figure that would raise the blood of any heterosexual male. That was before I met Karl, who women probably found equally attractive. He was around six foot four, broad shoulders, lithe rather than bulky with short blond hair and milliperfect stubble. They both wore a tan like it was their natural skin colour. They could have been Scandinavian sex gods. Turn heads? You bet they did.

As for me. I'm one of those Brits - yes, I still call myself a Brit despite being fourth generation - with the sort of ancestry that throws up some surprises. Somewhere in the past there's a little bit of Jamaican that voodoos me with a mischievous streak and gives me my recklessness, but damns me with the occasional turn of uncertainty. My Indian heritage is physically more noticeable with jet black hair and light brown skin, though strangely I burn very easily. This is where I get my aloofness and arrogance from.

I'm actually neither but the appearance has had its uses. Dominating both these is my Irish blood giving me the gift of the gab and a little ruggedness to dull down that Asian beauty, leaving me with a face that leads people to assume I'm Italian. I can live with that.

I took my intended leak, with rather more attention to my surroundings, and, before making my way back to the camp, spent a few moments inspecting the tiger again. You see them on TV but you never appreciate their true size. I'd been pretty stupid and swore to myself I'd not let Abigail down again. In my defence the tail pattern was not that different from a Mark II Quant, and the tail was the only deviance.

A clear August sky was growing lighter and the cacophony of bird calls, silenced by the roar of the hunting rifle, had started in earnest again, although the smell of cordite still hung in the air. There seemed a foreboding amidst the sparse oak woods that, I decided eventually, was just a result of my recent experience.

When I entered the camp Karl was cooking breakfast on the portable stove, and the smell of frying bacon could have made me smile had Abigail not been sitting on a fallen tree trunk nearby, her Magnum M98 Mauser already broken down and being meticulously cleaned and oiled. She looked up and shook her head, but it was Karl who spoke.

"You were damn lucky, Tony." He didn't turn or raise his voice but I knew he was furious with me the way he held his shoulders. "Don't leave the camp without telling us. Lucky we heard you go and that Abigail was looking out for you. Make sure the magnum's with you at all times." I patted an empty hip where the .357 Centurion should have been sitting within its holster.

"At least you'd have had half a chance with that." He'd pulled my revolver from his waistband and threw it hard. I caught it against my stomach forcing out a sound of fear rather than pain as he added. "Keep that with you at all times. Don't underestimate the dangers here, Tony." He went back to shuffling the bacon in the pan.

I felt about six inches tall, and one hundred per cent the city boy.

Then still smaller when he added quietly. "And make sure that's loaded." Sure enough, the cylinder was empty. I should have know he wouldn't have thrown a loaded gun at me.

"I'm sorry guys. I owe you, Abe. I've learned my lesson."

"I don't suppose you have." He looked at me hard then, and I realised for the first time that he didn't really want me there, maybe didn't even like me. I'd made an uncharacteristic assumption but it had been Abigail who had made the offer and in my excitement I must have missed the signs.

We'd been out for an evening meal a month earlier, the three of us and a single friend of theirs called Honey, who I think Abigail was trying to match me with. Karl was thrilling us with his stories from the park so much that I just couldn't stop myself from asking what chance there was of going with them on a "tour of duty". We were on our fourth bottle of house red which Karl had predominantly consumed. Even so, it had taken me quite an effort to persuade him and, in hindsight, he may only have agreed so that I would shut up, although Abe had seen how much I wanted to go.

"We can take him on the first leg just for a few days. He can fly back from Stansted."

"Is that still operational?"

"Atmosphair have taken over running day trips to the tree houses in Hatfield Forest, and Stansted is ideally placed. The Park's always had a presence there."

"I know, but we shouldn't be allowing sightseers in at all!" I was surprised at the strength of Karl's feelings and felt immediately ashamed that I'd asked, yet angry that he felt this way about anyone not involved with the park.

"Stansted's not that far off our tour. We can arrange to pick up more supplies once we drop Tony off. He'll be with us, Karl." She laid a hand on his arm. Just for a split second he stiffened but then relaxed and forced a smile in my direction.

"Looks like you've got a supporter, Tony." He looked at Abigail. "Can you sort out the papers Monday."

She kissed him on the cheek then. "It'll be fine Tony. Don't worry."

The evening had ended with Honey coming back to my place, but, while she was quite attractive, there just didn't seem to be any chemistry between us and after a coffee and stilted conversation I rang her a cab. I fell asleep thinking about Abigail.

👾👾👾

I'd flown into London City Airport on a full jetprop Nevada. I think I was probably the only tourist. Most of the passengers wore purple fleeces emblazoned with the British Wildlife Park's flourished elephant-trunk emblem and slashed lettering. There was a bunch of UN soldiers in black fatigues noticeable by the blue berets tucked into their epaulettes and a dozen or so troops from the crack European Attack Team in traditional British camouflage.

For some reason this surprised me. I'd expected the plane to be packed with sightseers. I felt completely out of place and somewhat uneasy the whole flight but when Karl and Abigail met me at the airport I relaxed immediately. They had already spent a fortnight working their way up from Brighton and we'd be heading North-East in the morning.

Like most other towns and cities in the UK, London had been raised to the ground with just a few of the main historical buildings preserved. London City Airport was therefore a bit of a misnomer, yet there was quite a sprawl of hotels and park administration buildings that made it a surprisingly large settlement.

Basic as it was the hotel had proved comfortable enough, though I'd hardly slept through excitement. We set off the following morning in the BWP's Invader, a custom wide-wheel-based Land Rover, with me sitting in the middle of the bench seat. Karl was on my left doing the driving and Abigail sat on my right, the butt of a rifle resting on the floor between her legs and its barrel wavering in front of her face; unloaded I was later informed. We all wore multipocketed khakis with baggy knee-length shorts, courtesy of the BWP, though mine only carried the park's logo on the left breast pocket, no ensignia for me. You could have sat another two people in the cab quite comfortably, the vehicle was that wide. The compound led straight out on tarmac road through woodland.

"Don't look disappointed, Tony," Abigail reassured me, "roads like this only go out about five miles from London then it's dirt track or cross country."

Karl turned his head in my direction. "We'll be stopping before then though. There's a UN range near here. Need you to get used to the Mauser. Have you fired a rifle before?"

I shook my head but he'd already turned back to watch the road. "No," I told him.

"Any gun?" asked Abigail as if she knew where Karl's questions were leading.

My head shake was spotted this time. "I play paintball in the Diablo League," I said cheerfully

"Oh my god," mumbled Karl.

"He could be a natural," Abe tried to reassure him. In fact, it turned out I wasn't at all bad. I'd teased them about not having used firearms of course, although Karl didn't see the funny side of it. While they knew I was a salesman they'd never asked me what I sold. That's not as strange as it sounds. Tell someone you're a salesman and most will avoid asking what you sell for fear you'll try to sell them something. I'm fine with that though. Funnily enough I'm not exactly proud of selling guns; pleased of having my own gun business yes, but then I don't like to make a big thing about that either.

My interest in guns started back when I lived in the Afro-Brit ghetto sandwiched tightly between China Town and the Asian quarter. So tight that we were the brunt of anger from gangs of youths from both.

My grandparents had done the best they could following my

parents' death at the hands of a terrorist bomb when I was just six. My playmate and second best friend after Devon was Johnny from next door, whose involvement with the local triad gangs had eventually led to his death in my mid teens. A bullet through the head. In broad daylight. Right outside our appartment. It was this moment that led both to my hatred and fascination of firearms. Guns weren't going to go away but I believed we could exert more control over them. Naïve youth.

I'd made it my business to be able to strip down and clean any firearm I sold, but I rarely got to fire a gun on a range. Uncomfortable as it was the Magnum revolver lumped into the holster on my waist belt gave me a certain feeling of assurance, not to mention smugness, as I had scored higher than Karl with it, although both he and, particularly, Abigail had impressed, and knocked spots off me, me with the Mauser. I was going to appreciate that more than I realised.

As we left the range, and the small UN outpost, along a gravel track that was fast becoming overgrown, Karl answered a question I'd wanted to ask.

"These UN outposts are dotted all around the South East. Kent and Essex mainly. That's the nearest one to London. Supposed to stop pet dumping. Designer pets that is. Resources are too stretched though. Patrol boats do their best but there's only so much coastline they can cover. The inland sites are little more than a political gesture. Governments can say the national community is upholding their end of the Birmingham Convention when in fact the UN couldn't give a fuck."

"Karl!"

"Tony's not stupid. I think he knows more about the park than he makes out."

"Only what I read in the papers," I told him honestly, thinking that he was just annoyed at my tease earlier. "I'm not really up on the Birmingham Convention. Enlighten me."

Abe looked across at Karl before she answered. He shrugged as if to say, go ahead, but he knows already.

I held my protests in check and let Abigail respond to my request.

"Before the UK was re-forested ..."

"De-populated ," Karl interrupted.

"Whatever."

Abigail's response was unexpected. I'd never seen this side of them before. They were always such a perfect couple. I knew it was childish of me but I quietly enjoyed this show of disaffection.

"... It had become a major crime centre and haven for terrorists. There'd been a great deal of lobbying for the transformation of the UK mainland into an International wildlife park, but at that time there'd been no plans to include species from other countries, or regened animals. It was at the Birmingham Convention that this was agreed and the twenty-four City Neuvo principal accepted."

We all know how successful the Cities project was, the flip side of depopulating the UK and almost as controversial. I don't think we could imagine ever doing something like that again though. But I've an aunt, lives in New London, who reckons she doesn't want for anything, and loves the California weather. Nowhere near as warm in Faircity, although the Irish parklands certainly give it more of a spacious feel.

"So," I interrupted, "you believe that the billions spent on the new cities left little to be spent on the park."

"Nothing to be spent here. It's ..."

She hesitated. Scratched her chin on the end of the barrel. "It's not for me to say."

"Sorry I brought it up," Karl said, avoiding a fallen tree with an exaggerated swing of the steering wheel. "I sometimes wonder what we're doing this for."

I decided not to press the conversation. It seemed clear to me that they both felt they had said too much, but what that was eluded me.

Our journey had stalled to a snails pace. Although Abe announced we were on the outskirts of Epping Forest it didn't look much different to me apart from the density. Without the GPS on the dashboard I'm pretty certain Abe wouldn't have known either. We were obviously following a track of some kind else we'd not have been able to negotiate the Invader between the trees.

Apart from a group of chimpanzees, that disappeared even before Karl had time to stop to watch, the morning and early afternoon proved uneventful. We lunched on French stick and sliced ostrich by the side of a swift-flowing river where swans and mallards seemed to be prolific. It could have been any park in France accept for the apes we had seen, but this was the country where my great grandparents had been born. I still had that feeling of foreigness that I get anywhere other than Paris.

"Make the most of the bread," Abigail advised me. "We'll be on dried food in a few days." I raised my eyebrows at that as the back of the vehicle seemed crammed with equipment. "It's not really necessary. Just a discipline we like to maintain."

A little later Karl had been working the Invader through the undergrowth when, from her single bandoleer, that parted and accentuated her breasts, Abigail eased out a bullet and slid it into the chamber using a slick movement of the bolt. With a quick proficiency she hauled herself off the seat and was resting her forearm on the rim of the sun roof before Karl could ask, "What do you see?"

"Variant," was all she said.

I barely heard Karl's mumbled response, "Not this far south," and couldn't make out if he was questioning what Abe had seen or was just surprised.

Karl stopped the Invader, it's low-noise engine lost in the rustle of leaves from a westerly breeze that hinted at a change in the weather.

"Lost them," Abigail told us as she sat back down with the rifle between her legs again but this time she slipped the barrel into a clip on the dashboard. "I'd rather blow the windscreen out than my head off," she said to me, obviously having noted my concerned looks earlier.

"What did you see?" I had to know.

"Variant," she said again.

"What type?" I asked, aware that some animals were gened to heighten their predatorial instincts, not their docility.

"Let's just say it's dangerous. And, to be this far south, either stupid or very confident."

"You sure Abe?" Karl asked.

"I'm sure." She sighed, but not unkindly. "Let's get going again. We need to be in open woodland before we set up camp for the night."

I was still none the wiser as to what type of animal Abe had seen but from the way they kept checking the side windows and looking out the back I imagined it to be something like a rhinoceros. They didn't close the sun roof so it was unlikely to be a leopard, but by the time we stopped I had become quite concerned, and said as much.

"I think is was just a chance encounter. No need to report it to central." I didn't realise the significance of this remark until much later.

Once we'd set up the tent Karl sat in the back of the Land Rover making his report while Abigail set to work heating dinner over an open fire. I could hear mumbled words from the truck and a jumble of static but nothing specific.

Abigail seemed quite relaxed now so I tried to emulate her mood. As the spectator on this safari I was less inclined to start conversation and Abe was either wrapped up in her own thoughts or trying to listen to Karl on the radio. By the time he rejoined us with a cool beer each I was feeling much more comfortable.

"Have to get our priorities right," Abe said with a smile, raising the can in a "cheers" gesture.

Sitting on fold-up chairs around a flaming fire, and staring into it as if we were meditating, we ate a beef stew in silence. Not because we had nothing to say but, I think, because we were hungry. I for one wasn't used to the fresh country air and it had given me a real appetite. A shallow stream splashed its way over a stony bed nearby adding further to the restful atmosphere. It was the smell of fresh coffee that finally brought me out of my revere and stimulated the conversation once again.

"E, A, T will have chopper patrols out in the morning Abe," Karl informed casually. "Another warden has spotted variants. Near the Norfolk border. Wasn't much point in telling them about the loner though." Then added for my sake, "That's the European Attack Team. They sometimes help out with their helicopters with this sort of thing. Gives them practice."

"They don't just use the park for manoeuvres then?" Before my flight to the UK I hadn't even known that the European Attack Team had a presence here, but had gathered from our occasional and brief moments of conversation during our journey that this was the case.

"Generally just manoeuvres." Karl studied the grindings at the bottom of his cup. "But they sometimes use these opportunities to practice their trade."

Abe noticed me looking out into the growing darkness.

"Don't worry Tony. Karl's set up the security cone. If anything gets within twenty metres of the camp we'll know about it."

We'd chatted for maybe another half an hour. Abigail told me what they had planned for the next day, the second of what had finally been decided would be a 10-day tour. Apparently a small herd of elephants had broken through the Suffolk perimeter fence. All wardens in the East Anglian region had been tasked with locating them.

I'd not realised before that the park was zoned, but to sustain certain species it was necessary to keep them apart. Elephants could strip an area of foliage in no time and culls were required on a regular basis despite the help of poachers.

"Why do we never get to read about all this?" I asked incredulously.

"Who wants to read about the plight of a few animals," Karl responded. "It's just not going to sell newspapers."

"You're joking! Most people seem more concerned about animals than anything else. Until I met you I'd almost forgotten the park existed, but when I was a kid it was my dream to visit the park. I couldn't get enough animal programmes. Why isn't this place publicised any more?"

"Open your eyes Tony." My tone had obviously aggravated Karl. "Do you really think the EAT are here to play zookeepers?"

His anger was perplexing and his explanation of EAT's presence confusing.

Abigail looked daggers at him. "Forget it," he snapped. She looked at me and shrugged as Karl changed the subject.

"So, your a gun retailer?"

"I've three shops now. Don't sell on the internet although I get a lot of hits on the site." I was soon wrapped up in the details of my little empire. As I mentioned before, not many people inquire about my business so, given the opportunity, there was no stopping me. They were genuinely interested and their knowledge of firearms was improportionate to their own personal use. When we got down to costs they seemed surprised at the markup and, it seemed, disappointed for me.

Eventually I pulled myself into the sleeping bag feeling exhausted but anticipating an exciting next day. A flimsy canvas partition separated Karl and Abigail from my quarters. I eventually fell asleep, childishly disappointed that their relationship hadn't deteriorated. At least it didn't sound that way.

You're already aware of how my morning started: badly. It seemed I was going to be in their bad books for the rest of the safari. We took it in turns to wash in the stream and generally freshen ourselves up. They were, however, more mature than I'd given them credit for because once we'd started out on our journey again their professionalism took over, treating me no differently than they had the previous day.

"Did you notice?" Karl asked, glancing passed me at Abigail, just ten minutes into another slow, bumpy ride.

"The tiger had disappeared," she stated. He nodded.

"I thought one of you had moved it!" I'd taken a quick glance as I clambered into the Land Rover, just assuming, rather stupidly I suppose, that they had hidden it.

Abigail was loading her rifle. "A 400 pound tiger? We leave nature to look after itself. Scavangers do the tidying up for us."

"What took it then?" I asked, trying to imagine what sort of animal would be able to drag such a heavy beast from under our noses.

"That type," replied Abigail rising from her seat and bracing herself against the back of the sun roof opening.

I still couldn't see anything. Bracken and ferns covered much of the forest floor. I was disappointed my vision wasn't as sharp as Abe's. I looked up at her, trying to follow her aim. Could still see nothing as she let off a shot.

I heard a satisfied "yes" and the methodical clunk of the bolt as she slid a second round into the chamber.

"Careful, Abe," warned Karl. "There has to be at least half a dozen to have moved that tiger so quickly."

"What are they?" I demanded in frustration. But even as I said it I watched them rise up in the undergrowth and peal off in several direction.

"Fuck, Abe! So many!" The tone of Karl's voice didn't help my anxiety.

I closed my mouth slowly, having let it hang open.

"They're variants?"

Abe shouted confirmation through the roof.

"But they're human!"

"Humanoid, Tony. Don't be fooled. Not like you were earlier." Karl rattled his words of quickly. Glanced at me to make sure I realised he was serious. His eyes did that on there own. I'd never expected to see fear there. "Get in the back. Open up the black trunk. Here. Here's the key."

I clambered over the seats awkwardly as the Invader wobbled and bumped across the uneven terrain. Fumbled to get the key in the padlock.

Cursing at my ineptitude I finally yanked the lid open and was astonished to find an arsenal of weapons and ammunition.

"Pass me the Uzzi quick," Karl yelled. "We need to scare them quickly else they'll attack."

There was a thump of confirmation on the side of the Land Rover that startled me. Distracted and confused I handed Karl the weapon.

"Load the fucking thing, punter!" he screamed throwing the Uzzi back at me. "And grab one yourself if you value your life."

Another arrow whacked the side of our vehicle. Abe fired off three more rounds, may have been four, before she sat down suddenly with a sigh.

Karl turned and grabbed the gun off me just as I slammed in the magazine, his other hand tight on the steering wheel.

I checked on why Abe had stopped firing. Must have made an odd noise because Karl, who'd raked his side of the forest only once, looked round.

"Oh sweet M'hammed no!"

"Fire!" he screamed at me as he threw himself across the seat to his wife, the Invader lurching to an unceremonious stop.

Reality for me took a back seat in those moments. With the second Uzzi I'd found, I stuck my hand over the rim of the sun roof and strafed in a circular pattern around our stationery vehicle. I didn't want to look down and see again the barbed metal tip of an arrow protruding from Abigail neck; pushing out her skin like pouting lips, the only blood loss a gurgling splatter from her mouth and nose.

I could hear Karl talking to her so I guessed she was still alive. I emptied the magazine with another burst of sweeping fire, snapped another on, and, with a little more bravery stood through the roof to get a better view. Tall undergrowth could have hidden an army and I'd not have seen them. All seemed quite though.

"How is she," I called down, still not wanting a second look at Abe's wound. It had looked serious to me.

There was no answer. I glanced down quickly. Abe was staring straight ahead, a surprised look etched on her beautiful features. While I was firing Karl had slipped out her door. I'd not seen him go. I suddenly felt useless, vulnerable and more afraid than I'd ever felt in my life before.

Stealing myself to lean across the fresh corpse of Abigail I pulled the door to, only to be pinned as her torso fell forward on top of me. Quickly I pulled myself free, aware of her body against mine, a hug in death that I'd never been able to experience in life, yet I shunned it.

Right then I was more concerned about my own safety and, starting up the Invader, edged slowly forward looking for a place to turn. Going back the way we'd come seemed the obvious thing to do. I felt little guilt about leaving Karl. He was still alive though. I could here the intermittent chatter of an Uzzi with the occasional crack of a revolver.

I began to panic when that stopped, crying out in fear and surprise when he stepped into the path of the Land Rover. I hardly recognised him at first. Blood splatters covered him from head to foot. None of it seemed his.

I'd expected to find frenzied madness in his eyes but saw only despair. Tears streaked his face. When he opened the passenger door they fell freely again, washing paths of sadness down his cheeks.

He pulled Abe's body upright with a handful of shirt at her shoulder, studied her face for a minute then hauled her out the cab onto the grass, climbing back in and slamming the door.

I looked at him incredulously.

With a stare that could have frozen hell he turned to me and hissed between gritted teeth, "She's here." He thumped his chest in salute, thumbed out the window. "That's just her physical host." If he'd wanted to say it was my fault he couldn't have put it any better. I couldn't meet his accusing eyes, although I shouldn't have felt guilty. My throat was constricted but the "sorry" stuck there, saving me from insulting him with an unnecessary apology.

"Drive."

I did. For maybe half an hour. With eyes imagining variants behind every tree, I maneuvered the invader along what seemed the obvious, and only, route. Karl said nothing. Stared ahead at nothing. Rolling with the uneven surface where Abigail had sat. How quickly life can be taken away, I thought. How cheap it is.

Memories flooded back from my youth. Seeing Johnny die. He'd not been at school that day so when I saw him through our lounge window walking across the concrete bridge from the opposite block of flats I made for the front door to catch him before he went into his own house. Three other youths, probably no more than thirteen years old, were running along the other side shouting: "Heh, Johnny Lo!"

Ignoring them at first Johnny carried on walking. I could hear them still shouting as I reached the front door. Call it instinct, call it self preservation, call it cowardice if you like, but at the last second I hesitated at the door handle. Something was about to happen that I didn't want to be a part of. Johnny had stopped on the balcony that ran the length of the block right outside my grandparents door. Despite the net curtains and frosted glass I squated down to avoid being seen. As I did so the roar of a gun sent me spralling down the hallway and an ominous thud against the door was followed by two further shots and the sound of disappearing feet.

It was likely no more than seconds before the alarm sounded through the flats but the silence engulfed me like a time tunnel in slow motion. Irrationally I was sure that one of those kids was still outside waiting for me.

I'd never let my memory take me back there before but cold sweat brought me back to the present and Abigail. Delayed nausea crept up on me and I fought against the shakes, but eventually I braked and retched out the open door. A shadow suddenly fell across my vomit. Karl had walked round the front of the four-track.

"Get in the other side. I'll drive now." Despair was still in his eyes. A permanent feature I thought. It was hidden somewhat by a conflicting look of sympathy and contempt. He didn't know my past was haunting me, my fears overiding years of avoiding the truth.

I felt like a child who'd been chastised but promised a sweet if he was a good boy. Any other time I'd have protested, but just then I was neither in the mood or felt I had the strength. I must have looked as pathetic as I felt.

We topped a hill, coming out of the trees, about an hour after Karl had taken the wheel again. A wide valley spread out before us, not particularly deep, but enough to make you appreciate the enormity of the forest. A sea of multi-toned greens spread away to the horizon, an occasional mature tree reaching up to spoil the carpet-like effect.

Thrumping just above this canopy, below us but heading in our direction, were five dark green attack helicopters in a V formation, defying gravity like ballerinas in mediaeval armour.

I expected Karl to brake, jump out and start waving madly. We did stop but he just watched impassively as they rose up from the valley and flew over. Not even a nod. We could see them scrutinising us from their cabins as they zoomed over our heads. I was almost as surprised at myself for not reacting.

Karl turned to me; studied me with eyes even more startlingly blue through the congealed streak of splattered blood.

"Thanks," he said simply. For what, I didn't ask, and he didn't give me the opportunity when he added, "I need to explain some things to you."

I waited, nodding like a convict on death row who'd just been told his time had come. But the moment was broken by the now familiar sound of a helicopter coming in low from the left. One of the attack choppers had decided we were worth investigating some more.

Nose dipped, it hovered about 30 meters in front of us. This time Karl gave the ok with his thumb in the air and I followed with a raised hand. Sunlight filled their cabin and we could see the pilot and co-pilot speaking into microphones attached to their helmets. Our faces were in the shade. Their sunglasses would have made Karl's ghoulish features less easy to define. I doubt it was a minute before the chopper peeled away, with the side gunner giving us a salute, but it had felt like an age.

"Couldn't they have helped us?" I asked. "Did you kill all the variants?"

"I don't really know about the variants, Tony." Not an answer to my questions, but an answer. "Abe," he lingered on the name, extracting a new tense to be used when speaking about her, "was convinced they are the results of experiments." He sounded exhausted, picking each word with an effort in excess of requirements. "It seemed the only explanation. You've seen them, Tony." He looked at me as if he expected confirmation, but I'd only caught a glimpse of them, so when I didn't answer he went on, "Our first sighting of them was a couple of years ago. Up in the Lake District. We thought they were E A T troops on some sort of survival test. They were real aggressive though. I took a spear in the leg that day and we'd not even fired a shot. After that we heard that other wardens were being attacked. Then E A T sent over more patrols and UN sent in observers. Whatever they are they're savages, Tony." I hadn't needed any convincing, but Karl's eyes were on me again, pleeding. Wanting me to agree, conversly sowing doubt where none had been. How he had hauled Abe's body from the cab came to me again. My sympathy for him suddenly changed to disdain.

"They're human," I sighed.

"They killed Abe." He hissed this through gritted teath. Hatred was the only strength he seemed to have. "They deserve to die."

"No one deserves to die, Karl," I whispered assertively, knowing I was tempting an argument, a reaction that I would regret. His look cut through me but I stared him out surprising myself with this sudden spark of inner strength.

"Fuck you," denied me more explanation of the variants. That would come later. For now he ripped the gears into grinding first and pulled away into the line of trees just off the hillocks summit.

I took a quick look out the back, from some kind of instinct, and made out two circling helicopters as many miles away. Karl seemed oblivious. Was he following the wardens' code or had he become a maverick. It didn't fit my own beliefs, but then this was all new to me. I had a feeling I was going to find out soon enough.

For someone keen to see wildlife I should have been disappointed. Apart from seeing, rather too closely, a tiger, albeit a wild-born variant of a domestic pussy, I'd had a lifetime's share of excitement in the last two days. Pleasant it hadn't been. Our journey continued uneventful and in silence. Well, I'd asked Karl once what his plans were, only to be told he had a job to do, but I felt like a hostage rather than a friend.

There were few option open for me. In a fight I wasn't sure I'd come out on top. And, while firing blind into undergrowth is one thing, pulling the trigger on a person you can see was something I avoided thinking about. It just wasn't an option for me.

Karl had wallowed in a shallow pond early in the afternoon to wash away the memory of his rampage while I stood guard with an M16 carbine. I wondered why they'd had such a large arsenal, completely unnecessary, I thought, for a safari. It dawned on me that they might have had a hidden agenda on this tour of duty. Something of this ilk might have been anticipated but, probably, not until after they'd dropped me off. It was just one of a multitude of answers I came up with, but none of them made sense.

It also dawned on me that my desires in Abe's direction had been infatuation. I was disappointed at losing a friend and felt cheated that I'd not been given the opportunity to discover if she fantasised about me the way I had about her. Stupid to ponder on, I know, but that's me I suppose. Shame. I did feel shame. With such strong feelings for her I should have felt more regret. Karl's reactions had stunned me. How could he have left her the way he did. I just couldn't understand.

We set camp late. The sun was setting; a beautiful red sky that silhouetted the trees around us. With my eyes closed I could picture Abigail's lifeless eyes staring ahead, then Johnny's equally lifeless eyes as I eventually opened my grandparents front door, a dribble of blood like a river tributary splitting into each corner from the fatal forehead wound. But even that didn't stop me from falling asleep. Once, just after midnight, we were woken by the security cone, and the nightmares of the preceding day came back to haunt me for the rest of a sleepless night. We found nothing. On checking the gadget it had recorded a small rodent.

From the puffy red eyes of Karl the following morning I guessed little sleep was just one problem he had suffered. It confirmed the stifled sobbing noises I thought I'd heard, which, at the time, had almost convinced me that the previous day had all been in my imagination and that Abe was once again enjoying sex with her husband. Bad joke.

We ate breakfast out of necessity. Quietly and avoiding eye contact.

As we climbed back into the Land Rover after packing everything into the back Karl broke the silence.

"I didn't radio in last night. Chances are those choppers will be on the lookout for us."

"Can't you do it now?" I asked innocently.

"Why?" He looked across at me from the drivers seat, grinding the Invader into first gear. "To report Abe's death? To report killing twenty variants? Tony, we're not going back. We're on the run. They'll be looking for us."

I wanted to protest. To say that I wasn't a party in this. That he had brought it on himself. But, for a number of reasons I didn't.

Mainly, I think, it was my little bit of Jamaican recklessness. Instead I asked, "What's the plan then?"

"You're only with me because you might be useful with a firearm." Sinister undertones made me check out his eyes. I decided not to challenge him. At least not yet. But maybe I needed to reassess my ability to murder, because that's what it would be. And that went against everything I believed in.

"Keep your eyes peeled," he told me.

I tried to get a glimpse of the sky through the thickening foliage above us.

"For variants!" he snapped.

I hadn't expected that. Karl's slaughter the previous day had convinced me we were free of the humanoid terrors. I felt useless and stressed. My vision was no match for Abe's and we were passing through a particularly overgrown section, quite unusual given the canopy above.

"It's not just animals that have been gened." Karl had an annoying knack of answering questions that I'd decided I wouldn't ask. "The Scottish highlands have some fantastic pines for instance. Not straight like you'd expect. Picture a forest of gigantic bonsai trees clinging to the side of mountains. But don't go there. They're inhabited by equally large spiders. About our size."

He glanced at me with the first smile I'd seen. But it was a smile that saw humour in trying to scare. It revealed that the trauma he'd gone through had stripped away his charismatic good looks. Underneath, and what worried me, was manifesting itself in his outward appearance. His juvenile taunt didn't bother me, after all when was I likely to go to Scotland, his manner certainly did.

Eventually the trees spread out again but the tall grasses gave us little hope of spotting any animals, which was my reason for being there, or any variants, which was a good reason for not.

By midday we were moving out of the trees, coming onto the

outskirts of a wide expanse of grassland interspersed by stubby shrubs and the occasional copse.

"The fens," Karl informed me in his usual manner. "We'll stop here for a break."

I left the vehicle and stretched. Walked around but didn't stray too far, keeping a wary eye on Karl. Then we heard it at the same time. A single one, by the sound. Distant but heading our way, just above the tree tops.

"Grab the case!" Karl called out to me. I ran back to the Land Rover and helped him drag the mini arsenal out. We carried it about a hundred metres away - I couldn't have carried it any further - before the helicopter came into view.

"Down!" I had no option but to comply as he pulled me with him into a thorny shrub, and at that moment I didn't have the energy to protest.

How they didn't see us I don't know. It banked tightly as it passed overhead, eventually hanging in the air in front of our vehicle. A hovering tank, mat green armour-plating defying its ability to stay in the air. I expected a rocket to burst from the pods beneath but after a couple of minutes it twitched then slowly descended, settling gently into the tall grass with a slight bounce on the suspension.

Karl had been scrabbling in the heavy box and, as I turned to see what weapon he was planning on using, was amazed to see him preparing a missile launcher.

"You can't ..." I began to say, but realised he had every intention of blasting the helicopter. Without thought of the consequences I threw myself at him, trying to hold him down.

As I've mentioned before Karl was fit and stronger than me. He had the determination of a madman on his side too. I don't know what I thought I could do but I'd barely grabbed the launcher before I felt a blow to the head. All thoughts of stopping him left me as I was devoured by excruciating pain.

Consciousness might well have left me for a moment because, when I squinted my eyes open, Karl was levelling the launcher on his shoulder. Flat on my back as I was, with maybe three meters between us, I did the only thing I could and crab-walked forward kicking out as I collapsed.

It wasn't enough to stop him firing, or maybe I caused him to fire, but the roar and hiss of the rocket didn't end with a might explosion. I didn't hear it anyway. Karl swung the launcher round furiously. I didn't even feel any pain this time, not until I started to come round.

I was face down in a bed of flattened grass. My left eye, adjacent to the area of most pain, wouldn't open. Insects scuttled about in and out of view. It hadn't been just my head Karl targeted. As I rolled over pain shot through my back and chest taking my breath away.

"You ok buddy?"

I didn't open the only eye that worked, but I was relieved that my safari was over. Karl had obviously been overpowered, or shot, and hopefully I wasn't going to be implicated.

"I'm not sure." My voice sounded distant. "Don't think my rib's broken."

"Here, let's take a look." A female voice this time.

Pain shot across my forehead as I tried to glimpse who was speaking; caught a brief blurred image of short dark hair.

Gentle hands unbuttoned my shirt after touching the side of my head. My muzzyness dissipated somewhat, the ache receding.

The medic felt across my abdomen, moved up and around my side, across my chest and over and around on the other side. It was almost a caress.

"You're fine. You'll have some mighty fine bruising though. Here, let's take a look up top." She gently helped me to a sitting position.

I felt a cool damp cloth wipe the side of my temple, following the contours of my face across my eye. A strong smell of antiseptic seemed to give me renewed energy as she cleaned and swabbed my wound.

"Not as bad as it looks. Mostly congealed blood. Try opening the eye now."

Anticipated pain didn't overwhelm me. In fact I could open both eyes with surprising ease. What I saw confused me for a moment, then, for clarification I asked: "Going undercover?"

"What?" The woman was quite pretty. Her dark hair wasn't short, but tied back. Quizzical dark brown eyes began to drown me. Behind her a man, similarly dressed in what appeared rags, stood looking around like the bodyguard of a senator, glanced at me quickly, then back to his almost furtive watching.

"Variants," I said. "You're dressed as variants."

"Hear that, David?" Although she didn't turn her head, the guy behind responded.

"Sounds a bit derogatory to me."

Maybe the knock on the head had dulled my wits, but the obvious still didn't dawn on me.

"Here, let me help you up," the girl suggested. She grabbed my outstretched hand firmly and pulled me to my feet in an easy motion. Her breasts wobbled beneath the rough linen sack-shirt, cut halfway up her stomach, leaving ten centimetres of flesh showing between matching trousers. Irresistible. Was I that easily smitten? So soon?

"Where's the warden," I asked, with less interest than I'd intended, hoping I wasn't telegraphing my desire. I was finding it hard to think. "What's your name?" I insisted.

"Bo."

"Bo what?"

"Just Bo … "

"Deeker," interrupted the bearded guy behind, still keeping his vigil. "It's Bo Deeker, buddy, and she's having fun at your expense. She's a witch and she's charmed you."

"Awe, David, don't be a spoilsport. Here."

She held her right hand palm flat against her forehead and whisked it down passed her chin. I stumbled back.

Moments before, she had been an attractive, desirable girl.

Now she was, well, plain, streaked with dirt or fading cammo paint; more muscled than sleek, and maybe five years older than me.

"Party trick. Sorry. I won't charm you again unless you ask."

I studied her then. Could see what I'd seen before in the angles of her cheek bone, the contours of her face, in those deep, heart-sucking brown eyes. No, she wasn't plain at all. There was a presence there that I couldn't deny. Witch? I'd seen similar trickery in Parisian clubs. In my weakened state I'd probably been a prime target for autosuggestion.

"We need to leave now," David insisted.

"Where's the warden?" I asked the question again a little more forcefully, watching Bo looking at me.

David's answer wasn't exactly equivocal: "He's still alive." Then with a glance my way: "He's one of us, you know."

"European Attack Team," I confirmed, surprised, yet showing I understood.

"How about variant?" Bo suggested. Then, looking at my reaction, "Should've saved that bit 'till later I think, Dave."

I was staring open mouthed at the both of them. They weren't EAT, but variants. Karl wasn't a warden, he was variant too; had slaughtered twenty of his own kind. It also told me that Karl was a liar, if I was to believe my two new acquaintances. They had killed Abigail. I was their prisoner. Yet they seemed, well, normal.

"You have a name?" she asked, as if I was some sort of alien.

Moments ago I had felt comfortable with these two, felt that I could even like them. This new revelation had just sent my brain into overload. Conflicting emotions and fears overwhelmed me. I've never done this before or since, and maybe it was just the bang on the head - and I'd prefer to think that, than my survival instinct had failed me - but I passed out.

I guess it was concussion. It must have been some time before I came round. When I did I was being bounced up and down on a makeshift stretcher. Not so makeshift, I realised, as I rolled my head to the sides.

Four male Variants each held single-handed the end of a pole, little more than two roughly hacked branches, across which were tied shorter branches and animal hides. And that's what I was lashed to. I could lift up, turn my head either side, but nothing else. From the speed at which foliage passed above me they were running at the sort of pace I could probably maintain for 100 metres, but they didn't slow. On either side I caught sight of similar stretchers piled with what I assumed were provisions, as single hides were lashed over to cover them. There were others running free of baggage. Many others. All carried bows, some also short spears, a handful guns.

It was like a great herd stampeding through the trees, yet that implies chaos, and this seemed to have a purpose. Karl hadn't hinted that there were so many. I'd assumed his bloodbath had purged this area of most, if not all Variants. How wrong I had been.

A shout suddenly went up, spreading through the group, slowing the pace to a brisk walk. David and Bo appeared by my side then. David smiled, said I'd be ok, that she had laid some magic on me, then they were gone again, but not before Bo raised suggestive eyebrows, neatly plucked, I noticed for the first time, like you might expect of a real woman. It'd be hard to argue she wasn't.

Jolting diminished at the new pace, in fact the movement set me to dozing often. Abigail came to mind once, but like a distant memory, as if my feelings for her had died with her, having never had the chance to become tangible. Johnny's death followed close behind, but that was one memory I was familiar with.

Although I was being helped by these people there was no doubt in my mind that I was their prisoner. Why that was, and why they hadn't killed me was a mystery. Escape seemed a ludicrous idea. Where was I? Where could I go? Wild animals roamed the countryside, and while I could still feel the holster I was sure the revolver was no longer there.

I woke at one point to find I was on the ground. My bearers squatting at their allotted corner. One of them put a finger to his lips, pointed forward. As best I could, I raised my head, was surprised when the two nearest Variants helped support me. Not the sort of treatment I'd expect from captors, particularly this uncivilised

Ahead of us, little more than eighty metres away were at least a dozen elephants feeding on the trees.

"African," whispered the variant to my right. "We'll have to go round. So many of us will make them nervous."

"I wonder how they escaped from their compound?" added one of the others near my feet, which started some restrained laughter, shushed by nearby bearers.

We moved off to the left, skirting the animals quite closely. I kept a watchful eye, more out of awe than fear. They didn't seem to feel threatened by our presence though a huge bull followed our movements with a bellow of defiance as an ordered shout set everyone off at the faster pace again.

An appetising smell dragged me awake, after a deeper sleep, to find my bindings had been removed. My stretcher was flat on the ground again in flickering semi darkness. Until that moment I hadn't studied the others that closely, assuming them to be all around the thirty mark -my estimated age for Bo and Dave. But one guy, who was watching me must have been at least 50, probably nearer 60, hair pulled tight to his head in a ponytail, yet he'd kept pace with the others, no problem, something even I couldn't have done

I expected to see a massive encampment of Variants but I was close to a single fire around which sat my four bearers plus David and Bo, all engrossed in eating.

Fading light didn't help in locating other Variants but their fires ought to have been visible.

"Here. He's awake," Bo exclaimed to the others, as I rolled over to sit up. Then to me: "Sleep's a great healer."

"Where are the others?" I asked, sweeping my hand around, trying to disregard the feeling of wellbeing, and my paranoia. It made me wonder if I had been drugged.

"As visible to us as we are to them. They're out there."

There wasn't much else to do but believe her. Perhaps I believed too easily, or was just supposed to, so that I wouldn't consider an escape attempt.

"That smell's good," I said, as innocently as my grumbling tummy would allow.

"Here," Bo said, grabbing a metal plate and ladling a large portion of stew on to it. "Rabbit, potatoes and onions.

My hunger overrode my fear of the Variants and I leant across. "Thanks," I said, only to be denied the plate from the witch.

"Here. Come and sit with us. We're full. We're not going to eat you." There wasn't a hint of sarcasm to her voice, though I'm sure it was intended.

I edged over reluctantly. Ponytail showed an outward distrust while the others paid me no particular attention, in what I assumed was a gesture to put me at my ease. I sat cross-legged next to Bo, took the plate and spoon. The stew was delicious. I finally raised the plate to my lips to drink the last of the gravy totally engrossed in eating. They were all looking at me now with varying degrees of grins accept for the older guy with the ponytail sitting furthest away from me.

"Great," I told them, raising the empty plate. They laughed then, a sneer from ponytail, and, despite my misgivings, I laughed too. And it felt good.

Bo put her hand on my arm. "Here, laughter's the next best healer to sleep."

Here: A word which rolled off her lips like a bad habit, yet it carried more. It could easily have become annoying. What it did do though was alert you to the fact she was going to speak.

Necessary, I would think, if she were planning some sort of suggestive remark, or charm as her partner would put it.

"You're not a warden," David suddenly stated. Bo was watching me closely. It was clear from the following silence that I had to interpret that as a question.

"I was a guest. A tourist if you like."

A grunt of disbelief wasn't lost in the crackling fire, a stare from ponytail that made me feel very uncomfortable. Bo daggered a look his way.

I was still very confused. From the first couple of days, Karl and Abigail had instilled in me a fear for Variants, even before I had known they were humanoid. It was difficult to break free of that fear. Ponytail was managing to reassert it.

My answer had inspired a few raised eyebrows and exchanged looks and, with a boldness I didn't fee,l I said: "I'd like to know about you."

"Karl didn't tell you then," from David without hesitation, a reminder they'd told me Karl was one of them but not what had happened to him. I shook my head. "He was born here. Not Freeborn though. Some of us are Freeborn now. Most of us are ... not." He didn't elaborate. "No doubt he made us out to be savages when many of us are merely Roamins." My quizzical expression stimulated an explanation. "Roamins: Gypsies, new-age travellers, pikies, whatever you want to call us ... And some true Romanies too. Not sure I like Variants, although you could argue everything is a mutation of sorts."

"How did you get here?"

"Some of us never left. At least our ancestors didn't. Do you really think they could have completely cleared the UK of inhabitants? Others escaped here. Others are actually dumped here. Experiments gone wrong." David paused for effect. "Don't look so surprised. Some scientists just aren't happy with animal gening, still seem to be searching for the perfect human - whatever that is."

"Or the perfect soldier," cut in ponytail.

David continued: "The way they set their experiments free isn't humane. It's usually so that someone like you can hunt them down."

"I've never shot anything in my life," I protested, glancing at Bo. "I maybe a firearms salesman, I own gun shops in Paris." Telling them what I did for a living didn't seem to matter to me this time. "But I don't advocate the use of guns for anything else but target shooting and licensed hunting."

"Licensed by whom, and for what? Sport?" David asked. The others around the fire were still watching me, their grins of minutes earlier replaced by a grim seriousness, yet I only felt truly threatened by ponytail.

I could see where this was heading but I always felt I could justify what I did. "Licensed hunting has to be better than allowing everyone the right to being armed for their own protection. Anger can be a strong motivator to pull out your gun. It can make a weak person feel stronger."

"You say this from the heart," Bo said, her glance to David a confirmation of what I was saying. "We're not condemning the use of guns or condoning ownership. Yet licenses are granted to those wishing to hunt us. Do you approve of that."

"Of course not." I responded too quickly. Doubt tainted my words. I felt guilty.

"Karl and Abigail had licenses." She said this as if she were forgiving them. Watched carefully as disbelief then uncertainty washed my features; my face, I know, revealing more than I wanted.

Dave interjected with his, by now, customary show stopper: "Karl is Bo's twin brother."

"Where is he?" I blurted, as if the question could hide my confusion. I couldn't help staring at Bo, recognising the slant of the cheekbone, the strong chin line, the slight raising of the left side of her top lip as she spoke, but her eyes weren't blue.

"He's still out there somewhere." Bo waved her hands casually in a wide gesture. "And he's one of several 'twins' of mine."

"Bo's from Sizewell." David carried on their story. "Up near the lakes. There's a gene research lab there. Don't look surprised. There is at least a dozen we know of dotted around the UK. Officially they don't exist. Anyway, the Sizewell lab dumped twelve 'experiments' on the top of Scafell Pike twenty years back. Just ten years old they were. Left them for a week then sent out hunting parties to track them down. Licensed. It helps to fund new research. Rich folk seem to enjoy the 'sport'. Rich and perverted. Paedophiles mostly, with dart guns."

"That was about the same time we felt we had a strong enough base to change things." This with passion from Ponytail, who alone still showed hostility towards me. "And a leader, in Munro Huartson, with the charisma to unite the wandering bands of Roamin."

"So," Dave took up the story again, I think, to ease the change in the atmosphere that the older guy had somehow introduced, "the hunters became the hunted. As far as I know their bodies never were found. Thankfully for our community the authorities must have assumed they died of exposure along with the children."

"But we'd managed to save eight of them," cut in the old guy with a smugness that was not in the others repertoire. "And they were a talented bunch." His smile towards Bo was her cue.

"But Karl had been given special privileges at the institute. He'd experienced what you might call 'the civilized life'." There were chuckles around the fire which I found uncomfortable. How did they know what it was like to live outside their world? Bo emulated one of Karl's traits, "Forman," - she nodded to the old guy -"is Professor Raymond Forman, formerly of Genomics International." Ponytail actually nodded.

"Preacher." Bo indicated the ginger-haired guy sitting on Dave's left. "Is the Reverend Diamond Grace who somehow got to hear about us and thinks we need Christianity."

"Took me two years to find them," Preacher informed me with

the typical enthusiasm I'd come to expect of a theologian. "Or should I say, before they revealed themselves."

"This here with the broad-shoulders is Sarge." Bo slapped the back of the bearer who held the left pole at the rear. "Ex EAT. Lost on patrol. Well, actually he broke his radio and leg in a bad fall. We fixed his leg and he decided we weren't the animals he'd been brainwashed into believing. Took a while though."

"And I never even made Corporal let alone Sargent." A deep soft voice belied his size but not his almost-jet-black skin.

"That's Jo-Jo." Bo frowned at the last of the bearers. "He's been with us for just six months. Claims to be from Glencoe - We do know there is a gene research lab there - and spent five years surviving on his own before he came upon us. He blocks my inquisitiveness ..."

"Telepathy," Jo-Jo corrected.

"Inquiry gene I prefer to call it. It's only telepathy when there's more than one of you with the gene. Like my brothers and sisters."

"Mind reading then."

"... so he's obviously been gened. But was that so he can infiltrate us safely or because he is what he is, like us twins? Remember, we were failed experiments. Our inquiry genes barely scratch the surface of someone's mind. It's generally no more than a mere feeling we get." She spoke again as if Jo-Jo wasn't there. "We're still not sure about him yet."

It looked as if Jo-Jo was about to protest but he dropped his eyes to the fire, his fists tightening in his lap, and let out a sigh.

"So you see," she hesitated where she would naturally have slipped in my name, "we do have an inkling of your world, albeit coloured by personal experience. It seems inclined to want to interfere too much in ours."

"But you shouldn't be here. The UK is just for animals."

"Then why the research labs?" Forman this time, who must have had his own answer as an ex-professor.

"Animal research."

"Is that all I am?" Bo asked. "An animal."

"And me and David?" Jo-Jo's support for her.

What I kept asking myself was how had the situation in Britain remained a secret. How could something as big as this have stayed out of the press for so long? The answer had sinister implications. But I wasn't going to win this argument. I changed tack. "Where are we going?"

Forman, a.k.a. Ponytail, this time, almost with glee, "We're going to Stansted Mountfichet. Then we are going to take Stansted Airport."

Despite the amount of sleep I'd had the previous day I still slept well. Bo gently shook me awake in the halflight of dawn with a cup of herbal tea.

"Here, Tony." She sat down next to me.

I'd given them my name, eventually. It felt like giving up my soul, like giving up my final anchor with the other world. Strange. But that's how I perceived it.

"Thanks."

"I know this is hard for you," she said as if carrying on the previous night's discussion, meaning how I felt about them. "You can't comprehend how anyone would want to live like this let alone fight for it. We are hunters because there is an abundance of wildlife and because crops are easily seen from the air. "

I sipped the tea, cross-legged on my stretcher watching her over the rim of the enamel mug.

"You don't have enough faith in yourself to have faith in people generally, but you are stronger than you think. Your principals verge on fanaticism." She cut off my objections with a raised hand. "Despite our way of living you have probably experienced more than any of us here. Your reaction, giving your beliefs, to our freedom, is understandable. We are a contradiction to what you live for."

It was necessary to consider what she said. I'd have been cheating them had I done otherwise. She was watching me intently. "I accept I have strong feelings about guns and their use, perhaps even passionate, but it's certainly not fanaticism."

She put a hand on my arm. It was like I'd never been touched before. To describe it as electrifying sounds corny but the thrill that ran through my body then was a totally new experience. Those brown eyes drew me in, mesmerised me. We were kissing before I realised she was so close.

It was like a twilight dream. Total abandonment. She freed me for that moment of lovemaking from any inhibitions I had. That others were close by, could see us, hear us, meant nothing to me then. I gave them no thought. My other self would have baulked at the situation: People around; a woman I didn't know, who was a product of sick science; out in the open. If this was being charmed I wanted more. It couldn't stop.

We climaxed together. She'd gripped me at the last second so I came deep inside her, tingling all over. After regaining my breath I opened my eyes; looked up at her — that's how we had finally ended up. Those brown orbs were studying me like she was reading my thoughts, she frowned.

"I'm not property, Tony."

It was my turn to frown as she continued.

"That was good. I hope we can connect some more. Here, some might take partners, but monogomy isn't the norm." She gently lifted herself off, sat back on my legs. Some of my chest hairs stuck to her shiny torso, the paleness of her skin emphasised by her tanned face; always-exposed midrift and arms accentuating the porcelain quality. Sweat trickled between her breasts. Excitement began to overwhelm me again like I'd been drugged with some euphoric substance.

"Here." She had my attention. "I'll say it differently. Here, jealousy is a punishable crime. Processions are too. Individuals are given the right to be what they are. Whatever they are."

In a swift motion that surprised and disappointed me she lifted herself away emphasising her words rather than her body, though my animal instincts appreciated the latter as much as my civilised consciousness understood the former.

Exposed — the sky was clear and brightening by the second — my self-consciousness suddenly overwhelmed me. The others were nearby. But none were looking save Jo-Jo, who turned away quickly when Bo followed my glance. She looked back at me and winked, completing my confusion. Until fifteen minutes earlier I'd assumed Bo and Dave were partners but he was taking no notice, was helping to break camp.

We dressed, smelling of each other's sex. Despite what she'd said, Bo smiled at me often during that day and touched me at every opportunity, and in places that got the reaction she wanted. A tease that I admit to enjoying. Foreman didn't seem at all pleased with this.

It became apparent we had camped close to the airport, a two-hour walk — it could have been anywhere as far as I was concerned — and, by midday, had taken and secured the area without the need for force. There were three thousand Variants in the war party and growing. Stansted's security team - one hundred and twenty - working ten-hour shifts, decided their lives were worth more than their jobs.

It was a huge area for anyone to protect from that many savages, even if they were primitively armed, although I had noticed several Variants with guns, mainly semi-automatics. Whoever would have expected such an attack when animals were generally the only danger? I would love to have been a fly on the wall when they first picked up the hoard on their CCTV system. There was little doubt a message of their impending fate had been made to their headquarters.

Bo told me that once we had taken our main objective a call would be made to CNN and BBC, not to mention an ultimatum to the UN and EU, but I wondered if Munro suspected the influence the genetics industry might have over the authorities and the media.

As Foreman had said Munro was indeed a charismatic figure.

Well over six foot he carried himself like a humble messiah, a ten-strong band of lieutenants, advisors and bodyguards walked at a distance that enabled him to talk with other Variants without intimidating them.

It was mid afternoon when he came to see me. Our little group was sitting beneath a thick chestnut tree, some two hundred meters outside the airport's perimeter fence, drinking a light but tasty beer that had been an integral part of the armies' supplies. Until that morning I'd not appreciated that that's what it was, an army.

We made to stand when we saw him coming but he called: "Don't get up for me."

From a distance, with his long white flowing hair, he looked an old but agile man. His clothes were made long and loose giving the effect of robes, unconsciously perhaps mimicking the imagery of Jesus. Before he reached us though I could see deep pink eyes and transparent eyebrows. I had never seen an albino before. He sat down beside us.

"Just thought I'd introduce myself. So you can have someone to blame for all this."

"Blame? You are fighting for your freedom. Why should I want to blame anyone?"

"Freedom? We have that already." He looked thoughtful for a moment. For affect I'm sure. "Recognition. Recognised as being human. Recognised as existing at all. It's only the powerful, the influencial, who know of our existence, and they use us. They treat us worse than animals. They hunt us down. They murder us or worse." He glanced at the others. No they'd not told me this. "Experiment on us. Sometimes they come for one of us. One of us who has escaped or who has been allowed to escape or who has been left for the hunters. They fit trackers at the labs at an early age, there's no scar. We don't know when they'll come for us. This might not be our country, but it's our home. If we could choose, which we can't, most of us would prefer this life. We were safe when there were fewer of us, but eventually the authorities decided we might become a threat. That's backfired on them."

I was allowing this to sink in when Bo screamed "Karl!" and dived across in front of me. Her head exploded, splattering my cheeks with a warmth that I refused to accept. I was aware of a rifle crack a split second later. All hell broke loose then.

At the time, I was only aware of Bo's body lying like a rag doll with red stuffing oozing from the cavity in her skull, but later I was able to recall everything in detail, like a part of my mind was recording events while the other part grappled with the horror and disbelief.

As soon as Bo moved, I guess having sensed her "twin's" intention, Foreman threw himself across Munro, while Jo-Jo pinned me to the ground in a similar fashion. I just kept screaming "No!" This just couldn't be real, it couldn't be! Not now. I started crying too; a mixture of sadness and rage, I think, as I was able to stand despite Jo-Jo clawing at me, imploring me to keep down.

Another shot rang out. My legs took me in that direction — sprinting. A third. Others were running my way too. A fourth shot. Then I was tackled from behind, sending me unexpectedly sprawling into ferns.

"Stay down you fool. This isn't your fight." It was Jo-Jo again. "Remember what Bo said and learn!" I struggled to turn over only to have his forearm jammed across my windpipe. "What did she say?" He was shouting in my face. There was an emotion in his eyes that were mirrored in mine. He recognised my feelings or it could have been his own. "What did she say," he persisted, "once you'd finished?"

If I didn't give the right answer he wouldn't let me reap my revenge. He saw that too. "Karl is a marksman. You haven't even got a weapon. Don't let her have died for nothing. What did she say?"

I considered that. Relaxed a little, which Jo-Jo did too. I resisted my instincts to take advantage of that, to throw him off.

I remembered. His face changed to Bo's. I watched her mouth the words, heard my own voice repeat them: "Here, jealousy is a punishable crime. Processions are too. Individuals are given the right to be what they are. Whatever they are."

"Here ..." It caught in his throat. A grin stretched the irony across his face, yet he repeated it: "Here, you can't afford to be possessive. Jealousy. Envy. These are things you have to let go. We avoid partnerships because they can be so brief. Sure, we grieve for our fellows, but to survive we stay alone. I have to do that with you." He emphasised with increased pressure on my throat. "I'm doing it with Bo. Do you understand me?"

I nodded. I think I did understand. He'd loved her too. She'd sacrificed herself for me.

"No she didn't." I'd said nothing but Jo-Jo had refuted my thoughts. Like Bo had done, like Karl. "She was saving Munro."

That jolted me more than anything else he'd said. I struggled to believe it.

There was a final shot. Jo-Jo winced, gasped. He lifted himself up dragging me to my feet with the front of my shirt, looking me in the eye as he did so. "Karl's dead too. Shot himself. I'd have done that too. They'd have torn him apart."

They? Wasn't he one?

"I'll die for them," he told me. "Bo was right not to trust me, at first. But I'm as much a Variant as anyone else here. Given time, even you could fit in, perhaps." He looked to the sky as though listening, as though waiting for something to fall on him. Then he straightened up and took my arm gently. "Come on. I need to find Munro."

Jo-Jo had sensed the impending attack, as had others. His talent wasn't unique. But I don't think anyone anticipated the ferocity or scale of what was to come.

Munro prepared as best he could. What I didn't realise then was that this was by no means a last stand, though to me it felt like a martyr army.

What the EAT did best, they did. There was no warning.

Barely seconds, as the sound of the first missile salvo put everyone's mind straight about how the attack would be played out. The main buildings, where Munro had advised the authorities he had imprisoned the airfelds security, were raised to the ground by several massive explosions. An indication that no quarter would be given, and no one without military clearance was going to survive to tell what was to happen here.

Barely had the sound died away before a wave of bombs, almost certainly dropped from altitude, peppered the entire site, hinting at how the islands cities might have been sent back to nature at the inception of the British Wildlife Park; the enormity and cost.

Munro's people kept their positions. No more than a dozen Variants had been guarding the buildings, the rest were well away from the perimeter fence, way out in the trees, in terrain they knew best.

And so, the battle began, but we didn't make it easy. We'd split well before the ground troops came in on their gunships, bringing armoured vehicles and bulldozers that would have horrified Karl and Abigail. There stood an enigma with how my feelings were leaning. Whatever made those two wardens choose, not just my kind of life, but to want to kill their own people? Then it dawned on me. It didn't really matter how these people came to be Variants or how different they might be. They were human, yet they seemed free of prejudices. Untainted almost.

I was beginning to feel an affinity with the Variants, or at least an empathy for them. They had resilience and determination in abundance, giving me reason to be ashamed of my selfish feeling. I realised that a lot of my anger was at losing something, not for the something I'd lost.

Jo-Jo smiled with that Variant resolve, followed by a frown as my fear of intrusion became evident to him.

During the following days I virtually became an accepted part of the group that had first carried me on the stretcher. We'd been given a name by Munro for saving his life; apparently a true honour among their kind: Iceni. An ancient British tribe which had virtually been wiped out by the Romans. Very apt.

I trotted this way and that over the next week. Joining to form larger bands — attracting the EAT — then splitting to ambush their troops when we could. Hitting their camps at night. Worrying them to death. Guerilla tactics was all we were capable of but effective nonetheless.

At all times we worked towards London, our final destination, if fate allowed. Never obvious. Sometimes we'd backtrack. Other times we'd push on with speed.

We were into the second week since Bo's death. I was becoming fitter by the day. It'd be months before I could sustain their speed and distance, but they worked around my handicap.

Sacrifices were made for the Variant cause like lambs to the slaughter. Modern weapons were no match for hand-made bows and spears, but determination wove through the Variant army beyond anything I could comprehend. The losses seemed to make them stronger, and their methods evolved to utilise whatever they had and were capable of.

The Iceni were still intact under David's command with three successful night raids under our belts. Traversing the woods at night was scary on it own without worrying about troopers. We'd all acquired flak jackets while Sarge hefted a backpack filled with grenades and ammo for the various assault rifles he held in hs massive hands. I'd reluctantly accepted a pistol which sat unused in the holster I'd sentimentally, I assume, kept from my time on the safari. That seemed such a long time ago. I had killed though. A knife across a throat. Just a silhouette. Just a silhouette...

There'd been about twelve troopers camped out beside an armoured MTV and Jeep. Have no doubt, our missions were purely to kill. Preacher's only show of religion was to bless us before we went in.

Variants seemed to have excellent night vision though Sarge

said the sentries would most probably be wearing enhancement goggles. Jo-Jo assured me I wasn't a coward, in his usual unabashed prying, and that eveyone felt the same. I couldn't believe him though.

It had been early on in the attack. I had held back as usual. Reluctance and fear mainly. Yet this allowed me to save Foreman's life. The sentries had already, to use a heartless term, been despatched, and the other Iceni were silently going through their gruesome business. I was hoping to arrive when it was all finished as I had on previous occasions but maybe Jo-Jo's looks of disappointment were getting to me. There was actually a thirteenth trooper we'd not counted who had been in the MTV. As I reached the edge of their camp I saw him climb out no more than three metres in front of me with the intention of shooting the professor in the back which would also have awakened his friends. Instinctively I'd used the knife I was holding to terrible effect. I'd made little sound but Foreman turned as I let the body slide gently to the ground, and only as I did this, as I felt the body slide through my hands did I realise the trooper had been a woman.

I'd been fascinated by guns since Johnny's death but I soon realised that there were many other ways to snuff out that precious spark of life, and I'd used one of them. I could see why Preacher attracted little groups to worship together when we joined with other Variants. Strangely he never pushed Christianity at his own group.

Killing other humans sickened me, as I was surprised to find it did the others.

"I joined the EAT for a better life," Sarge told us one night in his deep reverb. "While the City Neuvos might be a design and social success, the ghettos of New York haven't changed much over the last century. I guess it's a bit like joining the French Foreign Legion back in the early 1900s, accept these days you don't really expect to have to fight. These boys may have enjoyed playing at war but I doubt any of them have seen real action before. Highly capable though, don't forget. But it's a might different facing an enemy that bites back."

Mid-afternoon, on a day nearing the end of the third week, I found myself in familiar territory: The firing range where I'd shown my proficiency with a pistol. It was deserted now but seen by Munro as a strategic point from which to make the last push on London.

Not even four hundred Variants made it that day, out of three thousand, yet Munro was in a buoyant mood.

"We've achieved something this last month that will go down in our annals as the root of our freedom." His speech echoed within the compound's high-ceilinged sports hall delivered to the remnants of his army seated on the polished wood floor.

"We rest here tonight. Tomorrow we take London."

Munro wasn't a person of many words. It wasn't necessary. His charismatic personality punched whatever he said to the heart of whatever you wanted to hear. Amazing man.

We were prodded awake around four in the morning to the smell of cooking. Word spread quickly that a further seventy or so Variants had straggled in and more arrived during a breakfast of porridge and bacon, somehow concocted from the store and stolen provisions. Most Variants were clothed and armed as the Iceni: with acquired Flack jackets, assault rifles, several helmets, even a few with shades; quite bizarre.

There was a predominance of women, which I happened to mention.

Foreman chose to respond with a grudging respect that he'd had since I'd covered his back. "Most are infertile. Bred to be. There are ways, in some circumstances, to reverse that." He spooned gruel into his mouth, checked for assent from the others before continuing. "Back home," he thumbed north, "we have families."

I was genuinely taken aback. No one had mentioned children before or that these Variants, this army wasn't the total Variant population. Strangely I had assumed this was the complete nation. Everything took on a different dimension at that point. With a totally altered perception I looked anew at the people in the hall.

While I had been going through the motions, these people had more than just Munro's words to sustain them. I felt ashamed.

Jo-Jo, who had looked out for me during raids, had become a friend and confidante, not that I needed to say anything, put an arm around my shoulders. "Tony, there's no need to feel that way. You are worthy. You have already had a hand in helping them."

"Through this? Through all the killing?"

"The world wasn't even going to hear us let alone listen. This way we have a chance of being recognised."

"You think so?" I said, wondering if news of this attempted island coupe had actually reached the channels."

"I have to." Then he started suddenly, as several others did in the hall. "They're close!" he shouted scrambling to his feet, the shout going up all around. "That way!" to exits preferred. This was unplanned; went against the great scheme. The Variants couldn't afford to be caught here.

I grabbed Sarge's arm, stopped him following the others, gripped the barrel of a carbine. "Plus plenty of ammo," I demanded.

As the ex-trooper looked down at me I noticed Jo-Jo turn his head. He waved, then gave me the thumbs-up as he squeezed through a doorway with the others, disappeared outside.

"You're staying."

I nodded though Sarge's words hadn't been a question. He let me take the gun then rummaged in the haversack for me, brought out a dozen full magazines.

"Best I can do, Tony." He pulled me into a hug, which I wasn't expecting. "That's from all the Iceni." Then corrected himself. "All of us."

I turned and ran to the other exits, joining maybe twenty

others, who like me, had chosen their fate that day. We moved through the outbuildings taking up strategic positions to meet and halt the EAT advance. We didn't have to wait long.

With a fearlessness that spread an ironic smile across my face, I raised my rifle confidently to aim, for the first time, at another human being. I felt purged of my past, recalling Johnny's death from the perpetrators' viewpoint, victims themselves. The ghettos were places of despair. The designer metropolises of the City Nueva project had created safe environments. They had been a resounding success, but at what price to the old cities? And here I was living another life altogether.

They moved cautiously towards us but I dropped the leading trooper easily, taking the life of another about six seconds later. A part of me felt betrayed, but I doubted I could ever really fit in with the Variants. I believed they felt I had done the right thing staying here. If Bo had still been alive I think she could have helped me to live amongst them. But, maybe, they'd underestimated the change I had gone through. I liked to think so, because going back to my old world wasn't an option.

Then a sound from behind and a familiar voice. "Duck!" I did, instinctively. A bullet ricocheted off the sill above my head as I swivelled in my crouching position to face Jo-Jo and a Variant I didn't recognise. "Mellisa's got precog." he said. "A better chance to keep your tally going. Give her the gun."

Remembering how convincing he could be in an argument, I barely hesitated. But I wasn't leaving out of cowardice. In that moment I knew I could help the Variants more alive than offering the ultimate sacrifice.

"Munro needs you." We moved out the back still keeping low, flinching at the increasing gunfire. "He thinks your knowledge of firearms could be invaluable."

They had accepted me after all. I hadn't realised it meant so much to me.

"That and he's only just been told your surname. Thinks he may have known your parents. IRA weren't they?"

"I doubt it." But cogs started rolling in my childhood memories. The meetings in the back room late into the evening, sometimes through the night. Maps left unrolled, held down at the corners with condiments. Wires, chips, timers and tools filling one of the kitchen drawers. It could be true. And then there was their deaths at the hands of a terrorist bomb. Their own bomb?

"Never mind," Jo-Jo encouraged, as if he'd not picked up my thoughts. "I'm pleased you're staying with us."

For the first time in my life I felt that what I really wanted and fate were teaming up. It was going to be an awesome partnership.

True Blue

Another novel spin-off. **True Blue** is set in a future following the 150-year-long Gene War, won by the Pure. A treaty was signed with the Made. But like all treaties, someone comes off worse. Royston Benson makes a few discoveries, not least about himself.

True Blue

Benson is close.

Tiken's message scrolled across Serina's vision as her mount's dive brought a gasp up from her stomach. The harness cut into her thighs and shoulders as her buttocks left the saddle briefly. Would she ever get used to sudden descents, even when expected?

How close? she thought.

Just across the water. He's blocking mindmail.

Benson ducked behind lichen-clad rocks on seeing the dragon glide gracefully over the Old Man of Coniston and swoop down to the water directly opposite. At first he'd thought it a part of the hallucinations that now plagued him. He could accept a Red from the SAS, but a Blue this far North of London sent conflicting emotions through his weary body. So, after three months of fleeing the capital, Special Branch had found him.

Resigned to his fate yet determined not to be caught, he raised the rocket launcher to his right shoulder and sighted his target through the digital scope.

Three months earlier, a thick fog stinking of dead fish, and creating yellow halos around the gas lamps, had crept up through the old moorings by the Thames to suck warmth from the concealed officers on their all-night vigil. No movement had been detected in the arched lock-up where blackened brickwork desperately held on to its Industrial Revolution heritage. Above it, the derelict station on the Waterloo archipelago had seen no trains since the start of the Gene Wars a century and a half earlier, and, with the rising river flowing either side, would never be a bustling place of transit again.

Chief Inspector Royston Benson yanked hard on Tiken's tether to get her attention. Snorting flickers of flame, the dragon turned from the nearby male. Even Benson's physiology reacted to the pheromones gushing from Tiken's glands. It was that time of year.

I need you fully alert, he thought.

The heads-up display of, *Yes, Boss,* hovered directly in front of his tired eyes for several seconds, showing Benson she meant it.

Having foregone a banquet on the strength of this raid's success, he too had found it hard to concentrate. All night he'd imagined the women who would have been vying for first place in his bed. After all, he was the Met's most decorated and successful officer. His tall aristocratic bearing — practiced rather than hereditory — was well-suited to the leather flight jacket, skull cap and goggles; the publicist's dream. Failure wasn't an option.

There were twenty officers in the vicinity, and five discreetly placed dragons – as discreetly placed as any forty-foot Blue could be – affording maximum communications. Riders received mindmail from only their own mounts while it was a dragon's main mode of interaction. While Benson had ordered an airwave silence, using the link with the dragons and their riders as the main form of communication, all officers wore satphone headsets as backups.

He was about to call off the operation when Tiken's sent image had him peering into a misty lightening sky. This wasn't what he'd expected, and he sensed the dragons' unease. Someone, not

Flying Squad, was riding a Blue. Yet Blues were confined to Special Branch. It was at the root of The Sweeney's history. How the hell could a Blue be involved with Made terrorists?

Serina was questioning her own judgement at that moment. But she'd known, the day her group had stolen the dragon chick, five years earlier, that someone had to stop the killings and reprisals; someone had to show the Pure they were no more pure than the Made, that the difference between the two wasn't... well, wasn't a difference at all. Years of interbreeding had meant a blending of the gene pool, and leaked documents proved that it wasn't only the Made who had genetically created their own creatures during the Gene Wars. The Pure had too. Discovering that dragons carried human DNA was the final piece of evidence. She had to act.

Kenti. That's what the dragon had called itself; even as the group had fled from the breeding pens in the Black Country of Wales in a battered methane-driven van that might once have been a Rover pick-up. Surprisingly there had neither been publicity about the raid nor any reprisals. Either it was believed that no-one else could raise a dragon or they had been too scared to notify higher authorities. Maybe a bit of both. Kenti flourished on the group's Cornish farm-come research base and matured into a magnificent creature bonding mentally with Serina. Given a choice, bonding with a dragon would have been her last wish. It was Kenti's though..

And now, here she was, flying into a trap her own group had orchestrated. It was hoped Kenti's presence would confuse the waiting force, if they'd actually acted upon the tip-off. Of that she'd know shortly. Her group had also informed the media that something momentous was going to happen. If they didn't follow up the lead then all this was for nothing. The revelation of Kenti's affiliation to a Made group, would rock more than just Britain's little world.

"What's going on?" Benson shouted through his mouthpiece.

This was the last straw. "I specifically instructed mindmail only!"

"Sir." It was Hide's voice. He was the new recruit; young and arrogant. "There's a dozen reporters disembarking a pleasure steamer down Leake Street. A TV crew too." There was a moment's hesitation before he continued. "Most of them are Made."

He'd reprimand the kid later about breaking silence. His mind was on the rogue Blue. No way could the media get a hold of this. "Do what you have to."

"Er. Yes, sir."

Kenti's wings whirlpooled the moisture around them as they dropped through the fog. She allowed the dragon's superior senses to guide them to the lock-up.

She expected to feel pain, and realised she didn't want to die, when the sudden chatter of automatic fire from close by sent Kenti veering away to the left. She gripped the saddle bars tighter as her dragon slew to either side. It wasn't supposed to happen like this. She was a naive fool!

Go! Get us out of here!

Kenti's fear was almost as strong as hers, and his flight was already in progress when a haunting harmony of pain hammered in her head: *K... E... N... T... I...*

Hide stood to attention in front of Benson's antique desk. Benson leaned wearily on a mahogany bookcase watching him through blood-shot eyes. Commander Clarque had spent the last ten minutes screaming his disappointment at the young officer's trigger-happy response but Benson was thankful their operation hadn't been a total washout. He knew how Clarque's mind worked, so wasn't at all surprised when on dismissing Hide he winked at the new recruit and said, "We need more officers like you."

Totally confused, Hide closed the door behind him.

Clarque looked across at Benson, who held up the London

Post with the headline, "Police thwart insurgents," and the subheading "Fourteen press die in terrorist crossfire."

"Right, Roy. Let's go meet this Made bitch."

Serina awoke in a white cell that could have been the white of heaven if not for a throbbing headache, bruised ribs and a nauseous mixture of citrus disinfectant and bleach. The rough futon was cold to her skin. There was a small ceramic basin in one corner — its lone tap dripping — a toilet with no seat or lid in the other. She was cold.

After hearing the gunfire she didn't remember much, but she did know that several dragons had somehow subdued Kenti. The Flying Squad weren't renowned for asking questions, at least not on a raid, so she was lucky to be alive. The door opened and a female officer squeezed through the gap, tazer-stick thrust out before her. Serina huddled sideways into the corner of the bed, suddenly conscious of her nudity as the woman threw her a pair of orange paper overalls.

She had one foot in the first leg when a short stocky officer, his insignia shouting Commander, and a much taller, familiar looking man, joined the policewoman.

"So, this is the Made scum that's given us so much trouble."

Struggling hurriedly to complete dressing, she fell back onto the bed, her vulnerability heightened by her nakedness. Finally, she Velcroed her modesty together and stood to face them.

Earlier, Benson had used his position to visit Serina's cell, before the red-head had regained consciousness. He'd studied her a long while, wondering how she could meld with a Blue. Unsure of what to do with her renegade dragon they had sedated it, and it was now being watched closely by Kiten and one of the older dragons in an old cathedral nearby.

He had been surprised by his feelings of arousal. There was nothing to suggest from her physique that she had Made genes. No doubt there had been some other genetic modification that set her apart from the Pure, but she had a natural beauty. Her skin was cream porcelain with a purity that eclipsed any woman he'd ever been with. The yellow-brown and purple welts around her ribs seemed to heighten her perfection. He allowed himself a moment of fantasy, imagining that CCTV wasn't fitted. Then he felt sick. She was Made. He'd never knowingly sleep with a Made woman.

Watching her lithe body now scrambling into the jumpsuit troubled him. He shouldn't feel this way about a prisoner; certainly not a Made prisoner.

When Clarque gripped her face with his pudgy leather-gloved hand Benson wanted to pull him away. Confused, he shouted from behind the Commander, "What's your game, little girl?"

She was taller than Clarque but he still managed to tip-toe her up against the cold plastered wall. He eased his grip then flicked her face to the side as he let go completely.

"Well?"

Her green eyes skipped to Benson then back to the Commander, but she remained silent.

"You will talk. We'll find out what you're up to." Clarque turned to Benson. "I'll leave her to you." And then strode out the room.

As soon as the Commander was out of earshot the girl demanded, "What have you done with my dragon?"

Each morning she was taken along an unpainted metal-walled corridor to a similar-walled room with just a table and two chairs; just her and the tall officer. The interrogations lasted for hours at a time and continued for weeks. Serina told the truth, but never divulged the identity of any of the other group, whom it seemed, had never gone to the lockup. Their plan had been foiled and her sacrifice had been for nothing. She was treated well and over the days she began to think that this bigoted womaniser – oh yes, she'd finally remembered who Benson was – had some compassion after all.

It was a month before Benson received the order to kill the girl's dragon. He hadn't expected that. Clarque was losing patience with his blue-eyed boy. The piece of paper burnt a hole in his pocket for three days before he took his prisoner from the cell to see Kenti one last time.

Serina was obviously not a city girl.

"Who could have built this?"

Her wonderment was infectious. He looked up at the dome as they climbed the steps to St. Paul's. It had been just a building to him. Now he saw the workmanship, could appreciate the architecture... and grandeur.

"They say it was designed by a bird-man."

"It's just fantastic," she said as they pushed through the doors and the vaulted ceiling rose above them.

At that moment Tiken's desperate and confused mindmail blotted out anything else,

We are Made!

Kenti wasn't sedated anymore; had been calmed by the presence of Tiken, who was now flattening rotting pews like an agitated zoo animal pacing its cage.

"What?" he exclaimed.

"You got the same message?"

He turned to Serina, seeing the hope that he'd never been able to quash, at the two dragons, accusing yellow eyes glaring at him , and considered his privileged life; his new-found feelings. All his life he'd hated Made. Dragons were a part of folklore, had been around for longer than man. At least, that's what he had always known. But now, his own dragon had announced Serina wasn't a liar, that his whole world was a lie. Tiken was a decendent of Made, as was Serena.

He'd come back for her that evening; said nothing; given her a set of tech flying wear and an unmarked flying jacket, and taken her back to the cathedral.

"They want Kenti dead," he said at last. "I can't let that happen."

He saddled up both dragons as she stood watching.

"I can't stay here now." He wanted to ask her if he could be with her, but he knew the government wouldn't rest until he was dead.

Fate wasn't on their side, or maybe it was. That night the Free Made Army chose to attack the capital. No more than a token battle really, but in the mayhem both dragons were hit and took to the ground. Benson scurried off alone, heading North on foot, not knowing the fate of Serina and their mounts. But finally the government forces had tracked him down.

Tiken's tail slapped the water occasionally and her wing tips sent up a fine spray across Serina's goggles, but she could still see the shoreline in front of them. Kenti was back in Devon recovering from his wounds; Tiken's partner now.

"My god. No!"

A sudden rise of vapour from a rocky outcrop told her the only weapon capable of taking down a dragon had been fired. A heart-seeking missile, designed to home in on the unique beat of the beast's massive pump. Why would Benson do that?

As the recoil sent him sprawling on the bracken covered ground a moment of recognition reached his addled brain.

"No!"

Nothing could stop the missile finding its target. He'd killed the only females he'd ever loved. His feelings for Tiken had been reciprocated since they'd bonded, since they'd met, and it was only at that moment that he realised he had fallen for Serina on their first meeting too. Only his ingrained prejudices had cloaked his love. How foolish he had been. And they had come looking for him together. Had risked their lives to find him. What irony, that fate had chosen him to end there's.

The two Reds that appeared over the top of the mountain

seconds before were still out of range. Rage and madness combined with his despair, but somehow his instinct for survival drove him to reload the launcher with his last missile, and hope that in taking down one Red he could wound the other.

Evasion!

Serina wasn't ready for the flip, and could only gasp as her stomach raced to her mouth. A gasp that first sucked air, then water. She fought the desire to cough, holding on to what oxygen she had, as Tiken dived deeper. Her ears felt like they would implode, but her mind was on the missile. It could travel through water. She'd seen the vids. Was she going to be torn apart by an explosion or was she merely going to drown?

He knew the SAS had been tracking him. There had been more than one occasion when a Red had passed very near to one of the many hiding places he'd used on his journey North. But, having failed with their searches they'd changed strategies and followed Serina instead. Only Tiken could have found him. He allowed himself a moment of thanks that Tiken had bonded with serena. It was rare that a dragon bonded with more than one human.

The explosion was taking too long, delaying his guilt, messing with his mind, and his ability to load the launcher a second time. The Reds would be in range by now. He fumbled the missile into position, knelt up and steadied his aim on the rock, just as one of the Reds exploded into pieces of flaming meat, along with its rider. The other Red screamed black smoke and veered left. There was no sign of Tiken and no time to think. He pulled the trigger again but this time the recoil sent him skull-first into rocks, and consciousness left him.

Coughing and retching as Tiken broke the surface, it took Serina a few moments to take in the scene. Pieces of burning dragon were hissing into the water around her, and a Red, heading towards Coniston Village above the west bank, realised another missile was heading its way and tried the same tactics as Tiken. But its evasive action came too late. Serena turned her head. Tiken banked right, flowing with the force of the explosion before coming back around to where they thought Benson would be.

Benson!

It wasn't for her mind. But the call was so strong. The emotion in that one word brought tears spilling down her cheeks. She knew then that she loved him too.

THE VAMPIRE GENE

The award-winning series from

SAM STONE

The trilogy

Standalone novels

The Young Adult imprint from The House of Murky Depths

DEAD GIRLS

The cult novel from Richard Calder re-imaged as an eight-comic series.